The Laura Black Scottsdale Mysteries

Books by
B A Trimmer

~~~~

The Laura Black
Scottsdale Mystery Series

Scottsdale Heat

Scottsdale Squeeze

Scottsdale Sizzle

Scottsdale Scorcher

Scottsdale Sting

Scottsdale Shuffle

Scottsdale Shadow

Scottsdale Secret

Scottsdale Silence

Scottsdale Scandal

Scottsdale Sleuth

~~~~

The Aloha Lagoon
Mystery Series

Hula Homicide

Homicide Honeymoon

Scottsdale Scandal

Scottsdale Scandal

B A TRIMMER

Editors: 'Andi' Anderson and Kimberly Mathews

Composite cover art and cover design by Janet Holmes using images under license from Shutterstock.com and Depositphotos.com.

Portions of HULA HOMICIDE reprinted courtesy of Gemma Halliday Publishing.

ISBN: 978-1-951052-34-8
Saguaro Sky Media Co.
060124pb

Email the author at LauraBlackScottsdale@gmail.com
Follow at www.facebook.com/ScottsdaleSeries/

Thanks to:

Katie Hilbert and Tony Tumminello
for their wonderful ideas.

Sherry Troop, for
suggesting the title.

*Thanks also to Cat Bertoldi,
Bonnie Costilow, Jeanette Ellmer,
Barbara Hackel, Millie Knight,
Judith Rogow, and Gail Shillito*

Scottsdale Scandal

~~~~
## Author's Note
~~~~

*Dearest reader, this book contains a fair amount of drinking,
some cussing, talking about sex, and plenty of action.
Bullets fly, grown men cry, and we'll have a happy ending.
If these sorts of things aren't your cup of tea,
it's probably best that you know now…*

Introduction

If you've never read a Laura Black Scottsdale mystery, you may want to start with *Scottsdale Heat*, the first book in the series. If you'd instead like to begin with this book, here are a few of the key people in the story:

Laura Black – A Scottsdale native with a degree in philosophy from Arizona State University. After working for a few years as a bartender at Greasewood Flat, she now works as an investigator in a Scottsdale boutique law firm.

Sophia Rodriguez – Laura's best friend, who works in the law office as the receptionist and paralegal. Sophie's a free spirit and former California surfer chick. She's currently exploring the concept of only having one boyfriend, Milo.

Gina Rondinelli – The law firm's senior investigator. She had been a detective in the Scottsdale Police Department and still likes playing by the rules. She's recently begun dating a former Navy SEAL named Jet.

Leonard Shapiro – Head of the law firm and Laura's boss. He's miserly and always pads his bills. He has limited people skills, but he usually wins his cases with the help of Laura, Sophie, and Gina. After a painful breakup with Elle, Lenny has started weekly training sessions in discipline and obedience with a dominatrix named Countess Carla, the Cruel.

Maximilian Bettencourt – Laura's boyfriend and the head of the legitimate side of the former DiCenzo crime organization. Before coming to Scottsdale, Max was a secret operative for the U.S. government, mainly in Eastern Europe.

Anthony "Tough Tony" DiCenzo – Former head of the local crime family, now retired. He's fond of Laura, and they have shared many adventures over the past year.

Gabriella – A former government operative from Eastern Europe. She currently works as a bodyguard for Johnny Scarpazzi. She's being hunted by Viktor Pyotrovich Glazkov, the head of an international crime organization based in Sevastopol, Crimea.

Johnny Scarpazzi – The new head of the criminal side of Tony DiCenzo's former organization.

Kristy Darby – A Scottsdale wedding planner who is having Lenny represent her in her divorce from her scummy soon-to-be ex-husband, Andrew.

Suzi Lu – A professor of computer science at Arizona State University who is also the professional dominatrix "Mistress McNasty." One of her clients is Johnny Scarpazzi.

Prologue

When I woke up, I was somewhere dark and cold. The side of my head pounded from where my assailant had struck me, and it hurt to the point of making me nauseous.

The night had been relatively warm, and I'd only worn capris and a stretchy cotton T-shirt. As I lay in the chilly darkness, I wished I had chosen something warmer.

I was lying on my back on something hard. My first thought was that I had been left on the floor in a dark room.

I carefully reached out and felt around on my left side. My hand came against a cold, smooth barrier about a foot from my body.

Jeez, they must have dumped me against a wall.

But when I rolled to get away from the chilly surface, I found another wall about six inches from my right shoulder.

Damn it. Where did they put me?

I seemed to have walls on either side and moaned in frustration. It was only then that I had a terrible thought.

With a sudden jolt of panic, I lifted my hand straight up. Less than a foot above me was another cold, smooth surface.

Oh no!

As I felt around at the sides and top of my chamber, I

found similar smooth walls at my feet and above my head. I then started to recognize the pungent aroma that was a cross between rotten meat and a high school biology class.

That, more than anything else, let me know where I was. After knocking me out, they must have stuffed me into one of the mortuary vaults in the autopsy lab.

In a total panic, I pushed on the top and sides of my enclosure. The stainless-steel panels were cold, smooth, and completely unyielding.

I felt around on the locker door. Unfortunately, the exit was tightly locked, and I didn't feel any type of emergency release latch.

With a fresh wave of fear, I realized there was no reason they had placed me into the locker legs first. If the bad guys had stuffed me into the vault by my head, the door to escape would be at my feet.

I wondered if there was enough room to turn around so I could search the far end of the enclosure. I twisted my body and tried to reposition myself with my head where my feet were.

It was a tight fit, but I thought I could make it. Unfortunately, I became stuck halfway through the turn.

Crap.

Unreasoning claustrophobic panic hit me. Not only was I locked in a mortuary locker, but I was now bent over double, twisted like a pretzel, unable to move.

I lay like that for maybe two or three minutes, shivering with the cold, trying to calm myself. But my leg muscles were already tight from not moving, and I knew they'd soon start to cramp.

How did this happen? I asked myself. *I was only helping a client find a missing dead body.*

Chapter One

"What does Lenny want?" I asked Sophie as I walked up to her desk in reception. "I swear, if it's another cheating spouse stakeout, I'm going to throw up."

"Wow," my best friend said, relief in her voice. "That was a close one."

"What are you talking about?"

"I emptied my trash can and put a new liner in it this morning. If you don't think you can get to the bathroom in time, make sure to throw up in that."

"Noooo," I moaned, stamping my foot like a three-year-old. "You're serious? Lenny wants to give me another cheating spouse? I just got through with one. I think I'd rather pull my own eyes out than do another one of those."

"Naah, I'm only messing with you," Sophie giggled. "It's not a cheating spouse. It's some sort of dead-body missing person assignment. I only wanted to see the look on your face."

"Hey," I scowled. "Sometimes you're really a butthead.

"Yeah, I know," she said, giving me all thousand watts of her smile. "I'm sorry you have to deal with my wonderful sense of humor."

Although I tried to be annoyed, I was inwardly relieved. I

hated the thought of spending the next couple of weeks trying to film naked people having sex.

"Do you know *anything* about the new assignment?" I asked.

"Not really," she said with a slight shake of her head. "According to what the client said on the phone, the county medical examiner lost her brother's body. She wants us to find it. She'll be here at ten-thirty."

"Jeez, that sounds almost as bad as a cheating spouse. Gina's the one who's trained in missing persons. Shouldn't she be the one to get this?"

"Sorry, girlfriend, you know how it is. Gina's still working full-time on the J. Barrett Knight assignment. We all know he's guilty as sin, so she has her work cut out. I think you're going to get all the crap assignments, for at least the next month or two."

"Fine," I sighed and shook my head. "But I won't be happy about it."

"Besides," Sophie said, "I don't know what you're complaining about. You're getting good at finding people, especially the ones who don't want to be found."

I looked at my best friend with my version of the Death Stare.

"At least this one's already dead," she laughed, ignoring my glare. "He should be easier to track down."

"Did you say Kristy Darby's coming in soon?" I asked, mostly to change the subject. "What's going on with her divorce?"

"She should be here in about fifteen minutes," Sophie said, looking pleased. "Her divorce is done, and she's coming in to sign the final documents."

"Really?" I asked. "That didn't take long."

"Yeah," Sophie agreed. "Her scummy ex-husband, Andrew, didn't do a thing to fight it. He even halfway admitted that he and his admin, Julie, had been more than friends for quite some time. Opposing counsel was pretty accommodating as well, all things considered. There weren't any kids involved, so it was mainly the standard paperwork back and forth. It pretty much flew through the system."

"That's great," I said, feeling a little relieved. "I like Kristy. I hope she comes out of this okay."

"The only roadblock was that she'd signed an ironclad prenup with her creep of an ex-husband," Sophie said with a frustrated sigh. "Lenny went to the judge to chip away at it, but he got shut down."

"So, Kristy will get her divorce but not come away with much of a nest egg?" I asked, feeling a little bummed.

"Well, she'll have half the marital property, mainly the house, minus what's left on the mortgage," Sophie said, looking a bit frustrated as well.

"There's some artwork, a savings account, her car, and her personal possessions. She also got half of Andrew's retirement account, which was almost two hundred thousand dollars. But his business was locked away behind a wall. Lenny wasn't able to touch it."

"I wonder if Kristy's ex is going to end up with Julie?" I mused. "Gina thought that might happen."

"Well, he's a jerk, and that Julie woman is seriously mental," Sophie said with a shrug. "I'd say they deserve each other."

Gina came up to the front about five minutes later. I hadn't seen her for almost a week, and she gave us an update on her assignment.

The client, J. Barrett Knight, had worked for several years as the head of Scottsdale General Hospital. While there, he'd uncovered an ongoing illegal narcotics operation run by his brother, Oswald, through the hospital pharmacy.

When Barrett tried to shut it down, he was threatened with death if he interfered. From that point on, he was merely the figurehead of the hospital while the drug distribution scheme occurred in the shadows.

"Barrett's still facing a dozen serious felonies," Gina said. "We're working to show that he had no choice but to go along with whatever his brother said to do, or else he'd have been killed."

"How are Lenny's negotiations with the prosecutor going?" I asked.

"The talks are going slowly, but I think they'll come around," Gina said. "Having Barrett testify against Oswald and Lillian Abbot will make it much easier for the state to get some serious convictions."

"Do you think he'll be able to get out of going to prison?" I asked.

Gina shook her head slowly. "No, he'll still serve time in a federal penitentiary. What we're doing is reducing the time he'll be there. Hopefully, he'll only have to serve two or three years before he can get out on parole."

As the three of us chatted in reception, Kristy Darby opened the door to the street and walked in. She was about my age, a little taller, and was dressed a lot nicer. She was slender and toned but not overly athletic.

She had a nice tan and softly curled honey-blonde hair that hung halfway down her back. She still wore several of her signature gold jewelry pieces but was no longer wearing a wedding set.

It had been a little over two months since I'd last seen her, and I noticed her makeup was a little more pronounced than it had been before the divorce. The changes were subtle but worked to highlight her deep blue eyes.

"Hi, Kristy," we all said in unison.

"Hello, ladies," Kristy said as she gave us her great smile.

"How have you been?" I asked. "The last time I saw you was at Grandma Henderson's wedding."

"I've been okay," she said as her smile faltered a little. "I know all of you have been divorced, so you know what I'm going through. I'm still a little in shock over the whole thing with Andrew and Julie, but I'm ready to move on with my life."

"How's the wedding planning business going?" Gina asked, trying to steer the conversation to something more pleasant.

Kristy shook her head and let out a snort of disgust. "That part isn't so good. After all the nonsense my ex's admin pulled, my new bookings dropped to nearly zero. I think every wedding venue in Scottsdale has been advising brides to avoid me."

"Can you continue the business?" I asked. I knew how good Kristy was after being with her through several weddings.

"Oh, I'm sure I could," she said, sounding frustrated. "Although, it would probably take a year or two to get back to where I was."

"That doesn't seem so bad," Sophie said.

"True, but after everything that's happened over the past six months, I'm ready to move on," Kristy said. "I've transferred the remaining weddings to a friend who's getting into the business."

"Wow," I said, a little shocked. "What are you going to do?"

"Well, that's my big news," Kristy said as she again broke out in a broad smile. "I answered an ad for a wedding planner position for one of the bigger resorts in Hawaii. I've been through three phone interviews, and now they want to fly me out to Kauai for a final interview and to look around."

Sophie started to squeal and jumped up to give her a hug. I also couldn't help myself and hugged her as well.

"That's so wonderful," I said. "I know you've always wanted to live on a tropical beach."

"I won't have a lot of money to start with," Kristy said with a slight grimace. "I'll get some for my half of the house and the retirement account. Plus, I've already sold my rings. I'm hoping it'll be enough for at least a down payment on something small out there."

"Don't make it too small," Gina teased. "We'll all want to come out and visit you."

"You're welcome to drop in anytime," Kristy said with a smile and a laugh. "But we should probably make sure I actually get the job before you start buying airline tickets."

"Of course they'll want you," Sophie said, her tone matter of fact. "I've been to your weddings, and they're lovely."

"Um, except for Grandma Henderson's, every wedding of mine you've been to was a complete disaster," Kristy said, slightly embarrassed, her eyebrows raised. "Remember?"

"Well, okay," Sophie admitted. "That's true. But I'm sure they'll be wonderful now that you don't have some psycho woman trying to sabotage them."

"If you need some additional references for the new job, have them give us a call," I offered.

"Thanks," Kristy said. "I may take you up on that. Only don't be surprised if they ask about Kristy Piper. I'm switching back to my maiden name."

Sophie asked Kristy to go into the conference room and called Lenny to tell him they were ready. His office door opened, and he joined Sophie and Kristy at the big wooden desk in the stately glass-walled room.

Right at ten-thirty, the door to the street opened. A woman in her late thirties holding a red file folder strolled in. Her dark chestnut hair was layered, with big bangs, and fell slightly past her shoulders.

She was nicely dressed, complete with a high-end Ferrucci bag and heels. Her clothes leaned more toward the sexy side, and she carried herself like she enjoyed showing off her fit body.

From the way her focus immediately went to Sophie, sitting at her desk, I gathered this was the new client. I could also see her suspiciously eyeing some of the stacks of folders my best friend had never gotten around to filing.

"Hi," I said as I walked over with my hand out. "I'm Laura Black, one of the investigators here." As I stepped toward her, I caught the delicate scent of Chanel.

"Kelsey Dawson," she said as we shook. "I'm here to see Leonard Shapiro."

"Hi, Kelsey, I'm Sophie," my best friend said with a finger wave. "We talked on Friday."

She glanced down at the phone on her desk. "Mr. Shapiro just finished a call. I'll see if he's ready for us. After we're through talking with him, I'll have some paperwork for you to sign."

Sophie picked up the phone and buzzed Lenny. "Kelsey Dawson is here." She listened for a moment, then hung up.

"Mr. Shapiro's ready for us now," Sophie said as she stood.

I walked into Lenny's office behind Sophie and Kelsey. Lenny solemnly shook hands with the client. He then offered her one of the short wooden seats in front of his desk, and I took the other.

Sophie took her usual seat by the open office door. This way, she could take notes and still be available if someone came into the office from the street.

Lenny briefly eyed the client, taking in everything. I knew he was doing more than simply admiring a beautiful woman. He was making mental notes of her body language, demeanor, and apparent level of wealth.

This is when Lenny will often give a nervous client a drink. But after apparently noting Kelsey's confidence and eagerness to get started, he didn't offer her anything. I looked over at Sophie, and she shrugged.

"Miss Dawson," Lenny started in his deep and steady lawyer voice. "How can we help you?"

"I'm having a problem with the county," she said, sounding frustrated. "I'm hoping you can help sort things out for me."

"We'll do our best," Lenny said with a smile and a nod. "What can we do for you?"

I had to admit, I was impressed by the look on his face. I knew he often practiced in front of the mirror to get the correct vocal inflections and facial expressions, but his game had gone up a notch after starting his weekly obedience sessions with Countess Carla, the Cruel.

"I'm looking for my brother's body," she said as her voice caught with emotion. "His name was Morgan West, and he died while traveling in Egypt last month."

"Oh, I'm so sorry," Lenny said. I could actually feel his empathy with each word. "Has your problem stemmed from that?"

"Morgan's body was supposedly returned to the Scottsdale offices of the Maricopa County Medical Examiner," Kelsey said after taking a deep breath to compose herself. "They were to run some tests and do an autopsy to determine the cause of death. The body would then be released to the Nesbitt and Sons Funeral Home on Hayden Road."

"When did you find out there'd been a problem?" Lenny asked with precisely the right tone of concern.

"The funeral home called last week to say there'd been a delay in receiving the body from the Medical Examiner," our client said, as her hands started to fidget. "They suggested I take the matter up directly with the county."

"I take it you've visited the Medical Examiner's office?" Lenny asked.

"I was at their Scottsdale office three times last week," Kelsey said, now starting to sound irritated. "I kept getting the runaround. Every person I talked to gave me a different answer for where Morgan's body should be. After several days of getting nowhere, I thought a more direct approach would be best."

Lenny had a yellow legal pad in front of him and took a few notes using his black Montblanc pen. I got the feeling these notes were mostly for show since he usually relied on Sophie to keep everything straight.

"If we could get copies of the paperwork you've gathered so far, it would help shorten the process," Lenny said.

"Certainly," Kelsey said as she held up the red folder. It looked like maybe a dozen pieces of wrinkled paper had been placed into it. "Everything I have so far is in here."

"Do you have a recent picture of your brother we could have?" Lenny asked.

Kelsey extracted an eight-by-ten photo from the folder and handed it to my boss. It showed a good-looking man in his early forties sitting in a restaurant. He was smiling and holding a bottle of beer.

"This picture is about two months old," Kelsey said. "He sent it to me the last time we talked on the phone."

Lenny handed me the picture, and I was able to study Morgan. He had a thin, handsome face, long, uncombed medium brown hair, and light brown eyes.

Lenny nodded slowly as if carefully considering all he had heard. "This is a fascinating case," he said with just the right tone of wonder and determination. "Thank you for bringing it to us. I want to get going on it right away."

Now that a game plan was being implemented, Kelsey visibly relaxed.

"Sophie will have some papers for you to sign," Lenny continued. "We'll also need a ten-thousand-dollar retainer to begin the investigation."

"I appreciate your starting on this as quickly as possible," Kelsey said without hesitation. "I hate the thought of my brother's body sitting in a morgue locker somewhere."

"Thank you, Miss Dawson," Lenny said, switching to his

sympathetic lawyer voice. "When you're finished with Sophie, Laura will need to ask a few background questions. We'll have the initial report ready in a few days."

Kelsey got up and returned to reception to wait for Sophie. Lenny motioned for the two of us to come to his desk before going out.

"Okay," he said thoughtfully. "Laura, this should be fairly straightforward. Go down to the Medical Examiner's office and see what you can learn. Most likely, this is only a government paperwork snafu."

He then turned to Sophie. "I can't see this one going anywhere. Give her a forty percent discount off the full hourly rate."

Sophie was about to take off when Lenny stopped her. "Hold on a minute," he pondered as he tapped his platinum-encrusted pen against the top of his desk.

"She didn't flinch when I told her about the retainer," he noted. "Funding doesn't seem to be an issue with this one. Let's only give her a twenty percent discount."

Sophie led the client into the conference room while I trailed behind. We then rearranged a couple of piles of file folders to clear a larger space on the big table.

"I'll need you to sign at the places indicated," Sophie said as she slid the new client paperwork across to Kelsey.

We watched as the client signed in the places my best friend had indicated with her little pink sticky notes.

"I'll also need to collect the retainer," Sophie said. "Do you want me to run a card?"

"No need," Kelsey said as she opened her bag and pulled out a stack of crisp hundreds. The original yellow-gold treasury band with the notation $10,000 was still tightly wrapped around the bills.

"I'll need a receipt," Kelsey said in an offhand voice as she tossed the stack on the table in front of my best friend.

Sophie raised an eyebrow and glanced at me. I shook my head and shrugged.

Why do I always get the weird ones?

"If you give me your folder," Sophie said, "I'll make copies of everything."

"Of course," Kelsey said as she handed Sophie the red file containing the paperwork.

I opened my notebook and started my interview to get the facts of the case. Sophie went back to her desk to prepare the receipt and copy the files.

"I'm sorry," I said. "But I'll have to ask you about your brother's death. It'll give me a starting point on where to look."

"Certainly, Miss Black," she said. "What do you want to know?"

"Oh, call me Laura," I said. "Do you know the approximate date your brother passed away?"

The question seemed to catch her off guard. "It was three or four weeks ago," she said, slightly confused. "I don't know the exact date. Do you think it's important?"

"It could be helpful," I said. "Especially if we need to contact the government officials in Egypt. Do you know what he was doing there?"

"He said a friend of his was traveling in Egypt, and this person wanted someone to go with them. Morgan is, or at least was, a bit of an adventurer."

"Do you have any idea who this other person was?"

"No, but knowing my brother, I assumed it was a woman."

"Did anyone mention the cause of death?" I asked, hating to bring up the subject. "Was it due to natural causes, or was foul play involved?"

"I'm really not sure," she said with a shaky voice, as a wave of sadness or regret passed over her face. She paused for a moment, and I thought she might start to cry.

"I got a phone call from a government official in Cairo that Morgan had died," she continued once she'd composed herself. "I guess my brother had listed me as his emergency contact. Unfortunately, the connection was lost before I could ask too many questions. I've tried calling them back, but I can't get ahold of anyone who knows the details."

"Did you get any other confirmation of Morgan's death?"

"There was also a call from someone at the Egyptian Health Ministry. They wanted authorization to arrange transportation for my brother's body back to the United States. They gave me a code. I guess you could call it a tracking number. It's what they gave to the airlines."

"And then the airlines transported your brother back to Arizona?"

"That's right. I have the paperwork for Morgan until he arrived at Sky Harbor Airport. All that's in the folder."

"Do you know what happened after your brother landed in Phoenix?"

"From what I've been able to piece together, the Maricopa County coroner picked him up from the airport,"

Kelsey said, sounding frustrated.

"Unfortunately, they seem to have lost him from that point on. He was supposed to go to the Medical Examiner in Scottsdale for an autopsy, but I don't think he ever made it there."

"Alright," I said. "I'm sure I'll have more questions, but this should be enough to get me started."

Kelsey rose and went out to reception to finish the paperwork with Sophie. The client was gone by the time I'd finished my notes and returned to the lobby.

"Hey," Sophie said from behind her desk. "I'm getting hungry and don't want to go down for tacos by myself. The guys always try to hit on me. I'd rather not deal with it now that I'm only dating Milo. Are you ready for lunch?"

"Sure," I said. "Tacos sound great. And don't the guys hit on you because you sit there and give them bedroom eyes the entire time?"

"Well, maybe," Sophie said with a shrug as she grabbed her purse from the drawer in her desk. "But it does get us free drinks."

The office phone rang, and Sophie rolled her eyes. "Why do people always have to call me?"

"Because you're the receptionist," I laughed. "Make it quick so we can get there before it gets too crowded."

"The next time you talk to Lenny," Sophie scowled as she picked up the phone, "remind him I need an assistant."

Chapter Two

After lunch with Sophie at Dos Gringos, I drove up Scottsdale Road until I made it to the airpark. I turned east on the Greenway-Hayden Loop, went a couple of blocks, then turned south on 78th Street.

The Scottsdale office of the Maricopa County Medical Examiner was in a nondescript one-story cinderblock building. Based on the unimaginative layout, I speculated that it had been built sometime in the eighties or nineties.

The only landscaping was a few mesquite trees and some stunted rosemary bushes. The parking lot was nearly empty, with four cars parked near a back loading dock. I drove to one of the six open spots near the front labeled *Visitor*.

As I entered a large lobby, I was directed by a sign to *Take a number and have a seat*. This was even though I was the only person in the reception area.

A middle-aged woman wearing a brown cardigan sat behind a counter and busily typed into her computer, ignoring me. The reception area was dead quiet, except for the clicking of her keyboard.

After several moments of standing at the counter looking at the receptionist, it became apparent she wouldn't help me unless I followed the rules. I went to the dispenser near the entrance and pulled out a ticket, *D-37*.

I looked at a large sign with glowing red numbers behind the reception counter. It was showing *D-35*. The receptionist hit a button near her keyboard, and *D-36* flashed on the screen.

"*D-36*," the civil servant called out. She looked at me, and I shook my head slowly. She then looked around the reception area to see if the ticket holder would appear.

She again pushed the button with a determined efficiency that I've only ever found in drug addicts and government bureaucrats.

"*D-37?*" she asked as she looked at me. From her slightly annoyed expression, it seemed that she thought I was trying to pull a fast one on her.

I held up my ticket, and her attitude shifted into a slightly more receptive mode.

"Can I help you?" she asked. From the picture ID hanging on a lanyard around her neck, her name was Dolores.

I couldn't quite place her accent. It was from somewhere back east. New Jersey, maybe.

"I'm here to ask about a missing body," I said. "Morgan West. He supposedly came into Arizona sometime within the last two or three weeks but has since gone missing."

"Are you his next of kin?" the receptionist asked.

"No," I said as I shook my head. "But I'm investigating at his sister's request."

Dolores calmly went to a wall full of cubby holes and extracted a multi-part document.

"As an agent for the next of kin, you'll need to complete this authorization form," she said. From the tone of her voice, she'd made the same speech hundreds of times before.

"Make sure to press hard when you fill out the information. All copies will need to be legible for the form to be valid. It will also need to be signed and notarized by the next of kin."

As she talked, she set the thick form on the counter in front of me. "Return the form once it's completed and notarized," Dolores said. "It's also available online if you prefer. But we would need four copies in addition to the original."

"No, this is great," I said, holding up the form.

"There's a five-dollar fee associated with this service," she continued. "Payment must be in the form of a cashier's check, money order, or business check made payable to the *Maricopa County Office of the Medical Examiner*. Once payment is received, I'll be able to give you access to the deceased's non-confidential medical records."

"But the guy is dead," I observed, trying to sound reasonable. "I don't think he'll care who looks into his medical records."

"I'm sorry," Dolores said in her official tone as she stiffened. "But we aren't releasing information on this case to the general public at this time."

Feeling annoyed, I walked back to my car. I've learned this sort of thing usually happens whenever I have to deal with county government. Still, it's frustrating.

As I drove toward the office, I called Kelsey Dawson. I had the top of the Miata down and used a pair of headphones to be able to hear her.

"Kelsey," I said. "I went to the medical examiner's office and picked up a records release form. Would you have time to sign it today?"

"Of course," she said. "Where would you like me to meet

you?"

"They need a notarized signature. Would meeting back at the office work for you?"

"Sure," she said. "I'll leave right away and see you there in half an hour."

My next call was to Sophie. "Hey," I said when she answered. "Would you do me a favor?"

"What is it?" she asked with a sigh. "Do you want me to drive you out to the middle of the desert again? If so, we'll need to get some gas first."

"Not this time. The county needs a business check for five dollars to access Morgan West's medical records. They also want Kelsey to sign a form before they'll give me the information. It needs to be notarized."

"You gotta love our county government," she said. "Is Kelsey coming back here for that?"

"She said she'd drive down right away. I'll be there in about twenty minutes."

When I returned to the office, Lenny was at a hearing, and Gina was still out on the J. Barrett Knight assignment. I chatted with Sophie in reception while I filled out the form for the Medical Examiner.

I told her I was going to Max's house for dinner. His mood had been off for the last few days, and I was hoping to learn what was bugging him.

Sophie said she was getting together with Milo after work. From the way she talked about the date, I couldn't tell if they were getting anything to eat or not. Sophie's main goal seemed to involve getting Milo over to her apartment as soon as possible.

The door to the street opened a few minutes later, and Kelsey walked in. Her outfit wasn't as extravagant as the last time she'd been here, but it was again form-fitting and revealing.

"Sorry about having you come back," I said. "But the county won't give me any information without the approval of the next of kin."

"Don't worry about it," she said. "I was halfway expecting a call from you. They had me fill out a form simply to tell me they didn't have Morgan's body. I guess I should have warned you about the bureaucracy beforehand."

After our client signed the document, Sophie took out her notary logbook and asked Kelsey for her picture ID.

"Wow," my best friend exclaimed as she looked at the driver's license. "I like your new look way better."

"Thanks," Kelsey said with a shrug as she signed the logbook. "That picture was from almost five years ago. My hair was chopped short back then, and I wore those horrible glasses. After my divorce, I decided I needed to change my style into something that would attract men."

I pulled into the circular driveway to Max's house a little after six-thirty. I didn't see his Mercedes in the drive, but I knew he sometimes parked it in the garage.

I walked up to the double wooden doors and knocked. After a few moments, I heard approaching steps, and Beatrice, Max's cook and housekeeper, opened the door.

"Come in, come in," she said, smiling as she waved me into the foyer.

"Am I too early?" I asked. I knew I was usually late, so maybe Max was starting to factor that in when he invited me over.

"No, Max call few minutes ago," Beatrice said in her thick Eastern European accent. "He say for you to have drink, and he be here by seven. I make you scotch with one ice cube, and you can wait."

Beatrice made the drink and offered to let me enjoy the scotch on the deck. I walked outside and made myself comfortable on my favorite oversized wicker loveseat.

As I sipped the scotch, I got a chance to relax while I looked over Paradise Valley. Max's house was on the south side of Mummy Mountain, and the deck faced westward.

The sun was poised over the horizon and gave the few clouds in the west a bright yellow glow. As I watched, the light slowly became orange and seemed to grow in intensity.

Over the many times I've been here over the last four months, I've come to regard the deck at Max's house as a peaceful oasis in an otherwise busy life. I can see why he chose this house and especially why he likes the deck so much.

As I looked out over the city, now turning gold with the setting sun, I thought about what it would be like to live here with Max. As always, the thought of moving in with him brought up a dozen conflicting emotions.

Fortunately, Max knew me well enough not to push too hard on the subject. He never mentions me getting more involved in his life beyond some gentle teasing.

I took the last sip of the scotch as Beatrice walked out to the deck. She had another drink on a silver tray with a white doily.

"Great timing," I said, taking the scotch. "Thank you. Although, this had better be my last one before dinner."

I expected her to return to the house, but instead, she stood and seemed nervous about something. I looked at her, and she started to speak but then faltered.

"Beatrice?" I asked, now concerned. "What is it?"

"Max say you private detective. He say you very good and help people solve problems."

"Well, sort of," I said, not wanting to go through the explanation of how I was an investigator at a law firm and not a private detective."

Beatrice looked at me, twisting her hands together. It was apparent she wasn't going to say anything until I started.

Jeez, I hate being pulled into someone else's problems.

"Um," I said. "Are you having some difficulties?"

This seemed to be what she was looking for. Her shoulders relaxed, and she started speaking. Her words came out in a quick flood, and I had to concentrate on making sure I understood her.

"Every year, I make cupcakes for baking contest at Scottsdale Cookie and Cake Club," she started. "I use my mama's secret trois chocolate mousse *prăjitură* recipe. This is famous recipe and has won our spring festival baking contest back home many times. But every year in Scottsdale, I lose to a devil woman. So, I think maybe she makes cupcakes better than me. But last year, I eat one of her cupcakes."

"How was it?" I asked. "Was it any good?"

"It tasted like dried-out *rahat de câine*," she said flatly.

"What's *rahat de câine?*" I asked, although I could likely guess.

"You do not want to know," she said.

"What's the name of this devil woman?" I asked, now growing curious.

"It is Kaitlin Kingston," Beatrice said as if the name left a bad taste in her mouth.

"What can you tell me about her?" I asked, leaning forward.

"She is young, maybe thirty-eight or thirty-nine. Skinny with curly yellow hair and big boobs. She wears tight shirt and short skirt. I think I know why head judge always let her win."

"Do you have any proof?" I asked. "If you have some evidence that she's trading sex for wins, it will make it much easier to figure out what's going on."

"No," she said as she shook her head. "No evidence. But I know how some men are. If you could expose judge and devil woman, I will be able to win this year."

"What's the judge's name?" I asked.

"It is Adam Jordan. There are two assistant cupcake judges, but Adam is president of club, and other two do whatever he says. If they do not, he finds someone to replace them."

"What kind of schedule do we have with this?" I asked.

"We have final club meeting tomorrow night," she said as she counted off on her fingers. "Open competition is on Saturday. Final bake-off is Tuesday after that.

"Where is the meeting tomorrow?" I asked, already starting to rearrange my schedule.

"Meeting is at seven at Max's Tropical Paradise Resort. If you come, you can say you want to join club. We have new members almost every meeting."

Beatrice then looked down, and I could tell she was embarrassed. "I have some money saved," she said. "Max pays me well. I have nice car, and it is all mine. I do not know how much money you want to help me. But I give you what I have."

As she said this, my heart went out to the woman. All my negative thoughts about taking on another person's problem disappeared.

"Please don't worry about money," I said. "I'll be happy to look into it, no charge. I can't guarantee I'll find a solution in only a week and a half, but I'll do my best."

Once again, relief seemed to wash over Beatrice. Her eyes sparkled with tears, and she mumbled something I took for a thank you. She then turned and quickly hurried into the house.

Five minutes later, I heard the sound of someone coming out to the deck. I turned to see Max walking toward me, a drink in his hand.

"I didn't hear you come in," I said, slightly embarrassed.

"I saw you out here watching the sunset," Max said in his smooth, baritone voice as he set his drink on a side table. "I know it's your favorite time of the day, and I didn't want to disturb you."

"You can disturb me any time you want," I said as I stood to give him a hug. As Max wrapped his arms around me, I felt a surge of safety and being loved.

"Hey," I said once we'd settled next to each other on the loveseat. "How are you doing? Something with you seems to be off the last few days. If it's only about work stuff, let me know, but you seemed troubled about something."

Max hesitated, then nodded. "Yeah, I do have something on my mind, and you should also know what's happening. It's about Gabriella."

I could tell something was wrong by his body language and the tone of his voice. Then it hit me all at once. "She's taken off after Viktor, hasn't she?"

"She left a little over three weeks ago." A look of frustration or perhaps guilt passed over his face.

In her youth, Gabriella had been a highly trained sniper in a special forces unit for an Eastern European army. Max had recruited her, convincing her to use her considerable talents for our side.

She and Max then operated side-by-side for several years. After they retired from government service, Max took a job with "Tough Tony" DiCenzo's crime family in Scottsdale. Gabriella came with him and quickly became Tony's personal bodyguard.

A few months ago, her location had been discovered by Viktor Pyotrovich Glazkov, the head of an international crime organization based in Sevastopol, Crimea. He had long vowed to kill Gabriella for her work against his organization in the past.

Familiar with Viktor's methods, Gabriella knew it would only be a matter of time before he sent someone to Arizona to kill her. Rather than wait for Viktor to send an assassin, she seemed to be going to Crimea to take him out first.

"Per our normal procedure, she was supposed to check in with us every three days," Max said. "At first, everything was going to plan, but then she went silent. We haven't heard from her in over a week."

"Is that unusual?" I asked. "I imagine that if she were

actively hunting Viktor, she might be unable to get to a phone for a while."

"Missing a check-in by a day or two isn't a big deal, but going silent for over a week is a sign of trouble. I told her we should go in together. That she'd have better luck with a two-person team. But she outright refused my help."

"I talked to Gabriella about this during Grandma Henderson's wedding. She said you'd offered to help her, but Viktor was her problem. She didn't want to drag you into it."

"She can be stubborn when it comes to things like this. Still, I wish she'd changed her mind before she took off. I didn't even know she was gone until she called me three weeks ago from Bucharest."

"I thought she was going to wait and come up with a plan before she went after him."

"I thought so too," he said with a slight shake of his head. "But apparently, the intel you gave her accelerated her timetable."

"I know we're talking about Gabriella," I said. "But still, I'm worried about her."

"So am I," Max admitted. "And honestly, if it were anyone but her, I'd say this would be a suicide mission."

"Is there anything we can do to help her?"

"At this point, I don't think I'll be directly involved," he said, sounding frustrated. "Johnny and Tony are also closely following events. If it turns out I'm needed, I may also need to disappear for a few days."

A knot quickly formed in my stomach as the implications of his words started to sink in.

"Gabriella's saved my life more than once, and I definitely owe her," I said. "Do whatever you need to do to help her. Take me along as well if I can be useful."

"At this point, it's likely I'd go alone. But I know your offer is sincere. Gabriella would know it as well."

"If you do have to go, I know you won't have time for a long goodbye or anything. Do your best to help her, then come back to me in one piece, okay?"

"I'll do my best," he said, leaning over and giving me a long hug. His arms felt great around me, and I didn't want him to let go, ever.

Chapter Three

I awoke the following day to the sounds of Max in the shower. I spent the next ten minutes lying in his bed, surrounded by his soft sheets, listening to the water run. The sound was both soothing and somewhat erotic, the perfect way to let me slowly wake up.

When I heard Max banging around in his bathroom, I got up and started my morning routine. Although joining Max in the shower would have been more fun, we'd quickly learned it wasn't a good idea, especially if we needed to be somewhere. Taking showers together in the morning resulted in us both being late.

I'd brought over a change of clothes, anticipating that I'd spend the night. After getting myself ready, I went to the kitchen to find Max munching on the breakfast spread Beatrice had already laid out.

As usual, there was French roast coffee, eggs, bacon, sausage, and toast. Although I was raised on white bread, Beatrice had insisted on making me toast with brown bread with dozens of different seeds.

At first, I wasn't too fond of it. The texture was somehow off. But now I craved the taste and crunch of Beatrice's morning toast.

"Where are you off to today?" Max asked as he sipped

his coffee. It was one of the French roasts I'd gotten him for Christmas, and I knew how much he liked it.

"I'm hunting down a dead body," I said, keeping my voice steady.

Max didn't say anything, but his eyebrow raised in surprise, and I knew he was suppressing a smile.

"The guy died in Egypt about a month ago," I continued, ignoring his look. "He was supposedly shipped back to the U.S. but never made it to the funeral home."

"Does your client have a guess where he ended up?" he asked as he took another sip.

"She thought he was probably still at the County Medical Examiner's lab in Scottsdale. But when I went there, they wouldn't tell me a thing until the next of kin signed a release. I got that yesterday afternoon, and I'm heading back to the lab as soon as they open."

"Well, good luck," Max said with a chuckle. "I do know how difficult dealing with Maricopa County can be. Just be glad you aren't trying to get a permit for a new golf resort."

I drove back to the Medical Examiner's office at the Airpark. As with the last time I was here, the parking lot was nearly empty. The only difference today was the presence of a maroon Chevy rental in one of the visitor's spaces.

When I entered the reception lobby, I had to smile. Dolores was handing a good-looking man a multipart form, perhaps even the same form she'd given me the previous day.

I hung back and listened as the clerk gave the same speech about pressing hard on the form to ensure all copies were legible. She then discussed the five-dollar fee. The man grunted an acknowledgment and walked to a cubby against the far wall to fill in the form.

Even though I was the only other person in the lobby, I'd decided not to fight the system. When she called my number, I approached the counter and handed Dolores the completed document and the fee.

The clerk entered several lines of information into her computer, took a page from her printer, and tore off the next to the last page from the form. She then returned the remaining four pages and handed me a receipt for the five dollars.

"You didn't need all of the pages?" I asked.

"We get the mint-colored page," she explained. The goldenrod page is for your records, and the other pages are for the other Medical Examiner's labs in the county. Although, you would need an additional five-dollar check if you visit another lab."

"Um, thanks," I said, not wanting to argue with her when I seemed so close to getting the information.

"Ah, yes," she said as she studied the form. "You're looking for Morgan West. He's been rather popular lately."

"What can you tell me about the body?" I asked. "Do you still have it here?"

Dolores began tapping on her keyboard. I assumed that pulling up the information would only take her a few seconds. Instead, she clicked the keys and moved her mouse around for almost two minutes before she could give me an answer.

"There was a delay in receiving the corpse from the main lab in Phoenix," she said in a monotone voice. "However, it appears it came in earlier today."

Finally, some good news.

"I'd like to see the body," I said. "I'd also like to talk with somebody to find out where it's been. I'm tracking it down for a client."

Dolores eyed me for another moment, perhaps to make sure I wasn't dangerous. "If you'll take a seat," she finally said. "I'll call someone to assist you."

Five minutes later, a bright-eyed man in his late fifties, wearing a white lab coat and carrying a clipboard, came to the front.

"Hello," he said as he held out his hand. "I'm Dr. Wilson. My official title is Deputy County Coroner, but I'm in charge of the lab here in Scottsdale. I understand you're here to see the remains of Morgan West?"

"That's right," I said, relieved to talk with someone who seemed to know what was going on. "From what I understand, there was some sort of delay in getting the body from your Phoenix office. He came into the country about two weeks ago from Egypt."

"I'm afraid our viewing room is currently in use," he pondered. "Would it bother you to go directly into the autopsy lab?"

"No, it's fine," I said, holding back a shiver of dread. "Whatever way is quicker."

I hope it's not too nasty in there.

Dr. Wilson led me to a sizeable cream-colored tile-lined room. Three stainless-steel dissection tables were lined up in the center of the overly air-conditioned space. Above each one was an enormous light on a movable arm bolted to the ceiling.

One of the tables had a body on it, but fortunately, it was covered by a sheet. The room had the nasty smell of rotten meat and a faint chemical odor that reminded me of my high school biology class.

Off to the side, a short, thin goth-looking woman in her mid-twenties was sorting through a pile of what looked like medical examination instruments. Except for her white lab coat, she was dressed entirely in black.

The woman wore tiny black headphones and bobbed her head to the music as she worked. She looked peaceful and happy as she hung out in the autopsy lab surrounded by dead people.

Go figure.

A dozen refrigerated mortuary lockers lined the back wall. Each had a stainless-steel door approximately three feet square. Dr. Wilson consulted some paperwork on the clipboard and went to a locker, two up from the bottom.

He pulled on the metal handle to unlock the door. It swung open, revealing two pale feet sticking out from under a white sheet.

Dr. Wilson checked some information from a cardboard tag attached to the man's big toe, then slid out the tray holding the corpse. He took hold of the sheet covering the body and prepared to pull it down so I could see the man's face.

"Let me know when you're ready," he said kindly.

I took a deep breath to steady myself, then nodded. Dr. Wilson pulled down the sheet slowly.

I bent over to look at the dead man's face. It didn't hit me all at once, but when I saw it, I knew there was a problem.

Crap.

From the picture Kelsey had brought in, Morgan West

was a Caucasian man in his early forties with medium-length brown hair. The man in the drawer was close to that in features, but there were some subtle differences.

Although the hair color and style were almost identical, this guy was closer to fifty. In addition, he struck me as having at least a partial Middle Eastern ancestry.

As I looked closer, I noted a faint strawberry birthmark on his left cheek, slightly below his eye. I didn't recall seeing that in the picture of Morgan.

Dr. Wilson continued to pull the sheet down to the man's chest. Above his heart, next to a colorful Egyptian-looking bird tattoo, was a discolored hole about the size of a nickel.

The injury appeared to have come from a large caliber bullet entering from the front. I hated to think what the exit wound looked like.

"Um," I said. "I don't think that's Morgan West."

"Really?" Dr. Wilson asked, perplexed. "Hold on. Let me check again."

The doctor examined the toe tag and compared it to the information on his clipboard.

"Everything appears to be correct," he said, sounding confused. "According to the paperwork, this man is Morgan West. Age forty-two, repatriated from Egypt."

I shook my head. "This man is closer to fifty. Plus, I was shown a recent picture of Morgan. His skin tone was somewhat paler. I also don't remember seeing the discolored patch on his cheek."

"Well, you're right," Dr. Wilson said as he looked closer at the body. "He does appear to be older than forty-two. But those sorts of mistakes don't happen. There are too many checks along the way. I'm sure there's a simple explanation for this."

"What's the usual procedure when a body's returned to the country?" I asked.

"After they're flown into Sky Harbor, they go through initial processing in the main Forensic Science Center in downtown Phoenix," Dr. Wilson said. "Then they're transferred to the branch labs for the autopsy. We got the notice of transfer probably a week and a half ago, but the body wasn't delivered until today."

"Is there a chance someone could have gone in and switched bodies in the meantime?"

"I've never heard of it happening," Dr. Wilson pondered as he flipped through some pages on the clipboard. "In theory, I suppose it's possible. But honestly, there's usually another explanation."

"What happens after the corpse gets to your downtown office?"

"They would have unsealed the casket to run checks on the body. As you can imagine, a great deal of paperwork and testing is associated with bringing a corpse into the country."

Still shaking his head, Dr. Wilson walked to the end of the lab where the goth-looking woman was working.

"Cricket," he called out and waved. She saw him gesturing and removed her headphones. I could hear the heavy metal music coming from them, even though I was a dozen feet away.

"Do you have a minute?" he asked.

"Sure, Dr. Wilson," she said with a smile.

I had to admit, Cricket had nailed the goth look. She had dark purple polish on her nails, several colorful tattoos, dark makeup, and multiple piercings. Half of her head was shaved short, while the other half had long, dark hair that hung past her shoulders.

"We got in a corpse this morning – Morgan West," Dr. Wilson said. "Were you the one to receive it?"

"Well," she said, eyeing the open locker and sounding slightly guilty. "I put him in the system this morning. But he's been here for a while. I was going to tell you about it."

"What do you mean?" he asked, sounding confused.

"I found him in locker twelve," the goth technician said. "The door on that one sticks, and we usually don't use it."

"How did you know someone was in there?" I asked as I stepped closer.

"I was cleaning the lab this morning and saw that the handle for twelve was covered in grime, chocolate maybe," Cricket said, rolling her eyes. "I checked the vault and found the corpse. He hadn't been logged in yet, so I entered him into the system and moved him to locker eight."

"Do you know why he wasn't received when he first came in?" Dr. Wilson asked, now sounding frustrated.

"Not a clue," she said with a shake of her head. "Maybe Brian forgot again. He's been processing most of our new arrivals lately."

As we talked, a set of double doors on the far side of the lab opened. A man in a wrinkled and stained lab coat wheeled a body on a stainless-steel trolley into the room. He went to one of the lockers and opened the door.

The technician was in his late thirties, had a body starting to go soft, and was slightly over six feet tall. He had pale skin, a scruffy goatee, and long dark hair pulled back in a messy ponytail.

Dr. Wilson and I walked to the man as he slid the body into the locker and closed the door.

"Brian, did you receive the remains of Morgan West?"

the doctor asked the technician. "Cricket found him this morning in locker twelve."

Brian glanced at Cricket and then at me. I could see his mind racing as he tried to think of something to say.

"Um, yeah," he finally said. "When he got here, we were full, so I put him in twelve. I was going to log him in, but I guess I forgot."

"Do you remember when he arrived?" the coroner asked, sounding irritated.

"Um, it was like a week ago, maybe a little longer," Brian said quietly.

I could see Dr. Wilson's jaw muscles tense as if he was gearing up to become angry. Instead, he sighed and shook his head.

"Alright," the doctor said. "He's in the system now. Please be more careful in the future. Breaking the chain of custody can cause serious problems."

Brian nodded his head, turned, and quickly wheeled the trolley out of the room.

"If the wrong body was delivered here last week," I mused. "Is it possible it was switched at the downtown office?"

"That would make sense," Dr. Wilson said. "At the very least, they might know more about what happened."

"Would it be possible for me to take a picture of the man in the locker?" I asked, pointing to the body.

I could tell Dr. Wilson wasn't too happy about my request, so I continued.

"We still need to find Morgan West's body," I said. "If I could learn the mystery man's name, it might help us find out what's going on. Even with the birthmark on his face, it'll be easier to track him down if I have a picture."

"I'm sorry," Dr. Wilson said as he pointed to a large sign mounted to the wall that read: *Absolutely No Photos.* "It's a firm rule here. Over the years, we've had too many pictures of corpses show up on Facebook and Instagram."

"Alright," I said, feeling frustrated. "I'll probably have some additional questions as I work through this. Would I be able to call you?"

"Certainly," he said as he extracted a card from his wallet. "Let me know what you find out. Mistakes like this aren't supposed to happen, but maybe they did in this case."

Dr. Wilson led me back to the visitor's lobby. "Here's my number," I said, handing him a business card. "Let me know if you find out anything on your end."

"Hey, Sophie," I said, calling her as I drove back to the office. Once again, I had the top of the Miata down and was using the headphones to be able to hear.

"How was the visit to the morgue?" she asked. "I don't think I'd ever like to visit a place like that. Being in the same room with all those dead people would totally creep me out."

"It smelled like the inside of a dumpster, but it wasn't as bad as I'd thought it would be," I said. "Fortunately, I didn't have to see anything runny."

"What are you up to now?" she asked.

"I'm heading back to the office. I'll need another five-dollar check. I'll be heading down to the main County Medical Examiner's office in downtown Phoenix."

"Do I need to call Kelsey to come in again and sign the

new form?" she asked.

"No, as it turns out, I can use the same form. I just need a new check."

"Do you know what a pain in the ass it is to cut these teeny-tiny little checks?" she asked. "I'll do it, but you're starting to owe me again. Besides, why do you need to go all the way over there?"

"When I got to the Scottsdale lab, they had a body labeled as Morgan West. I'll need to look at the picture again to know for sure, but I don't think it was our guy."

"Seriously?" she asked. "How can they mislabel a body? Are you sure it wasn't him?"

"The man in Kelsey's picture was in his early forties. I'm almost positive the guy in the locker was closer to fifty. Plus, the morgue guy looks sorta Middle Eastern and has a slight birthmark on his face. The Morgan in the picture was white with a dark tan and no birthmark."

"So, what do you think happened? Did someone switch bodies?"

"I don't know. It's either that or there's been some sort of paperwork snafu."

"That's what Lenny was thinking. Maybe he was right. In either case, it sounds like you're back to the beginning with finding the missing body?"

"Yup, and one other thing," I said. "It looks like the body in the morgue died from a gunshot wound. There may have been other things wrong with him that I couldn't see, but he definitely had a big hole in the center of his chest."

"How was dinner at Max's?" she asked, apparently not wanting to talk about the dead body anymore.

"The dinner was good, but I picked up another

assignment."

"Jeez, this happens to you a lot. I hope Max didn't talk you into doing something for Tony again. You know how Lenny almost threw a clot the last time that happened."

"It wasn't Max. It was Beatrice, his housekeeper. She's a member of the Scottsdale Cookie and Cake Club. They're having their annual baking contest this weekend, and she always loses to a woman who apparently makes terrible-tasting cupcakes. She asked me to look into it."

"I love cupcakes," Sophie moaned. "They're my favorite kind of cake, well, other than birthday and wedding cake."

Chapter Four

I arrived at the office and picked up the check from Sophie. Since there was now an issue with the identification of the body, I also grabbed the picture of Morgan that Kelsey had left with us.

"Hey," I said. "Are you doing anything tonight? I'm going to the meeting of the Cake Club. Do you want to come along? This isn't an official assignment, and I'd love some company."

"That depends," she said. "Do you think they're going to have any snacks? You'd think that being a cookie and cake club, they'd bake stuff for everyone to munch on during the meeting."

"I don't know," I said. "But if you don't go, I'll spend the entire week telling you how delicious everything was."

"Fine," she grumbled. "I'll go. But they better have something good."

I drove into downtown Phoenix using the navigator on my phone. After making several turns down crowded one-way streets, I found myself in an industrial part of the city that mainly consisted of light manufacturing and warehousing.

The Maricopa County Forensic Science Center was in an unassuming two-story government building on West

Jefferson Street. If it hadn't been for the sign out front, I wouldn't have given the structure a second glance.

Fortunately, the office was next to a massive parking structure. I found a space for my Miata on the third level and walked down to the offices.

This building's reception area was a lot more pleasant than the Scottsdale branch. I grabbed a number from the dispenser and was pleased that my number was already showing on the screen behind the counter.

"How can I help you?" The woman behind the desk asked as I walked up.

"I'm looking for information on a corpse that came through here about a week ago."

I could see she was gearing up for a speech, so I pulled out the notarized form and Sophie's check for five dollars. As she recognized what I had, she immediately softened.

"Morgan West," she said as she pulled out the pink sheet from the form and started to read. "That one sounds familiar."

"He was flown in from Egypt almost two weeks ago and was transferred to your Scottsdale office."

"Let me get you someone familiar with the case," she said as she typed into her computer. "I'll see if Dr. Beckman is available."

Five minutes later, a woman in her late forties came out to the lobby, wearing a lab coat and holding a folder.

"Dr. Beckman?" I asked as I walked up to her.

"Call me Latoya," she said as we shook. "You're looking for information on Morgan West?"

"That's right. I'm trying to track down his body. It seems to be missing."

Dr. Beckman gave me a strange look. "Sure," she said. "Why don't we go to my office."

She used her badge to buzz through a heavy wooden door and then led me down a long corridor. Her office was at the end of the hallway, and she offered me the chair in front of her desk.

"It sounds like you have an interesting story to tell," Dr. Beckman said. "What exactly do you want to know?"

"Don't you need to see my authorization first?" I asked.

"No need," she said with a chuckle. "I see the *Third-Party Release of Medical Records for Non-Commercial Purposes* form sticking out of your bag. It's one of the few five-part forms the county still has us using."

"Well," I started. "I'm trying to learn the location of Morgan West."

Dr. Beckman flipped through the folder. "According to the paperwork, his remains were delivered here from Sky Harbor Airport a little over two weeks ago. We performed some tests on the body to screen for infectious diseases. Everything checked out, and he was transported to the Scottsdale lab three days later."

"I was just there," I said. "They have a corpse with a toe tag that says Morgan West, but the body is for someone older with different physical features."

"Really?" Dr. Beckman asked. It was apparent I'd caught her off guard. "Mix-ups like this don't happen. The paperwork and chain-of-custody procedures are specifically designed to prevent it."

She again flipped through the paperwork on her clipboard but apparently found nothing unusual.

"It's the first time I've heard of something like this occurring," she mused. "There's a standard routine for bringing in a corpse from overseas. Before we transport, we go through a long checklist."

"Is part of that procedure verifying the body matches the name?"

"Of course," she said. "In this case, we pulled a copy of Mr. West's driver's license and compared the picture to the corpse."

She then showed me a paper with a blow-up of Morgan's Arizona driver's license. The picture on the ID was the same man as in the picture Kelsey had given me.

"The hairstyle and facial features of Morgan West and the corpse in the Scottsdale lab are similar," I observed. "I could see how someone could make a mistake if they weren't paying attention. It's possible that the body was switched before it came to your office. Do you have any idea how that could have happened?"

She blew out a breath, and I could see her thinking. Finally, she shook her head. "No, I'm sorry. If the body in Scottsdale isn't Morgan West, I don't have an explanation."

Great. Now I really am back to square one.

I returned to the parking garage and took the elevator up to my level. I'd almost reached my car when a man stepped out from between two vehicles.

We made eye contact, and I was about to ask him what he wanted. He then pulled out a small semi-automatic pistol and pointed it at my stomach.

Shit.

"Don't move," he said slowly with a deep voice. "I only

want to talk. If you don't do anything stupid, you won't get hurt."

It only took me a second to peg him as the man I'd seen earlier in the lobby of the Scottsdale Medical Examiner's office. At the time, he'd been talking with Dolores, the clerk, and she'd handed him a form.

He was maybe five-eleven with an average build, in his late thirties or early forties. He had short dark hair, a five-day beard, and a full mustache.

As with the corpse in the morgue locker, he seemed to have some Middle Eastern ancestry. I would have said he was handsome if he hadn't been pointing a gun at me.

"What do you want?" I asked as I glanced around the parking garage. Unfortunately, the busy structure had suddenly become quiet.

"Give me your purse," he commanded.

"You followed me all the way from the Scottsdale Airpark to rob me?" I asked, not even trying to keep the attitude out of my voice.

"No, but with that tight outfit, if you're carrying a gun, the only place you could hide it is in your purse. I've been having a horrible couple of weeks and don't want to take the risk that you'll shoot me."

Annoyed and feeling like I really did want to shoot him, I handed him my bag. I suddenly felt naked without my pistol.

"When I was in the Scottsdale office, I heard you were looking for Morgan West," he said as he lowered the gun. "They wouldn't let me see his body, but you apparently could."

I didn't say anything, so after a moment, he continued.

"When you left, I followed you to a lawyer's office in

downtown Scottsdale. You had an assigned parking space in the alley behind the building. I can only assume you work there."

"So, you're a creep who likes to follow women?" I asked.

"From your Scottsdale office, you came here," he said, ignoring my taunt. "It seems we're both looking for the same thing."

"Why do you care so much about Morgan West?" I asked.

"I don't give a crap about Morgan," he said with a bark of laughter. "If we're being honest, I'm just as happy that he's dead."

"Well?" I asked. "Then what do you want?"

"I'm only looking for the body, same as you. Do you know where it is? We should start working together on this. You know, partners."

"Partners?" I asked. "You're serious?"

"I have some information you'd be interested in," he said. "I'll even pay you to help me."

The situation struck me as funny, and I had to chuckle. "Sorry, I already have a client," I said with a shake of my head. "Besides, I have no idea where he is. They have a body tagged as Morgan West in the Scottsdale morgue, but I don't think it was him."

"Really?" the man pondered this information as if it were profoundly significant. "Did you see the actual body? Do you know who he was?"

"I've never seen him before. He was only a dead guy with a very large bullet hole in his chest."

"Anything distinguishing about the body? Did you see

any tattoos on his neck or chest?"

"He had a tattoo next to the bullet hole. It was a bird, like something you'd see in a pyramid."

"Was that the only tattoo on his chest?" the man asked.

"It's the only one I saw," I said. "But I didn't see any further down than the bullet hole."

"It wasn't Morgan," the man said with a tone that was hard to read. He was either relieved or annoyed. I couldn't tell which.

"There must have been a switch," he said, sounding discouraged. "We need to figure out who the dead guy is. That will give us a direction for finding Morgan's body. What else can you tell me about the man you saw? Give me as many details as you can remember."

I shook my head as I tried to recall the man in the morgue locker. "He was maybe forty-nine or fifty with short dark hair. His features struck me as Middle Eastern. Like I said, I didn't see any other tattoos, but he did have a faint birthmark on his face."

"Birthmark?" the man asked. His eyes widened, and he was suddenly alert. "Tell me about it."

"It was on his cheek, under his left eye."

"What color was it?" the man pressed.

"Sort of a reddish pink," I said. "Maybe the size of a quarter."

The man nodded and smiled. His body language made it clear he knew who I was talking about.

"Alright," I said. "I've told you what I know. So, you tell me. Who's the dead guy? What does he have to do with Morgan West?"

The man paused, as if deciding what to reveal.

"I first met the man you saw in the morgue about two years ago," he said slowly. "He called himself the Professor."

"Alright," I said. "How does this all fit together?"

"For the last couple of years, we've been trying to purchase some rather valuable objects coming into the private collector's market in Egypt. We've also been trying to find the original supplier."

"Who is '*we*'?" I asked.

"I'd been working with a partner for the last three years." As he said this, his voice caught. "She's out of the picture now, but we first met with the Professor about two years ago. Morgan West, his bodyguard or maybe his business associate, showed up five or six months ago."

"Were they looking for the source of the objects as well?"

"They were the sellers. As far as we know, the Professor might have been the sole supplier."

I shook my head. "Before we go any further. You'll need to tell me what's going on, all of it. No guns."

The man's cheeks flushed red, and he did look ashamed. "I'm sorry about pulling a pistol on you. But I'm pretty sure I'm being followed, and I'm still not sure who is who yet."

"Okay," I said. "If you want to be partners, tell me your name."

"My name is Mustafa Yousef," he said as he unzipped a black-leather hip pack he had strapped around his waist. He stashed the pistol, then pulled out a folded wad of hundred-dollar bills wrapped with several rubber bands.

"Here's eight thousand dollars," he said, pushing the money into my hand. "You seem to have more access to the coroner than I do. I want to hire you to help me get what I want."

"You're not specifically interested in Morgan's corpse?" I asked. "You're looking for something else?"

"That's right," he said with a nod. "The body is only a means to an end."

I thought for a moment about what I would do with this man. We already had Kelsey as a client, but she only wanted to find her brother so she could bury him.

Eight thousand dollars was a lot of money, and I was briefly tempted to pocket it and start investigating. But I've gone off on my own before, and it never works out. Too many things begin to overlap.

If this guy wanted to find something other than Morgan West's body, bringing him in as a client would be the easiest for me. Besides, I didn't think Lenny would mind taking his money.

"Okay, but we can't do it this way," I said, trying to give him back the money. "Come down to the law office. You can sign up as a client, and everything will be above board."

"No. You keep the money for now," Mustafa insisted as he returned my bag. "I want you to know I'm serious, and I also wanted to apologize about the gun. You can give me a receipt when I go to your office."

"Fine," I said, stuffing the money into my bag and pulling out a card. "Call the office number, and Sophie will schedule an appointment. I'll let her know what's going on, and she'll get you in right away."

He was about to say something else when I held up a finger to stop him.

"But, if I'm going to work with you on this, I'll want to know everything. You can't hide what you're trying to do and expect my help to amount to anything."

"I suppose that's fair," he said. "I'll tell you everything I can."

"Hey, Sophie," I said, calling her as I drove back to Scottsdale.

"How'd the visit with the Medical Examiner go?" she asked. "Do they have the right body down there?"

"No, their paperwork says the guy in the Scottsdale lab is Morgan West, and that's all they know."

"So, where'd the body go?" she asked.

"Not a clue, at least not so far," I said. "But something else came up while I was there. Another guy's looking for the body. He says his name is Mustafa Yousef."

"Morgan's turning out to be a popular guy," Sophie chuckled. "But why would Mustafa Yousef care about the body? Was he a friend?"

"Hardly, but he definitely had a connection to Morgan. From my description, Mustafa told me that the guy in the Scottsdale morgue locker was called the Professor."

"Professor of what?" Sophie asked.

"No idea," I admitted. "But this professor was somehow working with Morgan. They were in Egypt together, apparently selling things that Mustafa described as extremely valuable."

"Valuable?" Sophie asked. I could imagine her eyes opening wide as she sat up in her chair. "Any idea what kind of valuable things he's talking about?"

"Not a clue," I admitted. "But I get the feeling it will be easier to find Morgan's body when I find out what they are."

"So, what does Mustafa Yousef want from us?" Sophie asked.

"I think he wants me to help him look for the valuable things. Apparently, finding Morgan's body is only a stepping stone to getting to them. He gave me eight thousand dollars in cash as a retainer. He has your number and needs to come in right away to be set up as a new client."

"Eight thousand is a lot of money," Sophie mused. "Are you sure you want him as a client? For that much cash, you could freelance. I won't even tell anyone if you take me out to lunch a couple of times."

"Yeah, I thought about it," I said. "But I'd rather do it this way. I get the feeling that both assignments are going to overlap, and I don't want to have to deal with keeping everything straight."

"I don't know," Sophie said. "For eight thousand dollars, I bet you could figure out a way to sort everything out."

The rear cubicles were empty when I arrived back at the office. I walked up to reception, where Gina was talking with Sophie at her desk.

"Hey, stranger," I said. "Are you coming to lunch? We're going down the street for tacos."

"Definitely," Gina said. "I have a break between interviews today and thought I'd grab lunch with you two."

"It's about time," Sophie teased. "We were starting to think you didn't like us anymore."

"Did Mustafa Yousef get ahold of you to make an appointment yet?" I asked.

"Yup," Sophie said. "He called about fifteen minutes ago. I have him set up with Lenny at four o'clock this afternoon. Will you be around?"

"I should be," I said.

Lenny's office door was open, and he must've heard us talking. He came out and walked over to Sophie's desk.

It was a little odd, but when he got to the desk, he simply looked at the three of us and smiled. The silence was kind of awkward, and I got the feeling he was waiting for us to talk, so I blurted out the first thing I could think of.

"What do you think about our client, Kelsey?"

"What do you mean?" Lenny asked.

"Don't you think it's sort of odd that she opened her purse and pulled out a stack of brand new hundred-dollar bills? Who does that?"

"I couldn't care less if she gave us a bucket full of pennies," Lenny said as if it should be obvious. "As long as the bank accepts it, I'm good with her money, however she wants to pay us."

Lenny then went back to smiling. Unfortunately, this wasn't the comforting smile he used when dealing with a client. This was the creepy smile he used as a boss. It was a little disturbing, and the three of us looked back at him.

What now?

"Are you three heading out to lunch?" he finally asked.

"Um, yes," I said, hoping he wasn't going to invite himself along.

"That's great," he said. "Feel free to take your time

today. When you get back, I'll have a surprise."

I got a sinking feeling. Lenny's surprises never worked out well.

"What's going on?" Gina asked warily.

"It's mostly a surprise for Sophie," he said, suppressing a smile. "But it's something that will help out everyone."

Sophie cocked her head to the side. "Can you give us a hint?" she asked tentatively.

"You'll see soon enough," he said, obviously pleased with himself. "But I think you'll like it."

Chapter Five

We walked to Dos Gringos and sat in a booth along one of the open courtyards. It was a beautiful spring day, and I would've liked to spend the afternoon here, day-drinking Coronas on the patio and chatting with my two best friends.

Gina told us about spending Saturday night with her boyfriend, Jet. They'd driven up to Sedona and had stayed in a hotel overlooking the valley. I was glad to hear they were still getting along.

The waitress brought our orders, and we all dug in. "Do you have any idea what Lenny's surprise is going to be?" Sophie asked Gina as she munched on a carne asada taco.

"Not a clue," Gina said, sipping her iced tea. "The last time Lenny told us we'd get a surprise was when he gave everyone a bonus."

"That would be great," I said, crunching on chips and salsa. "But Lenny said this surprise would be for Sophie."

"Maybe it's something Countess Carla, the Cruel, is making him do to make up for being such a lousy boss," Gina speculated. "Suzie said this was something that could happen."

"Maybe he's going to replace the crappy carpet we have in reception," Sophie pondered. "Ever since he blurted out how old the carpet in the office is, I've been waiting for him to have it ripped up and replaced.

"Well, I hope it's not anything too horrible," I said. "You know how Lenny's surprises never seem to work out."

We walked back to the office and came in from the door to the street. As soon as we entered the reception lobby, we saw a woman sitting at Sophie's desk.

She was in her early sixties and looked pleasant enough. Her dark hair was done up in a poofy shag, and she had a pair of reading glasses hanging from a cord around her neck.

"What the hell?" Sophie muttered.

"Can I help you?" the woman asked as Sophie walked up to the desk.

"You're sitting at my desk," my best friend said, eyes narrowed.

"Oh, you must be Sophie," the woman said with a wide smile. "I'm Deborah, but you can call me Debbie. I started working here a few minutes ago."

"That's great," Sophie said, now sounding annoyed. "But you're still sitting at my desk."

"Leonard said you'd be moving to a cubicle near the breakroom," Debbie said. "Didn't he mention that yet? I think he's already moved some of your things back there."

As the words sank in, Sophie got a horrible look of confusion and sadness on her face. "No," she said so softly I almost couldn't hear her. "This is where I sit."

The door to Lenny's office opened, and our boss strolled out. Debbie stood and came around the desk to meet everybody.

"Great," Lenny said. "I see you're getting acquainted. This is Deborah Thompson. She'll be our new receptionist. She'll also take care of the billing and the filing."

"Hi, Debbie, I'm Gina," our senior investigator said as she shook Debbie's hand. "Welcome to the office."

"I'm Laura," I said as I waved. "Let us know if you have any questions."

"Oh, I've been an office manager off and on for the last thirty years," Debbie said confidently. "I hopefully won't have too many questions. But if I do, I'll be sure to ask."

"But she's sitting at my desk," Sophie said quietly.

"Well, sure," Lenny said with a friendly smile. "Now that you'll be our full-time paralegal, you can take one of the empty cubicles in the back offices for some privacy. I've already put your laptop and tablet on one of the desks there."

"But I've always sat up here," Sophie said weakly.

"I know how much having to deal with the clients has distracted you," Lenny said, looking around at the stacks of folders that had started accumulating again. "Plus, I know how much you hate to file. Sitting in the back offices will help you concentrate on your main job. Debbie will be able to take care of the day-to-day things."

"Oh," Sophie said quietly as she looked around the reception lobby. "Okay. Um, I guess I'll get the rest of my things then."

My heart went out to Sophie. Even though she'd been asking for someone to help her for months, I didn't think this was what she'd been looking for.

Sophie grabbed a few knickknacks and a coffee cup full of pens from the desk. She also picked up a tiny dragon tree in a colorful ceramic pot. Without saying a word, she walked to the door that led to the back offices.

Gina and I exchanged a glance. She could see what Sophie was feeling and shook her head slowly. I knew what she was thinking because I was thinking the same thing. *Be careful what you wish for.*

I stayed in reception long enough to be polite, then went to the back offices. Sophie sat in the empty cubicle next to mine as she looked around the back room.

"You know," she said quietly. "I've been back here hundreds of times, but I've never realized what a depressing part of the office this is."

"It's not so bad," I said. "The bathrooms are right here, and the vending machines are nearby. We're even near the back door, so you can come and go as you please."

"I'm going to miss watching the shoppers as they walk up and down the street," she said with a touch of melancholy. "It's always the most fun during snowbird season. Some of the outfits people from up north wear to Scottsdale are hilarious."

"It's not like you'll never go up to reception," I said. "You'll probably still be there four or five times a day."

"Oh, I know," she said with a sigh. "But it won't be the same. It's so beautiful up there, and it's the nerve center of the office. I don't know how I'll feel about being stuck back here all day, every day."

"But at least you won't have to file. I know how much you hate doing that."

"It's not like I was doing a lot of filing lately," Sophie said as she rolled her eyes. "But I understand what you're saying. And thanks for trying to cheer me up."

Sophie and I were in reception waiting for Mustafa Yousef to show up for his appointment. The longer I waited, the more uneasy I felt about working with someone who'd already pulled a gun on me.

Sophie was still alternating between ignoring Debbie and staring daggers at her. Although my heart went out to my best friend, I knew having Debbie here would benefit her. I hoped Sophie would come around and start to accept the new situation soon.

Two minutes before his appointment time, the door to the street opened, and Mustafa strode in. He was again wearing the black belt bag, and I assumed he was still armed with the pistol.

He saw me standing beside Debbie's desk and flashed me a broad smile. Once again, I was struck by how handsome he was.

I heard Sophie suck in a breath and watched her eyes slowly travel up and down his body with unconcealed interest. She then gave him a flirty half-smile and absentmindedly fluffed her hair.

"I'm Mustafa Yousef," he said to our group. "I believe I have an appointment with Leonard Shapiro."

"That's right," my best friend said, biting her lower lip. "I'm Sophia Rodriguez. Let me see if Mr. Shapiro is ready for us."

Rather than pick up the phone and call Lenny, Sophie slowly sauntered to his office. She made sure to pass close to Mustafa, and when she got to Lenny's door, she turned to ensure that Mustafa was looking at her.

After knocking on Lenny's doorframe and talking with him in a low tone, she turned to look at our new client. "Mr. Shapiro is ready for us."

As we walked into the office, Lenny stood in the middle of the room and extended his hand. Once the introductions were made, Mustafa and I sat in front of Lenny's desk. Lenny had moved Sophie's chair, so she now sat in front of the desk as well.

I've seen that with women, Lenny tries to exude an aura of support, and his tone is very soothing. When dealing with a man, he drops the quiet tones and becomes more aggressive. It's almost like Lenny wants to hear about the man's problems so he can get into a fistfight on his behalf.

I guess it's effective. The male clients seem to enjoy working with Lenny, and he rakes in an obscene amount of money.

"Mr. Yousef," Lenny started as he resettled himself behind his desk. "I understand that you're looking for the body of Morgan West. Laura tells me that you've already given her an eight-thousand-dollar cash retainer to get started on it. Can you tell me what your interest is in finding his body?"

"I'll be as open as possible," Mustafa said. "I represent a group in Egypt interested in finding and acquiring certain ancient artifacts that have been circulating in Cairo over the past two years."

"And you believe that if you can find the body of Morgan West, it will lead you to these artifacts?"

"Yes. I'm not at liberty to discuss how it will help me, but I believe it will."

"What would you do with the body once we locate it?" Lenny asked. "Are you proposing to dissect it or something along those lines?"

"No, nothing like that," Mustafa said, looking slightly shocked at the question. "I only need to take some pictures of the corpse. After that, I have no further interest in it."

"According to what you told Laura, the body in the

morgue labeled Morgan West is actually someone called the Professor. Can you tell us any more about him?"

"He was in the group selling the antiquities in Egypt. He was perhaps even their leader. Both he and the artifacts disappeared soon after Morgan was murdered. We'd assumed the Professor had fled the country or was already dead. Laura confirmed the death yesterday. My only concern now is finding the body of Morgan."

"I already have a client who has us looking for the body," Lenny said. "I don't see a conflict of interest, at least to this point. But if one develops, I must defer to my original client. Will that be acceptable?"

"I don't think you'll have a conflict," Mustafa said, waving his hand dismissively. "I only want to photograph the corpse. After that, I'll have no further interest in it."

"Very good," Lenny said. "You've given us the eight thousand, and Sophie will give you a receipt, but we'll need a total retainer of fifteen thousand to get started."

"I can have the remainder wired to you first thing in the morning," Mustafa said as if it were unimportant.

A gleam flashed in Lenny's eyes. He glanced toward Sophie, and she made a notation on her pad. I glanced down to see what she had written -- *Full hourly rate - no discount.*

After Mustafa left, I went back to my place. I had enough time before the cake club meeting to take a quick shower and change.

I arrived at the lobby of the Tropical Paradise about twenty minutes before seven. Sophie had beaten me there and was standing in front of one of the big aquariums, staring at the hundreds of brightly colored fish.

"Hey," I said as I walked up to her. I could see from her expression that she was troubled about something. "Are you ready to go to the meeting?"

"I've been thinking about that," she said, sounding slightly bummed. "After the whole Debbie thing today, I don't know how much fun I'll be tonight. I might only stay for a few minutes, then I'll probably duck out early."

"I understand," I said. "I could tell that Lenny bringing someone else on board had bothered you, a little bit."

"You know, I don't care so much that Lenny hired someone else to do the work," she said, sounding frustrated. "I'm all for that. But I'm still sorta pissed that he gave her my desk. I've sat there since day one. She even has my chair."

"Well, you know how bad Lenny's personality is. Maybe Debbie will get mad at him and quit after a week or two."

"I don't need her to quit," Sophie said with a shake of her head. "It'll be nice not filing anymore. But I do want my desk back."

We looked at one of the information monitors in the lobby and learned that the cake club meeting would be held in the Camelback Ballroom. We looked up the location on the resort map on the wall and made our way there.

The first thing that struck me when we got to the ballroom was how many people were in attendance. I'd assumed there'd be at most a couple of dozen bakers, but what greeted us was a crowd of at least a hundred and fifty people.

Most of the club members seemed to be middle-aged and senior women. But there were also a surprising number of couples, men, and people in their twenties and thirties. There even appeared to be several groups of kids who seemed to be high school age.

We both signed up at a table near the entrance. As we filled out the new member forms, I talked to the woman about the meeting.

"Is it always this busy?" I asked.

"Oh no," she said with an enthusiastic shake of her head. "Our monthly meetings are usually pretty quiet. But the annual cake show and bake-off starts this weekend. Tonight's meeting is the unofficial start of the event."

She gave each of us a lanyard with a colorful name badge dangling from it. We then went into the ballroom and looked around.

Classic rock was playing from a small stage at the front of the room, and there was a low buzz from so many people talking at once. A cash bar was off to the side, doing a brisk business.

We found Beatrice chatting with a small cluster of women. She broke away from her group when she saw us and led us to a relatively quiet corner.

I introduced Sophie to Max's housekeeper, and we started to chat. After a few moments, two women walked by our group. Both were eating colorful cupcakes.

"Those look so good. Where do you get the cupcakes?" Sophie asked as she scanned the room. "Never mind," she said excitedly. "I see them."

I followed her gaze to the back. A long table had been set up with ten or fifteen groupings of brightly colored cupcakes. Most of the cupcakes were displayed on tiny acrylic stands.

"It is tradition that the cupcake bakers provide snacks to sell at the meeting before main competition," Beatrice said. "I suggest you get one with brown icing and dark chocolate shavings. You should also get one with green icing and blue sugar crystals."

Sophie scampered off to grab a snack, and Beatrice pointed out people in the crowd.

"There is Adam Jordan, president of club and head judge," she said, directing me to a good-looking man in his late thirties. He was tall and broad with an athletic body.

Adam had a hundred-dollar haircut that showed off his long dark hair. His eyes were a pretty shade of light brown, and he had a great smile.

Beside Adam was a tall, beautiful woman three or four years his junior. She was dressed in a stunning sapphire blue silk dress. It was flattering, showing off her curves without being overly provocative.

"Who's the woman with the judge?" I asked.

"That is Naomi," Beatrice said. "They have been married for almost fifteen years. She used to be model, and now she is hostess for fancy restaurant in downtown Scottsdale."

From how they interacted, they didn't strike me as people with marital problems. It seemed that Adam and his wife were happy with each other.

As the couple worked the room, it was apparent that Adam was quite the politician. He'd greet a group of people, talk with them for twenty or thirty seconds, then skillfully disengage and go to the next group.

Adam seemed to be in his element, clearly enjoying the evening. From what I could tell, the other cake club members seemed to like both Adam and Naomi. The smiles, hugs, and handshakes seemed to be genuine rather than forced.

"There is Kaitlin Kingston, the devil woman," Beatrice hissed as she pointed out an attractive blonde in a low-cut pink dress. Kaitlin appeared to be in her late thirties, had a friendly smile, and seemed somewhat shy as she stood in a loose circle of other women.

Standing next to Kaitlin were a woman and a teenage girl. From their identical colored hair and similar facial features, all three apparently shared the same bloodline.

"Who are the women next to Kaitlin?" I asked. "Are they family?"

"The woman is her baby sister, Shirley," Beatrice said. "The girl is her niece, Beth."

Shirley was a few years younger than her more flamboyant sister. She was pretty but wasn't dressed as overtly sexy as Kaitlin.

Beth looked like a typical bored teenager of fifteen or sixteen years. She was chewing a wad of gum and typing on her phone.

Sophie returned, eating a cupcake with one hand and holding a backup cupcake in the other. From the blissful look on her face, she'd temporarily forgotten about Debbie.

"Well?" I asked. "What do you think?"

"This chocolate one is delicious," she moaned as she finished it. "It melts in your mouth and has tons of flavor without being too much. Honestly, it's as good as any you'd get from Sweet Dee's. And that's my favorite cupcake place in all of Scottsdale."

"That cupcake is one of mine," Beatrice said, a hint of pride in her voice. "Now, try the green one."

Sophie peeled back the wrapper and took a bite of the cupcake with the dark green icing. At first, she chewed enthusiastically, but then her chewing slowed. After a moment, she wrinkled her nose and got a slightly confused look. She then carefully set the uneaten half on the table.

"Well?" I asked.

"Um, it's a little dry," Sophie mumbled, her mouth still full of cupcake. "Like maybe it was in the oven too long. I was expecting it to taste like lime or something, but it's sweet to the point that all I taste is the sugar. It kind of makes the back of my mouth hurt."

"That is cupcake made by Kaitlin," Beatrice said with a touch of snark. "She can't bake, but she always wins."

"This one wins the contest over yours?" Sophie asked as she looked down at the half-eaten green cupcake, her eyebrows raised in surprise. "No wonder you're so pissed."

"What can you tell me about the contest?" I asked Beatrice. "How does it work?"

"Saturday is preliminary round, and anyone can enter. At the end of Saturday, judges will narrow each category down to the top six contestants."

"And when are the finals?" I asked.

"They call it the bake-off, and it is on Tuesday at five. Remaining contestants in each category compete for ribbons and prizes. The winners in each category are then eligible for Best of Group and Best of Show awards."

"Do you get anything if you win?" Sophie asked.

"For Best of Show, you get big ribbon and your picture in Scottsdale paper," Beatrice said. "You also get three hundred dollars. If you win Best of Group, you get ribbon and one hundred dollars."

I looked at my best friend and started to laugh. I tried not to, but I couldn't help it.

"What's so funny?" Sophie asked, narrowing her eyes at me.

I pulled a compact out of my bag and opened it to let

Sophie see herself in the mirror. When she caught a glimpse of her face, she gasped.

"Why are my lips green?" she asked, clearly unhappy.

"Kaitlin uses cheap food coloring rather than natural ingredients," Beatrice said with a grin. "It makes lips and tongue turn green."

Sophie stuck out her tongue and examined it in the mirror. Sure enough, it was bright green.

"I need to try this," I said, picking up the other half of the cupcake and taking a bite from the bottom, avoiding the icing.

As Sophie had said, the cake was dry and tasteless. As I swallowed the disappointing dessert, I hoped it didn't turn anything on me green.

"I'm going to get a drink and try to wash this off my lips," Sophie said with a scowl as she headed toward the bathroom.

Chapter Six

Beatrice returned to her friends while I grabbed two seats near the front. Sophie came back a few minutes later, holding what looked like a margarita and another of Beatrice's cupcakes.

Copies of the rules and schedule of events were available, and I'd grabbed one for each of us. As I flipped through mine, I was somewhat surprised at the number of categories.

The contest was broken into the major groups of cookies, yeast baking, non-yeast breads, muffins-scones, candy, pies, and cakes. They had eight subcategories within the cake group, including chocolate, spice, carrot, yellow, angel, bundt, frosted cupcake, and decorated.

"I wonder how you get to be a judge for the decorated cakes?" Sophie leaned over and whispered to me. "I'd be a kick-ass judge and wouldn't mind spending a couple of days doing nothing but eating birthday cakes. Wedding cakes would be my second choice if they wouldn't let me do birthday cakes."

The meeting started, and Adam quickly hopped onto the stage. He went to the microphone and went through the main points of order. There was a lot of discussion about the final details of the contest on Saturday.

From what I could tell, each baking category would be evaluated by Adam as the lead judge and by two assistant judges. The last part of the meeting was an introduction of the people who would judge the individual groups. In all, there must have been a dozen of them.

After the meeting, I pointed out Adam's wife, Naomi, to Sophie. They were stopping to chat with people but seemed to be making their way to the exit.

"Huh," Sophie said. "It looks like Adam did okay for himself. His wife's a beauty and has that sophisticated look about her. You wouldn't think he'd risk all that simply for a little action on the side."

As they walked to the exit, I saw that Adam and his wife would pass close to Kaitlin. I wanted to see what would happen, and I nudged Sophie to look as well.

When Kaitlin saw Naomi, she walked over and hugged her, which was returned with a warm and friendly smile. After chatting with Kaitlin for about thirty seconds, Adam and his wife continued to stroll to the exit.

Surprisingly, the look on Adam's face never changed. He seemed perfectly happy to have the two women interacting with each other.

What was that all about?

"Um, did that look right to you?" I asked.

"Not really," Sophie said, confused. "I've dated married guys before, and I've never gone up and given any of their wives a friendly hug. Either Kaitlin's a stone-cold bitch, or she's not having sex with Adam."

"Yeah," I pondered. "That's what I'm thinking too."

The meeting broke up a little after nine. I knew Max would be upstairs at his nightly meeting but wouldn't be done for almost an hour.

As the people started to file out of the ballroom, there was a low buzz as everyone chatted excitedly about the contest on Saturday. As we were leaving, we ran into Beatrice.

"Did you find anything suspicious?" Beatrice asked.

"Not yet," I said. "I didn't see anything that shows Kaitlin is involved with the judge, at least not so far."

"I know you will find something," she said, sounding confident. "Those terrible cupcakes winning for five years in a row is not normal."

"Is there a way to find out who won in all the categories over the last few years?" I asked. "Maybe Kaitlin isn't the only one who keeps winning."

"It is all on the cake club website," she said. "I think records go back ten or fifteen years."

I made it back to my apartment about ten. It had seemed like a long day, and I was ready to get some sleep.

I'd brushed my teeth, changed into an oversized T-shirt, and had started eyeing the bed when the theme to *The Love Boat* began playing through my phone.

"Hey, you," I said when I answered. "How was your day?"

"It was good," Max said. "I only had the usual three or four problems over here."

"Have you heard anything from Gabriella yet?" I asked.

"No," he said, sounding serious. "Unfortunately, it's gone past the point of simply being a minor communication issue. Something's happened."

"Are you going out to look for her?"

"I'm on standby," he said, sounding frustrated. "I still need to find out where she is. Your intel pointed her to Sevastopol as a starting point, but I'm not sure where she ended up. I'm calling in a lot of old favors, but it might take me a week or two to get a lead on her trail."

"Let me know what I can do to help," I said.

"Let's talk about something nicer," he said. "How did the meeting go tonight? According to Beatrice, the other woman's cupcakes are terrible."

"Sophie and I shared one tonight," I said with a laugh. "They aren't the best."

"Have you found anything to point to her coercing the judge?"

"Not yet," I admitted. "To be completely honest, the devil woman seems like a nice person."

"Well, I hope you can find out what's going on. Beatrice has been a nervous wreck the past month."

I awoke the following day feeling frustrated. I wasn't getting any closer to finding Morgan's body and wasn't sure what to do next. Add to that, I was getting involved in the cupcake thing, and it also wasn't making any sense.

I got up and made a pot of coffee while I went through everything I had so far on Morgan. From Kelsey's information, her brother had died while traveling in Egypt. This had been verified by at least two government officials.

Morgan's body had then flown to Sky Harbor Airport and had been picked up by the Maricopa County Coroner. The body was transported downtown and tested for diseases.

It was then supposedly delivered to the Scottsdale lab for an autopsy. When it arrived, there was a delay in entering the corpse into the computer system.

When we found a body labeled "Morgan West" in the Scottsdale morgue locker, it was instead a man identified as the "Professor" by Mustafa. None of this seemed to add up.

While going over this in my mind, I made a quick breakfast and ate it on the couch while I watched the local news. Even though I'd already fed Marlowe, he sat beside me and watched closely as I ate.

A little after nine, my phone rang with an unfamiliar local number. When I answered, it was Dr. Wilson, the coroner at the Scottsdale Medical Examiner's office.

"Miss Black," he said. "I promised to keep you informed on the missing body of Morgan West."

"Yes, Dr. Wilson," I said. "What have you found out?"

"I'd rather not do this over the phone," he said. "Would you mind coming into the office?"

"No problem," I said, happy to get some movement to the assignment. "I'll be right there."

I locked the door to my apartment and caught up with Grandpa Bob as he waited for the elevator.

"Hey, neighbor," he said as he turned toward me. "How's the detective business? Nab any bad guys lately?"

"I'm not a detective," I said, explaining my job for probably the fifth time. "I'm an investigator in a law office. You know, like Paul Drake in the old Perry Mason series."

"Oh, sure," he said in a distant voice. "I always watched

that show. Della Street was a real looker. She had a great pair of gams on her. I was always a little jealous of good ol' Perry, having her as his confidential secretary. I always wondered what they did together that she had to keep so confidential." He then chuckled a couple of times to himself at his joke.

The elevator opened, and we stepped inside. As the doors closed, Grandpa Bob turned to me.

"Watch out if you talk with Mary," he said, shaking his head. "She's in a mood today. I'm heading out to the store and waiting until she calms down."

"Really?" I asked, concerned. I'd seldom seen Grandma in anything but a good mood. "What happened?"

"The kids brought over some things from my old apartment last night."

"Is that what upset her?" I asked.

"I think so," he said. "It's hard to tell with women sometimes."

I went down to the parking lot and walked to my Miata. As I was unlocking my car, a tall skinny kid wearing a lightweight Arizona Diamondbacks jacket approached me.

He couldn't have been older than nineteen or twenty. He had long red hair pulled back in a messy man-bun. It looked like he was trying to grow a beard, but so far, all he had were a few scraggly whiskers.

As I was about to ask him what he wanted, he pulled out a black semi-automatic handgun and pointed it at my chest. From the huge opening in the barrel, it had to be a ten-millimeter, if not a forty-five.

Crap, not again.

I looked around the parking lot to see who else was there.

Grandpa Bob had already gotten into his car and was heading out to the street. Other than that, we were utterly alone.

"You need to come with me," the kid said, trying to sound tough. "There's someone who wants to talk with you."

"Who is it?" I asked, not moving.

"You'll find out, soon enough," he said with a smirk.

I could imagine him using the same tone while talking with his buddies in whatever high school he'd recently attended.

"I'm not going anywhere until you tell me who we're meeting with," I said.

"Do you want me to shoot you?" he asked with a nasty gleam in his eye. "Cuz, I'll do it. I've killed people before, you know?"

"If someone sent you to get me, don't you think they'd be upset if you shot me instead?"

I could see his eyes dart back and forth as he tried to come up with an answer. After maybe ten seconds, his shoulders slumped.

"Raymond Eckart," he said with a bit of a pout. "He's the one who wants to talk with you."

Raymond Eckart? Who the hell is that?

"Fine," I said. "How do you want to do this? Are you coming in my car?"

"Of course I am," he sneered. "And I'll have my gun on you the entire time."

"But I imagine you drove here," I said. "And I'm not giving you a ride back."

From the puzzled look on the boy's face, it was apparent he hadn't thought this all the way through.

"Fine," he said. "Follow me in your car. But you'd better stay tight on my ass the entire time. If you try to get away, I'll force your car off the road. I'll shoot you in the leg and then drag you to the meeting."

"You want to give me a hint where we're going?" I asked, ignoring his taunts. "I don't want to lose you in traffic."

"Here," he said with disgust as he pulled a piece of paper from his pocket and handed it to me.

It had an address on North Hayden Road. From the number, I guessed it was one of the big apartment complexes across from either Chaparral or Camelback Parks.

"Okay," I said as I got into my Miata. "Take me to Raymond Eckart."

The boy climbed into a blue Camry rental parked by the dumpsters in the back of my lot. He then led me to Hayden and Camelback. As I suspected, the address was one of the larger apartment complexes along the Greenbelt.

I followed the rental into the parking lot, and the boy got out. He'd put the gun away but was still wearing the jacket. The way his hand was jammed into the pocket left little doubt that he still had the pistol trained on me.

We took an elevator to the seventh floor, and the boy led me to apartment 710. He knocked twice, and a moment later, the door opened.

The man standing before me was not what I expected. In his late fifties, he wore a black three-piece suit and had a dark tan, as if he'd recently been living somewhere sunny.

He had short gray hair and intense hazel eyes. But the thing that most held my attention was his size. He was only about five-eight but must have weighed close to three hundred pounds.

He had a broad, weathered face, and his eyes peered at me with clever intelligence. He looked me up and down, and the corner of his mouth lifted in a slight smile.

The man held out a massive hand as I stepped into the room, the boy trailing behind me. "My name is Raymond Eckart," he said in a commanding voice with a deep British accent. "I don't believe that hiding my identity from someone I'll be working with serves any purpose. Who are you, my dear?"

"Laura Black," I said, shaking the big man's hand, even though he'd had me brought here at gunpoint. "What do you want from me?"

"Very good," Raymond laughed. "Straight to business. I like a woman who can get to the point without having to beat about the bush. As you wish. Have a seat, and we can discuss why you're here."

The big man waved me to a brown couch while he sat in a green upholstered chair. From the sparse and generic furnishings, the apartment seemed to be a short-term rental unit.

On a wooden coffee table between the couch and chair was a tray of oysters on the half shell. I could see that they had been on a bed of ice, but that was now mostly melted.

A third of the oysters had already been eaten, and there were wet spots all over the table from where they had dripped. The seafood was giving the room the pungent odor of the beach at low tide.

The only other thing of note in the room was a well-stocked wet bar. It stood against the far wall near the hallway leading to the back rooms.

Raymond looked at the kid, leaning against the far wall, still glaring at me and trying to look tough. "Owen," he said.

"Prepare two cocktails for myself and our guest."

Raymond then looked at me. "I have all the basics. What would you like?"

"Um, if you don't mind," I said. "I'll make it myself."

"Ah," he said as his face lit up, and he let out a small chuckle. "I see you are a cautious woman. Very good. You realize the world is full of people who would do you harm."

He swept his arm in the direction of the liquor. "Please, be my guest."

I walked to the wet bar and found an unopened bottle of twelve-year-old Macallan scotch. I cracked the seal and poured two fingers into a rocks glass.

A full ice bucket was on the counter, and I used the tongs to drop in an ice cube. I glanced over at Raymond and gave him a questioning look.

"Yes," he said. "That scotch is one of my favorites. But a few more ice cubes, if you'd be so kind."

I handed Raymond his drink, then sat across from him, automatically swirling the glass to mix in the water from the melting ice cube. We each took a sip, and I paused to enjoy the sensations from the scotch as it danced on my tongue and slid down my throat.

I glanced at Raymond. He seemed to be going through the same sort of pleasurable experience.

This doesn't make up for being kidnapped, but that was good.

I was about to take another sip when Raymond reached out and picked up a shell from the tray. As he moved it toward his open mouth, it dripped over the table.

He stuck out his tongue, tilted the shell, and the oyster began to slide into his open mouth. He made a loud slurping sound, and part of the oyster slapped against his chin, dripping juice down his throat.

The stench of the shellfish had already made me a little queasy. Watching Eckart as he sucked the mollusk into his mouth made my stomach twist.

Raymond chewed the oyster twice and then swallowed. His prominent Adam's apple bobbed up and down as he let out a sigh of contentment. He then dabbed a sizeable white linen napkin against his lips and chin.

"Now then," he said as he leaned close to me, smelling like an open can of Marlowe's ocean delight. "What would you say if I told you we are on the trail of more wealth than you can possibly imagine?"

"I'd say I have a pretty good imagination. What exactly are you talking about?"

"Let me tell you a story," he said with a sly sparkle in his eye. "It's a story of a man who keeps showing up in Egypt with ancient golden treasures from the tomb of Men-her Ra."

"And who is Men-her Ra?"

"He was a pharaoh, a king of Egypt during the eighth dynasty, some four thousand years ago."

"This man who keeps appearing with the treasures. Who are we talking about?"

"Ah, for the moment, let's just call him the Professor."

"Okay," I said. "What does this have to do with you?"

"I represent a select group of buyers, some domestic, some foreign, who desire such gold antiquities. When I first met with the Professor, he showed me several of the items he had to offer. Needless to say, I was quite intrigued."

"Did you purchase anything from him?" I asked.

"I did indeed," Eckart said as he held up his index finger. "At a fair price, mind you. The offers I made were actually rather generous considering that the sale of such antiquities is expressly forbidden under Egyptian law."

"If buying and selling the items was illegal, why'd you do it?"

"I'm sorry to say that Egypt isn't as stable as it once was," Raymond said with a touch of melancholy.

"The local authorities have become more concerned with lining their pockets than maintaining public order. It's become a land where every man must fend for himself."

"Okay," I said. "That makes sense. But why are you in Scottsdale? It's a long way from Egypt."

"A fair question," he said with a nod as he picked up a shell from the tray and slurped down another oyster. Rather than chewing, he seemed to swallow it whole.

"I'd planned on purchasing the remainder of the Professor's inventory when a rival of mine decided to take matters into his own hands."

"What did they do?" I asked. The story was starting to fill in some of the puzzle pieces.

"Three of his associates broke into the Professor's apartment in Cairo. From the police reports, the Professor wasn't there, but his partner, a man named Morgan West, was."

"What happened?" I asked, although I could already guess.

"Morgan was murdered," Eckart said as he sipped his scotch. "The Professor and the remainder of his inventory have since disappeared. I can't be sure, but I suspect the Professor is also dead."

"That still doesn't explain what you're doing in Scottsdale."

"The Professor said he was selling the items merely as trinkets to sharpen the appetites of the antiquities buyers in Egypt. He repeatedly claimed to know the whereabouts of the funeral mask of Pharaoh Men-her Ra."

"And that's valuable?"

"As a piece of history, it's beyond price. However, as an artifact, I would estimate it could be sold to the right buyer for over eighty million dollars."

"But if Morgan is dead and the Professor is missing, how do you expect to find it?"

"I won't lie to you, Miss Black. Recent events have made my task all the more difficult. I'm here in Arizona, tracking down a rather obscure lead."

"Really?" I asked as I processed the new information. "What kind of lead?"

"Approximately four months ago, I learned that the Professor gave Morgan a code, let us say, to let him access the rest of the items in his possession, including the Pharaoh's mask."

"Okay," I said, trying to keep up with the story. "You believe Morgan and the Professor had the funeral mask of an ancient pharaoh. You don't know where it is but think it could be obtained with a secret code?"

"Actually, I believe I know the general location where the mask is located," Raymond said with a smirk as he leaned back in his chair and took another sip of his scotch. "But you are essentially correct."

"Is that location something you're willing to share?" I asked.

"At the moment, I believe I'm the only one who possesses that knowledge. I'll need to keep that information to myself, for now."

I briefly wavered on telling Raymond about the switch of the bodies in the morgue but quickly rejected the idea. He was keeping secrets, so I'd keep a few as well.

"If both Morgan and the Professor are dead," I said. "How do you propose to get the code?"

"This is the interesting part of the story," he said, now with a twinkle in his eye. "I have it on good authority that Morgan West had a tattoo of the access code placed on his lower abdomen, in a rather personal area of his body."

"You're serious?" I asked. "Why in the world would he do that?"

"The why of the matter is unknown," Raymond said with a dismissive wave. "However, I can confirm that a good amount of alcohol was involved in the decision."

"But you're sure the tattoo is there? How do you know if you can't see it?"

"A perceptive question," he said with a nod. "I had an informant sitting next to him in the tavern when the idea of the tattoo was proposed. She overheard the scheme for a permanent record of the code to be inked onto Morgan's body."

"If it was that important," I said. "Maybe your spy should have followed Morgan to the tattoo parlor."

"That's precisely what did occur," the big man chuckled. "However, my spy was unable to observe the actual tattooing. Fortunately, I've since had the good luck to interview the tattoo artist. After speaking with her, I'm certain the code is indeed there."

"Did she remember what it was?" I asked. "If she'd

written it down, it would've saved you a lot of work."

Raymond frowned and shook his head. "More's the pity that she didn't have the foresight to record the tattoo. Morgan told her it was merely a cheat code for the video game Skyrim, so she ignored it. However, I've been able to ascertain that the code is fourteen to perhaps eighteen characters long."

"And?" I asked. "What else do you know about it?"

"Ah, you are quite shrewd," he said with a nod as he paused and took another sip of his scotch. "The tattoo artist also remembered that the code begins with thirty-two and solely consists of random numbers, no letters. She also stated that it contains at least one dash and two periods."

"But if Morgan was ever intimate with someone who knew what they were looking for, they'd be able to learn the access code."

"Indeed," he said slowly as he nodded his head. "Those were my thoughts as well. In that regard, I hired a rather attractive young lady to befriend and become intimate with Morgan. I'd hoped she would become acquainted with the areas of his body that are not normally displayed to the public."

"What did she find out?" I asked.

The big man scoffed in annoyance and shook his head. "After they'd spent the first week together, my spy reported that a piece of opaque medical tape had been placed on the area in question. The excuse given was that the tattoo was new and needed to be covered."

"Do you think Morgan knew it was a set-up all along?"

"I can't be certain of anything at this point," he said with a shrug. "I paid my femme fatale a great deal of cash to spend the next month traveling, partying, and having intimate relations with Morgan."

"I assume it didn't work out?" I asked.

"There was a rather unfortunate complication," Raymond said. "It seems that during the month my spy spent with Morgan, she developed feelings of affection, perhaps even love, for him. It seemed to affect her judgment, and Morgan apparently became suspicious that she was indeed after the code."

"What happened then?" I asked.

"Morgan became upset and kicked her out of his apartment. I then tried my deception again with another young lady. Unfortunately, Morgan apparently decided not to be intimate with any other woman unless he could convince himself that the initial encounter was a truly random happenstance."

"So, the Professor disappeared, Morgan was murdered, and you never got the code to tell you how to get the Pharaoh's mask?"

"Yes," Raymond almost spat out the word. "All of this occurred at a most inconvenient time. This isn't the first recent rumor of the existence of the Pharaoh's mask. Excitement about the piece has spread throughout the antiquities community. Several other groups have started to show themselves, and interest in the piece is quite high, especially among the Chinese and the Saudis."

I again thought about telling Raymond about the switch of the bodies at the Scottsdale morgue but decided to hold off. Once he knew Morgan's body was missing, I'd likely lose him as an informant.

"I saw a body labeled as Morgan West in the medical examiner's lab yesterday," I said. "He had what appeared to be a bullet hole in the middle of his chest."

"I'm glad you were able to locate Morgan," the big man said. "As you may know, the body has been missing for several days."

He then leaned forward. His eyes were eager with anticipation. "Did you happen to see the tattoo in question?"

"Not so fast," I said as I held up my hand. "If I did see the tattoo, why should I tell you?"

I saw movement from the back of the room. "Maybe you'd like me to take you into the bedroom back there and beat the information out of you," the kid spat out at me. He hadn't talked since we'd arrived, and I'd almost forgotten he was there.

"Owen," the big man snapped at the boy. "Behave yourself. I'll let you know when the time comes to give someone a beating."

"You'll have to excuse Owen," Raymond said as he turned to me. "He's loyal and quite handsome but somewhat inexperienced in the ways of the world."

The muscles in Owen's jaw bulged, and his face turned red with anger and embarrassment. He didn't say a word, but I could see he was livid with me.

"At this point, we aren't partners," Raymond said. "But it would be mutually beneficial for us to exchange ideas in a matter that concerns us both. Don't you agree?"

I thought about it and nodded my head. "I didn't see the tattoo you're talking about," I admitted. "The coroner only pulled the sheet halfway down."

Raymond's face fell, but instead of being angry, he nodded his head and let out a chuckle. "Yes, I imagine it's not standard practice for the coroner to expose the genitalia of the deceased."

Chapter Seven

After making vague promises to inform each other of our progress in finding Morgan, I left Eckhart's. I then drove to the Scottsdale Airpark and made my way to the Medical Examiner's office. I parked in the now-familiar visitor's parking space and went in.

As expected, the lobby was completely empty except for the clerk. I grabbed a number from the dispenser and walked up to the desk, holding the ticket out so Dolores could see it.

"Fine," she said, seemingly annoyed that I had thwarted her number system. "How can I help you?"

"I'm Laura Black, and I'm here to see Dr. Wilson," I said. "He called me earlier today and asked me to come in."

Dolores eyed me like I was fibbing, but she picked up her phone and punched in a number. "Dr. Wilson," she said, "Laura Black is here to see you."

She listened for a few seconds and hung up. "If you take a seat, he'll be right up."

Dr. Wilson arrived maybe two minutes later. From the look on his face, he seemed anxious.

He led me past the viewing room, which was currently empty, and then through the lab. I was relieved that no one was in the middle of an autopsy.

We went through a side door and ended up in an open area full of cubicles. Dr. Wilson had the only actual office with a door.

We went in, and he offered me a seat. On the wall behind him was a collection of diplomas and medical certifications in fancy wooden frames.

"Thank you for coming in," he began. "I know you're an investigator and have been trying to track down the body of Morgan West. You noticed the age and ethnic discrepancy with the corpse we have, and I thank you for that."

"Is there something new with the search?" I asked.

"We ran the fingerprints of the man we found in the locker. Your initial impression seems to have been correct. It turns out the man's name was Omar Nabil. He's a citizen of the United States."

"I see," I said. "Is there anything else you can tell me about him or Morgan West?"

"I wish I could," Dr. Wilson said, sounding frustrated. "I've been in charge of the lab here for almost a dozen years. This is the first time anything like this has occurred."

"Does anyone have a guess as to how the switch happened? I know you have procedures in place to prevent it."

"So far, everyone's drawn a blank," he confessed. "We've had to report the incident to the state of Arizona. I understand someone in the U.S. government has already contacted the Egyptian consulate to seek an explanation."

"How can I help?" I asked.

"Well," he said. "To be honest, that's why I asked you to come in today. Would you inform me if you uncover anything during your investigations that can point to what happened?"

"Sure," I said. "As long as it doesn't violate my client's privacy, I'll be glad to."

"Thank you," he said, relief in his voice. "I get the feeling the mistake happened before we received the body, perhaps even back in Egypt. But since we were the ones who broke the chain of custody, I imagine that all fingers will point to us."

We started to say our goodbyes when Dr. Wilson's desk phone rang.

"Go ahead and get that," I said. "I'll let myself out."

Dr. Wilson nodded and picked up the phone. I took off and ended up back in the autopsy lab.

The only person there was the goth woman named Cricket. She'd seemed friendly enough the last time I was here, so I decided to ask her some questions.

"Hi," I said as I walked up to her. "I was here the other day asking about the body you found in the locker."

"Oh, sure," she said. "Morgan West. What can I do for you?"

"I thought it was a little weird that the body was in a disused locker, and it wasn't logged in. Has anything else odd happened around here lately?"

"Are you kidding?" she asked with a sparkle in her eyes. "It's a coroner's office. Weird is what makes it fun to work here. Did you have anything specific in mind?"

"I'm not sure," I admitted. "It could be anything."

She shook her head slowly. "Um, the only unusual thing here lately was the creeper in the parking lot."

"What happened with that?" I asked as my investigator radar activated.

"I work late sometimes," she said, getting settled as she began her story. "The dissection lab has a great vibe at night after everyone else goes home. A guy was hanging out in the parking lot about a week ago when I left for the night. He started talking with me when I went out to my car."

"This creeper, what did he want?"

"He asked if I worked with the dead bodies," Cricket said with a lopsided grin and a shake of her head.

"That does seem a little odd," I agreed. "What did you tell him?"

"I said I only moved the corpses around and kept the place clean. If he wanted to ask about what else we do here, he'd need to talk with Dr. Wilson, the coroner."

"What did he say to that?" I asked.

"He said he wanted to look at a corpse in the morgue," Cricket said, chuckling and again shaking her head.

"A dead person in general, or was there a specific body he was interested in?"

"He didn't say which one. But he offered me a thousand dollars to let him examine one of the bodies alone for five minutes."

"Wow, what did you do?"

"I turned him down," she said with an eye roll. "I've worked here long enough to know there's a lot of sickos out there who want to mess with the corpses. A thousand dollars isn't worth my job."

"That sounds kinda creepy," I said. "Did you report it?"

"I told Dr. Wilson about it," she said with a shrug. "I don't know if he reported it to anyone above him yet. We get crackpots here every few months. I think it comes with the job. But the weird thing is the guy was back again last night."

"What did he want this time?"

"It was the same thing. He said there was a body inside, and he wanted to look at it. This time, he said he'd give me two thousand dollars if he could spend five minutes alone with it."

"But he still didn't say which one?"

Cricket shook her head. "No, we didn't get that far. I turned him down again. He didn't like that and seemed like he was getting angry, so I told him that after working hours, the doors to the building lock automatically, and I didn't have a way back into the lab."

"What did the guy look like?" I asked. "Was there anything distinguishing about him?"

"It was a little hard to tell. The sun had gone down, and he was wearing a hoodie and pretty much kept to the shadows. But I could tell he was tall, white, and maybe a little younger than me."

"How old?" I asked. "Any guesses?"

"Um, maybe twenty. I don't think he was too much older than that."

Owen? Someone else?

"Did you see what kind of car he was driving?"

"No," Cricket said with a shake of her head. "I didn't see any other cars in the lot. He must have parked somewhere nearby and walked over."

I pulled out a business card and handed it to her. "Thanks for the story. I'm not sure how, but it likely fits in with everything else happening here. Call me if you remember anything else or if something new happens."

I returned to the office, went in through the back security door, and found Sophie sitting in her cubicle. Her computer monitor showed a live video feed from the pier at Huntington Beach.

"Sophie," I said. "We've got a name to go along with the title of professor."

"What is it?" she asked, sounding annoyed. "I suppose you want me to use the secret software on it?"

"Well, yeah," I said. "Would that be okay?"

"I'm not sure about this," she said. "Ever since we got our visit from the Men in Black, I've been a little creeped out about using the government database."

"But why? They seemed happy with all the great intel you've been able to feed them."

"That's just it," she said, waving her arms up and down. "Now that I'm sure they're keeping track of what I'm doing, I only want to feed them good information."

"Like what?" I asked, confused.

"You know, international terrorists, high-profile drug smugglers, assassins, stuff like that."

"And you don't think a missing body from the coroner counts as a high-profile occurrence?"

"Not hardly," Sophie scoffed. "That's more like telling them how pathetic we are."

"But you've been running these mundane searches along with the high-profile ones ever since you got the software. If you suddenly switched things up, they might suspect something's wrong."

"Well," she wavered. "Maybe you're right. Give me what you have, and I'll see what I can come up with."

"The name is Omar Nabil," I said. "According to Mustafa Yousef, everyone called him the Professor. I did a Google search, and I think he might be a professor of history from Arizona State."

"Anyone else you need me to look up after I get into the secret software?"

"Yeah, we should probably get what we can on Morgan West. I'm not sure how, but he was caught up in something. Our new client, Mustafa Yousef, is also involved. We should figure out how he's tangled up in this."

"I'm going to need to look up how he spells that," Sophie said as she made notes. "Who else?"

"Raymond Eckhart," I said. "He's a criminal, or at least he gives off that feeling. He only seems to be involved with Morgan West from the side, but he's still involved."

"What about the judge from the cake club," she asked. "Adam Jordan?"

"Well, if you don't mind. It would be great to at least get some background information on him.

"Alright," she said. "I'll enter everything I have and let you know as soon as I get anything back."

~~~~

On the way home, I stopped by Filiberto's and got a carne asada burrito and a beef taco. I'd also gotten a bag of warm tortilla chips and munched on them the entire way home.

When I got to my parking lot, I saw Grandma Henderson pulling a bag of groceries from her car. I took the sack from her and walked with her to the elevator.

It seemed like she was quieter than usual. I remembered Grandpa Bob telling me she'd been in a bad mood after his kids had brought over some things.

We paused at Grandma's door as she unlocked it. I followed her in and stopped in my tracks. The living room was stuffed full of furniture and knickknacks.

There was clutter everywhere, with only a narrow path through to the kitchen and the bedroom. I even saw three new pictures hanging on the walls.

Grandma's apartment had always been neat as a pin. I knew when Grandpa Bob moved in, he was only supposed to bring one or two things from where he lived. Looking around the overstuffed living room, I counted at least five new pieces of furniture.

"Wow," I said as I gazed at the mess. "I didn't think Bob was going to bring this much over."

Grandma gave me a look that reminded me of Marlowe when I was late for his breakfast. "He wasn't supposed to bring anything," she said, a touch of hostility in her voice. "He told me his furniture was odds and ends, and he wasn't especially attached to any of it."

"What happened?" I asked.

"It seems like there were several pieces he suddenly couldn't live without."

I made it to the office a little before nine the following morning. Gina pulled into the lot at the same time, and we walked in together.

Since it was Thursday, I knew Lenny would be at his

weekly session with Countess Carla, the Cruel. It always made for a quiet office.

Sophie was sitting in her cubicle, looking like someone had forgotten the toy in their Happy Meal. She looked at us, and I could tell what she was thinking.

"Are you still annoyed about Debbie?" Gina asked. "You've been bugging Lenny to hire someone to take care of the office for years."

"Well, yes," Sophie grumbled. "But I was only looking for someone part-time to do the filing and maybe help stuff envelopes for the billing. You know, like when we had Annie here last summer. I didn't think he'd hire someone to take over everything I do."

"That's true," I said, "I didn't think he'd hire a full-time office manager, but at least this way, you can concentrate on the paralegal side. That part must be nice."

"That's just it," Sophie said, sounding downhearted. "Now that I don't have any distractions, doing the paralegal part doesn't take any time at all. I've spent most of the past couple of days sitting alone back here, playing video games on my tablet."

"At least when we start to get busy again next Thanksgiving, you won't be so overwhelmed," Gina observed.

"Yeah," Sophie mumbled. "You're right. But it sorta feels weird not doing anything. I'm not used to jobs like that."

Gina took off to the front offices, and I sat in my cubicle.

"Hey," Sophie said, perking up. "I got the first results on everybody with the secret software."

"That was quick," I said. "It usually takes you at least a full day to get everything back.

"I know," she said, sounding surprised. "It was freaky fast. I think the government bumped up my priority with the database."

"See, I told you they wouldn't mind you using it. What did you find out?"

"Well, Morgan is pretty much an open book. He went into the Marines after high school and spent six years there. He learned to be a welder somewhere along the way, and he's had several long-term welding jobs over the years. I guess those paid him enough to travel when he wasn't working because he's been all over the world."

"He seems like a normal guy," I said. "Did it show when he left the country and when the body came back?"

"Um," Sophie said as she flipped a couple of pages. "He left the country in early September last year. He's listed as being dead, and the cause was murder. The country of death was Egypt, but no additional information was given. His body came into the country a little over two weeks ago."

"Did you find anything criminal in his background?"

"Some," she said. "But only minor stuff. About the worst was a bar fight a few months after he came back from the Marines. He claimed to be protecting a woman from some ruffians and only got a slap on the wrist."

"What about the Professor?"

"According to the database, Omar Nabil really *was* a history professor at Arizona State here in Tempe. He specialized in the history of Arizona and the Southwest U.S. He's currently listed as being on an extended sabbatical. According to the software, he's been in and out of Egypt several times over the last two years. He last entered Egypt in July and left almost three weeks ago. After that, he seems to have disappeared."

"They don't have anything about him being dead?"

"Nope," Sophie said. "I imagine it's going to shock some people at the university when they find out."

"And our latest client, Mustafa Yousef? What about him?"

"He's more interesting. He's actually *Doctor* Yousef. He has a Ph.D. in art history from Cairo University and is listed as working for the Government of Egypt."

"Seriously?" I asked. "Does it say what he does there?"

"It says he works for the Ministry of Tourism."

"Huh," I said. "It sounds like that's a cover for what he's really up to."

"The shady one is Raymond Eckart," Sophie said. "The database lists him as an art dealer with ties to the black market and criminal underworld. He's wealthy and owns two houses in Egypt and one on the French Riviera. He's also been in prison twice for smuggling. I'd be careful with him."

"I think I'll need to be careful with all of them. What did you get on Adam Jordan?"

"He seems completely normal," Sophie said, sounding a little disappointed. "No arrests and never got into trouble at school. He comes from money, has political aspirations, and is listed on the ballot for the next Scottsdale city council election. Lenny probably knows him, so try not to piss him off."

I sat in my cubicle for the rest of the morning, going over the secret software printouts. Although the reports went into a lot of detail, I couldn't find anything that got me closer to finding out what was going on.

Chapter Eight

After lunch, I went up to check on Debbie and make sure she didn't have any questions. I had to stop and look around when I got to the front.

The entire reception area was spotless. All of the stacks of file folders had been put away. I looked into the conference room, and those files were gone as well.

"Wow," I said. "It looks great up here. It didn't take you long to straighten everything up."

"I don't mind filing," she said. "I'll probably spend the rest of the week organizing the file cabinets. Some folders were logged by case number, some by date, and others by client name. But I'll get everything into shape in a few days."

"It looks like you have everything handled up here," I said. "But let me know if I can help you with anything."

"Well, there is one thing I wanted to ask you about," Debbie said. "Leonard has a standing appointment on his calendar every Thursday morning. I know he's golfing, but when I asked if I needed to confirm his tee time, he told me not to worry about it."

"Yeah, Lenny takes his weekly golf appointments pretty seriously, so I'd avoid scheduling anything that interferes with that. You also probably shouldn't schedule anything for an hour or two after he gets back. Golf tends to tire Lenny out."

I was walking to the back offices when my phone rang with an unfamiliar local number. Hoping for a bit of luck, I hit the accept button.

"Hey, Laura," a pleasant woman's voice called out when I answered. "It's Cricket, from the MEs office."

"Hi, Cricket," I said, adding her as a contact. "What's going on?"

"You asked me to let you know if anything unusual happened. Well, the creeper was over here again. He was talking with Brian in the parking lot before lunch."

I remembered Brian. He was the disheveled tech in the dirty lab coat who'd forgotten to log the body of Professor Nabil into the computer.

"Do you think the creeper convinced Brian to let him in to look at the body?" I asked.

"I questioned Brian about it a few minutes ago," Cricket said. "He said he turned the guy down, but I get the feeling he'll let him in later tonight to do whatever he wants to do. Brian's always broke, and two thousand dollars might be more cash than he can resist."

"Are you going to tell Dr. Wilson about what Brian is doing?" I asked.

"No, probably not," she sighed. "Brian's sort of a basket case, but I've known his sister for years. I was the one who got him a job over here in the first place, and I sorta feel responsible for him. Honestly, I always try to keep an eye on him so he isn't able to mess anything up too badly."

"Any idea when they'd planned to meet?" I was already forming plans in my head.

"No, but Brian knows both Dr. Wilson and I sometimes

stay here until about seven. I imagine it would likely be sometime after that."

I thought about it and then had another question. "What kind of car does Brian drive?"

"He has an old Ford Escort," she laughed. "I'm surprised it still runs. Is that important?"

"I might be over there later tonight," I replied. "If so, it would be good to know if Brian is still in the building."

"Right, okay," Cricket said. "That makes sense. Hey, do me a favor."

"Sure, what can I do?"

"If you find out what's going on over here, would you let me know? Not just because of Brian. This feels a little strange, even for a Medical Examiner's office."

"No problem. I'll call you first thing in the morning to let you know what I saw."

"Good luck," she said. "I'll let you know if I hear anything else."

I had some time before I needed to head up to the autopsy lab, so I got on the internet and looked up the rules for shipping a dead body back to the U.S. I quickly found about a dozen documents on the subject, but none of them gave me any new insights into what could have happened to Morgan.

I then looked up some articles on black market sales of antiquities in Egypt. From what I read, it was still possible to go out to the old burial sites in the Egyptian deserts and find objects that were good enough to be sold.

This practice apparently still went on, even though it was strictly prohibited. You'd be looking at stiff fines and extended prison time if you got caught.

I hopped into my Miata, lowered the top, and headed up Scottsdale Road to the Airpark. It was about a quarter to seven when I got to the Greenway-Hayden loop, and most of the businesses in the area had closed for the day.

I spent a few minutes driving around, looking for the best location. I needed somewhere I could see the vehicles at the Medical Examiner's building but not be so close as to be obvious about it.

I ended up parking in an empty lot of a cable company's office, across the street from the county lab. The only car in the lot of the Coroner's office was a high-end black BMW convertible, and I assumed Dr. Wilson was working late.

The sun had dipped below the horizon a few minutes before I'd arrived, and I parked facing west. As I started my stake-out, I enjoyed the daily light show of an Arizona sunset.

I turned on the sound system and softly played some old Rolling Stones tunes. I munched on a bag of chips and sipped on a Diet Pepsi as the sky to the west exploded with shimmering reds, yellows, and oranges.

A few minutes after seven, I saw movement in the laboratory parking lot. But rather than Dr. Wilson, the black-clad figure of Cricket strolled out of the building.

Standing next to the BMW, she looked around at the businesses on the street. Her eyes came to rest on me, and she waved.

Climbing into her car, Cricket started the motor and lowered the top. I then watched as she adjusted some controls on the dashboard, still somewhat surprised that she owned such an expensive mode of transportation.

The convertible began to move and smoothly pulled out to the street. Rather than take off, Cricket drove into the lot where I was parked.

She pulled in next to me with the nose of her car facing the back of mine. I rolled down my window, and we could easily talk without having to get out.

"Hi, Cricket," I said. "I love your car."

"Thanks," she said. "It's fun to drive, but the insurance payments are a bitch. Yours is pretty, too."

"I got it a few months ago, and I love driving it," I said. "Have you heard anything more about tonight?"

"Not a thing," she said with a shake of her head. "It's been quiet in the lab today. Brian took off about two hours ago, and Dr. Wilson was in meetings in the downtown office all afternoon. As far as I know, if something's going to happen, it'll happen tonight."

"Thanks for the tip," I said. "I'm hoping to learn who else is interested in Morgan West. I'll let you know if anything unusual occurs."

"Good luck," she said with a wave as she took off.

Cricket pulled the convertible back onto the road. There was the sound of a powerful engine revving, and the sports car sped down the street, quickly disappearing from view.

Nothing happened at the Medical Examiner's office for the next three hours. After rocking with the Rolling Stones, I switched the music to the Talking Heads. After listening to two of their albums, I decided on some Taylor Swift.

A little after ten, I needed a bathroom break. Fortunately, there was a nice Shell gas station a few blocks away on Scottsdale Road, just south of the old CrackerJax. While there, I grabbed a slice of pepperoni and sausage pizza along with a fresh soda.

When I returned to my surveillance spot, a beat-up Ford Escort with faded silver paint was parked next to the back loading dock at the lab. From what Cricket had told me earlier, the vehicle belonged to Brian.

As I munched the pizza and sipped on the Diet Pepsi, a white panel van pulled into the lot and parked by the back entrance. Unfortunately, I was at a slightly bad angle and couldn't see who had gotten out of the vehicle.

I was somewhat taken aback by having a van arrive. I'd assumed whoever showed up would only want pictures of Morgan West's body. However, the presence of such a large vehicle indicated that they possibly wanted to take the corpse.

I got out and locked the Miata. I slipped my purse strap over my head, letting my bag sit nicely against my hip. Sliding my phone into the back pocket of my navy blue capris, I hurried across the deserted street.

When I arrived at the Medical Examiner's office, there wasn't a lot of landscaping to hide me. Fortunately, the moon hadn't yet climbed into the sky, and the streetlights along this part of the Airpark were widely spaced, casting several shadows near the buildings.

I pressed my body against a wall to be as invisible as possible. I then crept carefully around to get a better look at the loading dock.

From what I could tell, both vehicles in the lot were unoccupied. I used my camera to take pictures of the license plates, then slipped the phone back into my pants pocket.

As I glanced at the dock, I could see that the back door had been propped ajar by a cinderblock. Since the bad guys were apparently still inside, I took the open door as an invitation.

I casually strolled to the back entrance and stood against the building. I couldn't hear any voices, so I thought I'd try my luck and enter.

Easing open the heavy security door, I peered inside the building. All I could see was a wide hallway. The walls were covered in the same cream-colored tiles as the central dissection lab.

As I stepped inside and closed the door, the only illumination was from a couple of exit signs and some medical equipment that had been left powered up for the night. I heard voices coming from the direction of the autopsy room and carefully made my way toward the sound.

As I approached the lab, I could hear two people having a loud discussion. One sounded like Brian, and with the heavy English accent, I immediately recognized the second voice.

I reached a pair of large swinging doors that led into the dissection room. Each had a small window, and I was able to peer inside.

Brian and Raymond Eckart were standing in front of the racks of morgue lockers. They weren't actively arguing, but their voices were raised in frustration.

The vault containing the body of Professor Nabil was open, and the sliding metal tray holding the corpse had been pulled all the way out. The sheet covering the remains had been removed and was lying on the floor.

Next to the open morgue locker was a stainless-steel trolley table. Since its only function was to move corpses from one place to another, it appeared that Eckart had wanted to take the body out of the lab rather than simply take pictures of it.

The Professor's nude body looked waxy and somewhat yellow in the lab's fluorescent lighting. Even from across the room, I could see the bullet hole in the center of his chest.

"Look," Brian explained to Eckart as he pointed to the corpse's toe tag. "This is Morgan West. It says so right here."

"I don't care what the bloody tag says," Eckart barked out. "I know what Morgan looks like, and this isn't him. You'd better come up with the right body, and I mean now."

Since I knew they wouldn't be able to resolve the problem, I quickly formed a new plan. As I did, I started to back up slowly.

I'd go to the parking lot, get in my car, and wait for the van to leave. When it took off, I'd follow it to wherever Eckart ended up. I doubted he'd take the corpse back to the apartment. With any luck, it would open up a new avenue to finding Morgan's body.

Once I had that, I could relay the information to the police. They could then follow up on any crimes Eckart had committed.

I turned to go down the hallway when I saw the outline of a man standing directly behind me. He was in the shadows, but the size and shape of his body left little doubt about who it was.

"What the hell?" Owen growled out.

Crap.

With a sudden rush of panic, escape became my new goal. Knowing I had to get away from Owen, I pulled back my foot to give him a hard kick.

If I could connect with his knee, I could outrun him as I sprinted across the street. With enough of a lead, I shouldn't have any trouble getting to my car and taking off before he could reach me.

There was a sudden swinging movement from the shadows, and something hard cracked against the side of my head. My world became a sudden swirl of flashing lights and pain.

I tried to kick out, knowing it would be my one chance to escape, but bright lights flashed before my face, and darkness closed over me. I felt myself going down, but for some reason, I didn't remember hitting the floor.

When I woke up, I was somewhere dark and cold. The side of my head pounded from where my assailant had struck me, and it hurt to the point of making me nauseous.

The night had been relatively warm, and I'd only worn the capris and a stretchy-cotton T-shirt. As I lay in the chilly darkness, I wished I had chosen something warmer.

I was lying on my back on something hard. My first thought was that I had been left on the floor in a dark room.

I carefully reached out and felt around on my left side. My hand came against a cold, smooth barrier about a foot from my body.

Jeez, they must have dumped me against a wall.

But when I rolled to get away from the chilly surface, I found another wall about six inches from my right shoulder.

Damn it. Where did they put me?

I seemed to have walls on either side and moaned in

frustration. It was only then that I had a terrible thought.

With a sudden jolt of panic, I lifted my hand straight up. Less than a foot above me was another cold, smooth surface.

Oh no!

As I felt around at the sides and top of my chamber, I found similar smooth walls at my feet and above my head. I then started to recognize the pungent aroma that was a cross between rotten meat and a high school biology class.

That, more than anything else, let me know where I was. After knocking me out, they must have stuffed me into one of the mortuary vaults in the autopsy lab.

In a total panic, I pushed on the top and sides of my enclosure. The stainless-steel panels were cold, smooth, and completely unyielding.

I felt around on the locker door. Unfortunately, the exit was tightly locked, and I didn't feel any type of emergency release latch.

With a fresh wave of fear, I realized there was no reason they had placed me into the locker legs first. If the bad guys had stuffed me into the vault by my head, the door to escape would be at my feet.

I wondered if there was enough room to turn around so I could search the far end of the enclosure. I twisted my body and tried to reposition myself with my head where my feet were.

It was a tight fit, but I thought I could make it. Unfortunately, I became stuck halfway through the turn.

Shit.

Unreasoning claustrophobic panic hit me. Not only was I locked in a mortuary locker, but I was now bent over double, twisted like a pretzel, unable to move.

I lay like that for maybe two or three minutes, shivering with the cold, trying to calm myself. But my leg muscles were already tight from not moving, and I knew they'd soon start to cramp.

How did this happen? I asked myself. *I was only helping a client find a missing dead body.*

I did my best to relax, then carefully thought through all the steps I had taken to get myself into this position. Working backward, I started to push on the sides of the box.

My hands were slick with panic sweat, and getting traction on the slippery steel surface was difficult. At first, nothing happened as I tried to free myself, but after a minute or two of pushing on the walls, I felt myself begin to slide slowly.

I took a deep breath and pushed again. It was only through straining and twisting as hard as I could, along with a blind determination, that I was able to get myself loose.

Once I was free, I rotated myself back to my original position, flopping back on the metal tray. My heart pounded with terror as I tried to calm myself.

Wow, I won't do that again.

I lay where I was for maybe five minutes, chiding myself for being so stupid. The only positive was that the locker, which had felt so small at first, now seemed somewhat roomy compared to being unable to move.

Since I couldn't use my hands, I felt around with my feet against the far wall. I made sure to search the entire surface but didn't find any sort of release latch to help me open my prison cell.

As I lay shivering in the darkness, I thought back to the last time I'd found myself in a similar situation. That was when I'd been locked in the trunk of my old Honda, left for dead on the side of the road.

The issue then had been the summer temperatures. I'd passed out from heatstroke after notifying the police that I was trapped, and it was only good luck I'd been rescued before I died.

As I thought about how I'd called the police back then, a feeling of relief swept over me. I'd put my phone in my back pocket before entering the building. I could use it to call for help.

I reached around to the back of my capris, and my heart skipped a beat. My phone wasn't there. I quickly searched my other pockets, thinking maybe I'd somehow switched it, but it was gone.

When the guys were busy stuffing me into the vault, one of them must have noticed the phone. I again patted my pockets down in case I'd somehow missed the mobile the first time around.

Unfortunately, all I found was the key fob to the Miata. It was in my front pocket, and the guys must not have cared about me having that.

I experienced a slight spark of hope when I felt the tiny plastic flashlight that I'd attached to the fob. Finding the button, I switched it on.

As soon as I saw where I was, I regretted using the light. Until now, I hadn't fully comprehended how dire my situation was.

I was in a stainless-steel box, seven feet long by three feet wide. The ceiling was a claustrophobic-inducing ten or twelve inches above me. Now that I had a visual image, I couldn't shake the feeling of being buried deep underground in a shiny metal coffin.

Using the light, I examined the wall beyond my feet, then

carefully twisted around to look at the panel above my head. As I feared, there were no emergency latches for me to unlock the door from the inside.

I didn't have a watch and had no idea what time it was. My shivering had gotten worse, my teeth chattering against each other.

I didn't know how much air was in one of these lockers, but I remembered seeing a rubber seal on the door, meaning they were likely airtight. Even a best-case scenario would only give me a few hours before I suffocated.

I lay in my cell, and a feeling of desperation washed over me. It was at this point that I again started to panic and hyperventilate. I yelled for help, hoping someone friendly would come to my rescue.

Since I didn't know if I'd been placed in the locker with my head or my feet pointing toward the autopsy room, I had no idea which way to pound. I ended up hitting with my hands and kicking with my feet.

After three or four minutes of kicking and pounding, I realized I wasn't making enough noise for anyone in the lab to hear me. With a sudden inspiration, I pushed the silver button on the fob and slid out the metal car key.

I experimentally tapped it against the wall. The sound still wasn't all that loud, but it made more noise than hitting the wall with my fist.

While yelling for help, I hit the key against the panel above my head and kicked the end wall below my feet. After fifteen or twenty minutes of doing this, I was exhausted, and my throat was raw.

Not wanting to run down the battery, I turned off the flashlight. My head spun from the physical exertion, and the pain radiating from the point of impact on my skull steadily grew.

I'd been shivering, but between the panic and the kicking, I'd warmed up. Unfortunately, as I lay on the metal tray panting and scared, I started to shiver again.

I lay in the freezing darkness for what felt like two or three hours. The pain in my head continued to make me nauseous, and it was only through a focused determination that I didn't throw up.

Every fifteen or twenty minutes, I'd tap the metal key against the panel above my head thirty or forty times. I hoped it would be loud enough for anyone in the lab to hear.

I didn't think I'd ever been this cold, not even during my recent visit to the rooftop in Vail. This was even though I'd only been dressed in a bikini on that occasion, and the temperature had been in the single digits. Add to that, it had been snowing.

But my suffering on the roof had been short, and I'd soon found myself in a deliciously warm hot tub with Max. We'd sipped champagne and felt toasty, even as large snowflakes fell on our heads. That was a happy memory that I tried to focus on.

I wasn't sure how long I lay in the morgue locker, but the air was becoming stuffy and stale. I felt my lungs starting to tighten, and I found that I was beginning to pant like a dog.

I willed myself to stay awake but could feel my eyes getting heavy. Finally, in the cold darkness of the vault, I passed out.

Chapter Nine

When I regained consciousness, it took me a second to remember where I was. But the darkness and biting cold soon refreshed my memory.

I had curled into the fetal position and shivered uncontrollably. I felt a burning numbness in my arms and legs and was panting like I'd just run a race.

I'd lost all sense of time. In the quiet darkness, I felt like I was floating.

I groped around on the cold stainless-steel tray until I found the metal car key, then used it to hit the panel above my head. I also kicked out at the end of the box.

I'd already gotten blisters on my fingers from holding the key as I banged on the wall, but it didn't concern me at this point. I tried to call for help, but my voice was raspy and ineffective.

In my weakened state, I wasn't making a lot of noise. But I knew I had to keep trying until I passed out again, likely for the last time.

After ten minutes of signaling, the air was pretty much gone. I felt my heart racing, and my mouth was wide open. I frantically gulped at whatever remaining oxygen was still in the vault, like a fish tossed on a riverbank.

As I started to fade out, I wondered if I should scratch

out some final message to Max with the key. Maybe if I etched a heart in the stainless steel, he'd know it was for him.

There was a loud metallic sound and a sudden bright light. I felt a gust of warm air as the door above my head swung open.

I instinctively sucked in a deep lungful of the deliciously warm air. I let it out but quickly drew in another breath. After two or three more gulps of air, I felt my chest begin to relax, and my numb limbs started to tingle.

The sense of relief that swept over me was more than I could handle, and I started to laugh. I'm sure I sounded a little insane, but I couldn't stop the emotions from coming out.

The drawer slid out, and I found myself looking up at the face of Cricket. Her expression was a mix of amusement and concern.

"Laura?" she asked. "How in the world did you get in there?"

"Long story," I croaked out, squinting in the bright light. "Let me lay here for a minute. What time is it?"

"It's not even seven," Cricket said with a shake of her head. "I came in early to make sure nothing unseemly had happened here last night. It's a good thing I did. There isn't a lot of air in these lockers, and there's no way to open them from the inside."

"Yeah," I said weakly as I reached up to touch the lump on the side of my head. "I learned all about that."

"I found your purse and your phone in a trash can. I was

about to call the police when I heard you tapping."

My shivering gradually slowed, and I'd more or less regained feeling in my arms and legs. Cricket helped me off the stainless-steel tray.

I tried to stand, but my legs were still weak and trembling. I made my way to a chair and sat, grateful to feel warm and be able to breathe again.

"Are you going to tell me how you got in there?" Cricket asked as she brought me a bottle of water.

"Brian and a white panel van showed up in the parking lot last night, and the back door on the loading dock was propped open," I said in my raspy voice as I sipped. The water seemed to help with my sore throat. "I went inside and heard Brian quarreling with another man."

"Any idea what they were arguing about?" Cricket asked, her curiosity activated.

"The other man asked Brian where Morgan West's body was, and Brian told him it was the corpse in the locker and was pointing to the name on the toe tag. Apparently, it was the wrong answer because the man started making threats."

"It doesn't sound like Brian's going to get the money they promised him," Cricket observed. "I hope he's okay."

"I'd seen enough and was backing up to leave when, um, someone hit me on the head. When I woke up, I'd been stuffed in the locker."

"Wow, and I thought *my* job was unusual," Cricket laughed. "That's some kind of weird career you have. Maybe you could tell me more about it sometime."

"Did you see anything out of place when you came in?" I asked. "They were looking for Morgan, but they might have also been searching for something else."

"The only thing messed up here is you," Cricket laughed. "You were in the locker where Morgan West was being stored."

Gross.

"Okay," I thought out loud. "But if I was in the locker, where's the body?"

"That's a good question," Cricket said, frowning. "If they had the drawer open when you saw them arguing, I'd say they most likely snatched the corpse. They left one of our trollies next to the back door. That would make sense if they wheeled out a cadaver last night."

Maybe they put him in another one of the lockers?" I asked. I didn't think they had gone to the trouble, but it was probably worth checking.

"Sure. I'll look through the other vaults," Cricket said. "But I'd be surprised if the remains are still here."

I continued to sit and sip the water as Cricket opened each of the lockers. She checked all of the toe tags against a list she had on a clipboard.

She then searched the viewing room and the rest of the lab. When she returned, she verified that only the body labeled as Morgan West was missing.

"I'm going to have to call Dr. Wilson and let him know what happened last night," Cricket sighed. "He's likely driving in now, but he might need to inform the authorities."

"Yeah, you probably should," I agreed. "But, if you can avoid mentioning my involvement, I'd appreciate it."

"Don't worry," she said with a knowing nod as she handed back my purse and phone. "I don't think you're the bad guy in this, and I'm not someone who willingly spills other people's business to the police."

"Thanks," I said, knowing I'd likely dodged another bullet. "Would you let me know what happens? Also, give me a call if something else comes up."

"Will do," she said with a slight smile.

It was a beautiful Arizona morning when I walked out the back door of the Medical Examiner's office. The sun had climbed over the horizon, and the birds were still in the middle of their morning chorus.

I crossed the street to where I'd parked the Miata. Pulling the key fob out of my pocket, I used it to pop open the trunk.

I was about to return the fob when I saw the tiny flashlight. It was only a cheap plastic thing, but it certainly had proven to be helpful.

From the trunk, I grabbed an oversized sweater that I kept for situations like this. I was feeling more than a little grungy after rolling around in a mortuary locker all night. I didn't want to risk getting anything nasty on my car seat.

When I sat, the first thing I did was grab a bottle of hand sanitizer, squirt a glob of it in my palm, and rub it around. I ended up doing this twice before I felt clean enough to touch my steering wheel.

When I got to the office, Sophie must have just arrived. She was sipping a doughnut shop coffee in her cubicle and reading the Southern California Surfline reports on her tablet.

She was squirming and wiggling in her chair. After several moments of this, she reached underneath the seat and twisted one of the knobs. She paused for a moment, then began to wiggle again.

"What are you doing?" I rasped out at her.

"I can't stand the chairs we have back here," she grumbled. "When I came in this morning, I traded the chair from my cubicle for my old chair from reception."

"So, what's wrong?"

"Debbie's already adjusted it. It's taken me years to get it right, and now everything's messed up."

I glanced at the breakroom table and saw she'd brought in a box of pastries. I opened the fridge, took out a Diet Pepsi, and grabbed a chocolate doughnut.

I set everything down, then flopped onto the chair in my cubicle. Pulling open my desk drawer, I grabbed a bottle of Advil and shook out a couple of tablets.

I tossed back the pills, washed them down with Diet Pepsi, and then attacked the doughnut. I didn't realize how hungry I was until I'd taken the first bite.

As I stuffed the food into my face, Sophie looked at me with concern.

"Wha?" I mumbled as I lifted both hands, my mouth full of doughnut.

"Um, is it me, or do your hair and makeup look a little different today? And isn't that the same shirt you were wearing yesterday?"

"Yeah," I croaked as I got up to snag another doughnut. "I had a shitty night last night. I'm going to head home in a few minutes and get cleaned up."

"Really?" she asked, sitting up straighter and getting a gleam in her eye. "What happened this time? Weren't you supposed to go to the coroner's office and find out who was looking for Morgan West?"

"Owen was there, along with Raymond Eckart," I said as

I shoved the last of the doughnut into my mouth. "They had the body of Professor Nabil pulled out from his locker and were arguing about whether it was Morgan or not."

"Nobody had told them the body there wasn't Morgan's?" Sophie asked, her tone implying that the people in the lab weren't very bright.

"It doesn't seem like it," I said with a slight smile. "Owen then snuck up behind me and hit me in the head."

"You got whacked in the head again? Seriously? Did you get a concussion this time?"

"Maybe," I admitted. "But when I woke up, I discovered they'd stuffed me into the mortuary locker. I didn't have my phone and was trapped until Cricket, one of the lab techs, let me out this morning. There wasn't a lot of air in the vault, and it turned out to be a close call."

"Are you planning on going to a doctor this time?" Sophie asked, giving me a look. "You've been knocked in the skull like half a dozen times by now. You probably have some kind of funky brain damage thing going on."

"I hadn't planned on it," I said with a shrug. "But if I start to feel dizzy or anything, I'll make an appointment."

Sophie gave me a look that let me know she thought I was nuts.

"Fine," I said. "Keep an eye on me, and if I start acting strange, let me know. I'll go in and have myself looked at."

Sophie barked out a laugh. "And how would I know brain-damage strange from your normal day-to-day strange?"

"I don't know. If I stare into space and start drooling or something like that."

"Um, did they put you in the same locker where Professor Nabil was stored?" Sophie asked, a look of concern on her face.

"Yeah, it smelled like a trash dumpster in there."

"And that's what you were wearing while you were in there?" she asked, pointing to my shirt.

"Yeah, the vault was as cold as a refrigerator, and I wished I'd worn some long sleeves."

"But they didn't clean the locker before they shoved you in?" Sophie asked, with a look of growing shock.

"The bad guys were leaving me there to die," I said. "Why would they clean it before they stuffed me in?"

"Um, because the Professor had a bullet hole in him," Sophie said, now with a look of disgust. "His juices had been dripping out of him for days. Were you rolling around in that all night?"

"Um, probably," I said with a shrug. "I ended up with something sticky on my shirt. But at the time, I was more worried about dying than what I was lying in."

Sophie scrunched up her face and started to make gagging noises. For a moment, I thought she was going to throw up.

"Jeez," she said when she regained her composure. "You know, if I were you, I'd take a couple of long hot showers as soon as I got home. I'd also toss that shirt in the trash, and probably the sweater too. I don't know if they make a detergent strong enough to get out death juices."

As Sophie said this, I looked down at my shirt. Now that I thought about it, I did faintly catch the scent of the autopsy lab. The more I thought about it, the more intense the aroma became.

"You're right," I said with a sigh. "I guess I'm still a little groggy. I'll head home and get cleaned up. It's been a long crappy night. A shower and a change of clothes would likely do me a world of good."

I drove home and peeled off my outfit. My sweater wasn't so bad, but the back of my shirt was discolored with a pale pink stain.

I held it up to my nose to take a sniff and got the pungent aroma of the autopsy lab. This made my stomach twist, and I decided not to think about what I'd been rolling in all night.

I folded the shirt and laid it in the trash can. I had liked the top, and it looked good on me. It was a shame to see it go, but Sophie had been right. Wearing it again would gross me out, no matter how many times I washed it.

I tossed the sweater in the laundry and then climbed into the shower. The hot water felt great and helped me get ready for the rest of the day.

I'd finished getting dressed when my phone rang with the number I now recognized as belonging to the Scottsdale Medical Examiner's office. When I answered, it was Dr. Wilson.

"Miss Black," he said. "We had a break-in last night. The body of Professor Nabil is missing."

"Missing?" I asked, trying to sound surprised. "As in, somebody stole the body?"

"I'm afraid that's what it looks like," he admitted.

"Any idea how they managed to get through the door? Did they use a crowbar to jimmy it open?"

"Um, no," Dr. Wilson said, sounding embarrassed. "They used an active keycard."

"Seriously?" I asked. "Whose card did they use?"

"It belonged to one of the technicians who works here, Brian McCoy."

"What did Brian say about it?" I asked. "Did he lose his card, or do you think he was one of the men who stole the body?"

"I can't answer that yet," he said. "Brian didn't come in today."

"When was the last time anyone saw him?"

"Brian was at work yesterday. After that, he seems to have disappeared."

Something about the break-in had been bugging me, and I used this as an opportunity to ask Dr. Wilson.

"I have sort of a weird question about Brian. Do you think he knew that the body in the lab wasn't Morgan West but was instead Professor Nabil?"

Dr. Wilson paused as he considered my question. "No, I didn't specifically tell him. Honestly, I've been trying to keep the incident at a lower profile until we could explain how it happened."

"So, if Brian had been a willing participant in the break-in, is it possible he still believed the body in the locker was Morgan?"

Dr. Wilson again paused. "I'd say it was probable. When the break-in occurred, I'd just gotten the results of the fingerprints on the corpse. Other than my superiors and yourself, I haven't had time to discuss it internally with the staff."

I disconnected, and the phone rang maybe ten seconds later. I looked at the readout, thinking Dr. Wilson was calling me back, but the caller-ID was *Unknown.*

When I answered, there was a distant scratchy noise on the line. Wherever the call was coming from, it was a long way away.

"Laura?" a woman's voice asked.

It took me a second to place who it was. "Gabriella?" I asked, now concerned. "Is that you?"

"I might need sister," she said in her flat, steady tone.

"You need your sister?" I asked, confused.

"No. I might need you to come to Sevastopol and pretend to be my sister."

"Wait a minute," I said, my thoughts swirling. "Sevastopol is in Crimea. Right? That's where Viktor is, and it's not the most peaceful part of the world."

"No, it is disputed territory. Very dangerous."

Wow, what can I even say to something like that?

"Would it make more sense for Max to come and get you?" I asked. "He's good at rescues."

"Unfortunately, no," Gabriella said. "When he was Agent Kingfisher, Max and his team killed some members of the group here. There is still much bad blood between them."

"But that was like a dozen years ago," I insisted.

"They have long memories. I think I have good escape plan and should be okay. But if not, they will only allow family to come and get me."

"You know we don't look anything alike, don't you?"

"You can be step-sister, from Switzerland. That will be good enough."

I took a deep breath and tried to slow my heart rate. "Okay," I said. "Let me know what I need to do, and I'll be there."

"I won't know for three or four days," she said, and I heard her suck in a breath as if she were in pain. "But I send you what you need. Just in case."

"I'll be ready," I said. "Um, Gabriella, are you alright?"

"I was shot and blown up a little," she said. "But it's not so bad. I still have friends here, and they take care of me. Keep your phone on for the next week. I might call at any time."

"I'll be here," I said as the line went dead.

I made it back to the office a little after eleven. Sophie was still in her cubicle and looked at my new outfit with approval.

"Did you toss everything, or are you going to try to save the sweater?" she asked, genuinely concerned.

"I ended up tossing the shirt," I admitted. "But I'll keep the sweater. I keep it in the trunk for emergencies, so it doesn't matter as much."

"I guess," she said with a shrug. "But that's still pretty gross. It would need to be a serious emergency for me to wear that. Oh, you got a FedEx. It's on your desk."

I picked up the cardboard envelope and looked at the sender's address. Unfortunately, it only listed an account number.

"I'm about ready for lunch," Sophie said as I tore open the envelope. "Do you mind if Debbie comes along? I kinda felt bad about stealing her chair and already asked her."

I saw several things in the envelope and shook them onto my desk. Sophie watched what I was doing, and her eyes grew big.

"What the hell is all that?" she asked.

On a pile on my desk were several stacks of money. As I looked through it, some were European Euros, some were US dollars, and some were Russian Rubles. There was also a bright red passport, a plastic photocard, and several folded pieces of paper stapled together.

Sophie reached over to my desk, picked up a stack of 50-Euro notes, and used her thumb to fan through them. "Why did someone send you a pile of foreign money?"

I wasn't so concerned about the money. What had my attention were the other items. When I picked up the card, it looked like a driver's license and had *Swiss Identity Card* written across the top in five languages.

Oh, crap.

On the front of the card was my picture and my birthday. The name on the document was Laura Krovopüskov. I turned it over, and it looked very official.

I then picked up the red document. The words *Swiss Passport* were written on the front in the same five languages. When I opened it, my picture and birthday were laminated on the first page along with the Laura Krovopüskov name.

The passport was slightly frayed around the edges, as if it had been used several times before. I flipped through the pages, and it had half a dozen stamps. Two were from Egypt, two were from Canada, and two were from Ireland.

Sophie picked up the card and shook her head. "So, any idea why you have a passport and Swiss identity card under the name of Laura Krovopüskov?"

"Gabriella called a little while ago," I sighed. "She's in a city called Sevastopol, and she's been shot. She might need me to come over and escort her out."

"Why would she need an escort, and why can't Max do it?" Sophie asked, sounding confused. "He's the one trained in all of the spy stuff."

"She didn't say why, and I didn't ask. But she told me Max wouldn't be welcome over there because of what he did back when he worked for the government."

Sophie shook her head again. "Why do these things always happen to you?"

I tried to give her a Death Stare, but my mind was swirling, and I couldn't concentrate. I opened my top desk drawer and swept everything in.

"Let's go to lunch," I said. "I'll deal with this later."

We went to the front and gathered up Debbie. Sophie set the hands on the *Be Back Soon* sign to one o'clock and turned it to be visible through the window. We then went out through the front and locked the door.

We got to Dos Gringos, and Debbie studied the menu. She then spent a few moments looking around the restaurant with a look of nostalgia.

"Have you been here before?" I asked, trying to forget about the passport and the money. "It's one of our favorites."

"And it helps that it's only a three-minute walk from the office," Sophie added.

"I used to come here all the time," Debbie said. "But that was probably fifteen or twenty years ago when I worked down in Tempe. I've always liked their chicken Caeser salad, and being here brings back some happy memories."

Chapter Ten

We got back to the office and went in through the door to the street. Debbie flipped the *Be Back Soon* sign to the *We're Open* side.

The three of us stayed in reception while Sophie answered a question from Debbie about office procedures. Maybe it was only because Sophie had her chair back, but it was good to see my best friend starting to come around to having Debbie do a portion of her work.

I was about to head back to my cubicle and go through the packet Gabriella had sent me when the door to the street opened, and a woman walked in. She must have been sitting in her car, waiting for us to return from lunch.

I wasn't paying attention, but I saw Sophie stiffen. I then heard her mutter, "Oh, crap."

Curious about what had caused this reaction, I glanced over to get a better look at the woman. She was in her late thirties, medium build, with short brunette hair and large dark glasses.

I didn't see anything special that could have caused such a reaction. But then I looked closer, and it suddenly hit me. She was the spitting image of the woman on Kelsey Dawson's driver's license.

"Jeez," I said with a shake of my head, knowing the

difficulties this was going to cause.

"Yup," Sophie replied with a nod.

"I'm Kelsey Dawson," the woman said as she looked back and forth between us. We were both staring at her, and it seemed to make her uncomfortable.

"Um, how can we help you?" Debbie asked tentatively.

"I got some paperwork in the mail this morning," this new version of Kelsey Dawson said. "It said I had paid your law firm a ten-thousand-dollar cash retainer. There were also some papers that said I had signed up to be a client. I'm here to find out what it's all about."

Debbie looked confused, so Sophie took over.

"Okay," my best friend said, sounding flustered. "I'm sure we can get this cleared up. Let me see if Mr. Shapiro can see you now."

She picked up the phone on Debbie's desk and called Lenny. "Kelsey Dawson is here to see you," she said.

Sophie listened for a moment, then lowered her voice. "No, she doesn't have an appointment. It's a different Kelsey Dawson. We may have a problem."

Sophie led Kelsey and me into Lenny's office. He looked confused but offered her a seat. Sophie was also about to sit when Lenny offered the woman a glass of wine.

"Yes, please," she said gratefully. "That might be helpful."

Sophie opened the refrigerator at the wet bar, poured a glass of chablis, and handed it to the woman. She took a sip, and it seemed to relax her. She then lifted the glass and took a big gulp, draining about half of the wine.

"Now then," Lenny began, looking at the woman. "How can we help you?"

"Boss," Sophie said, breaking in. "This is Kelsey Dawson. When the other Kelsey Dawson signed the notary book earlier in the week, we commented on how much she'd changed from her driver's license picture. This is the woman in the picture."

Lenny paused and thought for several moments. He then sighed and looked at Sophie. "You'd better make me a Beam."

As Sophie got up and started dropping ice cubes into a glass, Lenny looked down at his desk drawer. I knew he was thinking about bringing out his pack of cigarettes.

Sophie brought him the drink, and he took a couple of long sips. He looked down at his desk drawer again and shook his head in frustration.

"We've apparently had a woman come in here representing herself to be you," Lenny said to the woman. "Do you have any explanation why she'd do this?"

"I have no idea," new Kelsey said, looking like she was on the verge of crying. "But I've been going through some major things in my life over the past few weeks. I'm only here to find out what's going on."

"Can you show us any identification?" Lenny asked.

"I knew you'd ask that," the woman said with a long sigh as she dug through her bag. "I have my birth certificate and passport. My house was recently broken into, and my wallet was stolen. These were in my filing cabinet and weren't taken. I've already ordered another copy of my driver's license. I'll get that in a few days."

She handed the documents to Lenny, and he carefully examined them. He then nodded and let out a sigh.

"Everything appears to be in order," he said, sounding somewhat discouraged. "Sophie, would you make a copy of these for the files? And, um, make us both another drink before you go."

Sophie made the drinks and took off. Lenny used the time to compose himself.

"Miss Dawson," my boss said as he leaned back in his chair and rubbed his eyes. "Something very odd's been going on. Would you be able to explain things from your side? Start at the beginning and don't leave out any details, even if they seem unimportant."

New Kelsey nodded and took a deep breath. This seemed to calm her to the point where she could begin.

"My life has sort of gone to hell over the past month," she said, pausing to take a long sip of her wine.

"About four weeks ago, I was notified that my brother, Morgan, had died while traveling in Egypt. They gave me a schedule for when his body was to be delivered to the funeral home here in Scottsdale, but he never showed up."

"Would that be Nesbett and Sons on Hayden Road?" Lenny asked as he looked down at his notepad.

"That's right," she said with a slow nod. "But when I called them to find out what was happening, they said Morgan's remains were still with the county coroner. Apparently, they needed to perform some tests and do an autopsy before they released the body."

"Did you go to the Medical Examiner's office to inquire about it?" Lenny asked.

"I went down several times," Kelsey said, shaking her head and sighing in frustration. "I started at their Scottsdale office, and they directed me to their downtown Phoenix headquarters. But everybody I talked to gave me a different answer."

"What did you do then?" Lenny asked. He seemed to

have pulled himself together and was talking in his concerned lawyer voice.

"I was at my wit's end," she said. "I was thinking about calling a private detective to have them find out what was going on. But then my home was broken into and ransacked."

"How long ago was this?" Lenny asked as he made a note on his legal pad.

"Maybe two weeks, I don't remember, maybe three," she said with a shrug. "They took my purse, my wallet, and all the papers I'd been gathering to bring my brother's body back to Scottsdale from Egypt."

"Did you notify the police?" Lenny asked. His glass was still half full, but he'd placed it on the side of his desk.

"Yes, but they didn't seem interested," Kelsey said with a scowl. "They said that it was likely neighborhood kids."

"What happened next?" Lenny asked.

"I thought that was the end of it," Kelsey said. "But then I received paperwork this morning that said I had given you ten thousand dollars in cash."

"Do you have any idea why someone would wish to impersonate you?" Lenny asked.

"No idea at all," she said with a shake of her head. "I can only assume it had something to do with the break-in."

"What can you tell me about your brother's trip to Egypt?" I asked.

"There isn't a lot to tell. Since he got out of the Marines, Morgan's fancied himself as an adventurer. A friend of his from ASU has been going back and forth to Egypt every few months, and he asked Morgan to go with him this time. I think it has something to do with hunting for an ancient treasure."

"Do you happen to know the friend's name?" I asked.

"It's professor something," she said. "Nabil, maybe. He teaches history."

"The woman pretending to be you had asked us to help locate your brother's body," Lenny said. "Why she wanted this is unknown. Actually, she's one of two clients we have who are interested in recovering Morgan's body."

"Is there anything else I should do?" she asked.

"You've already notified the police that someone has stolen your driver's license and credit cards," Lenny said. "I suggest you take the standard precautions of changing your card numbers and bank accounts."

"I already did," Kelsey said with a nod. "Until I got a copy of the receipt in the mail today, I'd assumed that whoever stole my wallet only wanted my credit cards. But it now looks like they were also trying to steal my identity."

"Since we're currently looking into the whereabouts of your brother's body, we'll keep you informed of our progress," Lenny said. "We'll also inform you if we learn anything more about the woman who tried to impersonate you."

"Thank you," Kelsey said. "It's been a hard few weeks. Adding this on top of it seemed to be the final straw."

We walked Kelsey out to reception. I got her contact information and gave her my card. I then told her to call me if anything else happened.

When the new version of Kelsey left through the front door, I felt a fresh layer of confusion descend on me.

"So, if she's the real Kelsey Dawson," Sophie said with a raised eyebrow. "Who's our client? I don't even know what to call her. Phony Kelsey, maybe?"

"I'm not sure who she is," I said, shaking my head and trying to fit everything together. "She paid us ten thousand dollars, which I suppose probably still makes her a client. But we'll need to find out who she is and what she actually wants."

I went back to my cubicle and called the woman who had impersonated Kelsey. I wanted to get together with her to find out what was going on.

Unfortunately, she didn't answer. I left a message asking her to call me right away.

While Sophie was still up front, I opened my desk drawer and peered inside. I was hoping that the money and the documents were merely part of a hallucination, perhaps caused by being repeatedly hit on the head. Unfortunately, the passport, the identity card, and the piles of currency were still there.

I picked up the folded stack of paper. There must have been ten pages stapled together. On the top was a typewritten note.

Laura, if you receive this package, I might be unable to leave Sevastopol without a family escort. If so, and if you are willing, I may need you to come to Crimea and pretend to be my sister. If I call to give you the go-ahead, travel to Bucharest in Romania using your U.S. passport. Take the train to the port city of Constanta on the Black Sea. Using the Swiss passport and identity card, book passage on the cargo ship Greifswald to Sevastopol. In port, take a taxi to Piratskaya Harchevnya restaurant on the Kokacheva Embankment. You will know you are at the right place because it looks like a pirate ship. Go to bar and ask for Polina. She will take you to me. I have full instructions and scheduling information on the attached pages. You are a good person and will do fine. Gabriella.

I flipped through the pages and found ship itineraries, detailed directions, and maps of Constanta and Sevastopol. Between the paperwork and the Swiss identity documents, I realized Gabriella must have been planning this for months.

Shaking my head that I had found myself in yet another awkward situation, I tossed the papers back in the drawer. I'd thought about taking everything home, but the back of a locked law office was probably better than my often broken-into apartment.

I sat in my cube for several minutes and rubbed my eyes. I knew I couldn't worry about Gabriella or traveling to Crimea while I still had other things I needed to do first.

The baking contest would be held tomorrow, and I still had no idea what was happening. That had to be the next thing to look at. I turned on my computer and searched for the Scottsdale Cookie and Cake Club website.

When it popped up, I first went to the club history page. I learned Adam had been the club president for almost ten years. He'd taken over from his mother, who had started the club back in the nineties.

I then went to the club bake-off page and found the listing of the past winners. I went back to the beginning and began searching.

Kaitlin's name didn't show up until five years ago when she got her first win. Her cupcakes won each year after that.

Everything else about the cake club seemed legitimate. There had to be something going on that would make Adam give Kaitlin the win each year.

Of course, I still had the same problem as Beatrice. Even

though I suspected some shady shenanigans, proving them would be an entirely different matter.

After work, I pulled into my apartment parking lot and raised the roof on the Miata. It had been a long week, and I looked forward to having a beer and getting to bed early.

As I got out of my car, a homeless guy got up from where he'd been sitting next to the dumpster and started walking toward me. The man was pulling a desert camouflage rolling duffle bag, the kind with two wheels and an extendable handle.

I casually put my hand into my bag and found my pistol. I wasn't actively being threatened, but it had been a crazy week, and I wasn't in the mood to take a chance.

"Excuse me," he said as he stopped ten feet from me. "Is your name Laura Black? I need to talk with you."

The man seemed familiar, and I tried to figure out who he was. He was in his forties, had short, medium brown hair, and a scruffy month-old beard.

I didn't think I'd ever heard his voice before, so he wasn't someone I'd talked with over the phone. It was more his face, particularly his eyes, that was causing the reaction.

I started trying to place him. I mentally added hair and removed the mustache and beard. As I did, an image sprang into view.

Oh my god.

"Morgan?" I asked. "Morgan West?"

The man's shoulders slumped, and he seemed to deflate. I could see I had guessed correctly.

"It figures," he grumbled. "You can still tell who I am. I guess changing my looks doesn't hide me as much as I'd hoped."

"Um, you're supposed to be dead," I observed.

"I know," he admitted. "But I'm in a tight scrape. I've tried everything I know to get out of it, but I have some nasty people looking for me. Right now, I'm only looking for a safe place to hide for a few days."

I thought about the wisdom of bringing him up to my apartment, but everything revolved around him and his body. I knew it would be the quickest way to learn what was happening.

"Come on," I said, still with my hand in my bag. "Let's head up to my place."

I led him into the building, and we stepped into the elevator. Once the doors slid closed, I realized this had been a mistake.

Whatever journey Morgan had been on over the last several days, it was apparent that a shower and a laundromat hadn't been a part of it. He smelled like a wet dog that had spent the day rolling in burnt garbage.

I let Morgan into my apartment and pointed to a chair at the kitchen table. I could tell he was exhausted, and I guessed he must also be hungry.

As he sat, I went to the fridge and pulled out a bottle of Corona from a fresh twelve-pack I'd bought a few days before. I popped the top and handed it to him.

Somehow I wasn't overly surprised when he downed it in four or five long swallows. "Aahh, that hit the spot," he said as I could see him start to relax.

"Do you want to tell me what this is all about?" I asked as I handed him another beer. I then took a seat in the chair next to him at the table. "You're supposed to be dead, and there was a professor in the morgue with your name on his toe tag."

"I know," he said in a tired voice. "That was Professor Nabil. I was working with him in Egypt."

"Look," I said, "if you want my advice, you'll need to tell me what's going on. Don't sugar coat or hold back on anything."

"I'll tell you everything I know," he said. "At the moment, I'm a little desperate and simply need your help. But I'll be able to pay you."

I could see how quickly this would complicate things and shook my head. "I already have other clients involved with this, and it's starting to cause some unusual conflicts of interest."

Ignoring me, he unzipped his duffle bag and began to search. As he pulled out dirty shirts and filthy socks, making a small pile on my kitchen floor, I could hear several objects bumping into each other. The god-awful stench wafting up from the bag was a nasty combination of a smokey campfire and a high school locker room.

Finally, he pulled out a bundle about the size of a football, wrapped in clear shrink wrap. The number *six* had been drawn on the outside with a black marker.

Morgan started by finding the end of the film and carefully unwrapping it. Underneath was a layer of bubble wrap.

After discarding the protective plastics, he unwound several layers of yellowed cloth that tore and crumbled as he removed it.

At the core of the bundle was a small figurine of a cat. It was five or six inches tall and appeared to be made of gold.

"Here," he said as he handed it to me. From the weight, it seemed to be solid rather than hollow. "Like I said, I'm in over my head and need your help. I'm not sure how much this is worth, but I imagine it will cover a week or two of your time and expenses."

How do I get myself into these situations?

I turned the cat over a few times, then set it on my kitchen table. It had several symbols carved into it that seemed to be Egyptian.

"Thanks," I said. "I appreciate the gesture, but you don't need to give me anything. You can stay here tonight, but I need to piece together what's been going on with you."

"No, you keep the cat," he said with a shake of his head. "It'll make me feel better about imposing on you. What do you want to know?"

"Let's start with Professor Nabil," I said. "What was your relationship with him, and how did he end up in a coffin with your name on his toe tag?"

"I've been friends with the Professor ever since I took his history class at ASU. He called me about seven months ago and said he was back in Egypt to sell some additional artifacts he had."

"Why call you?" I asked as I pointed to the cat on the table. "Do you have a background in these gold figurines?"

Morgan chuckled and shook his head. "The Professor said he was looking for a bodyguard and someone he could trust to help him conduct the transactions."

"Bodyguard?" I asked. "Is that something you've done before?"

"Not really," he said with a laugh. "But I spent several years in the Marines when I was younger. The Professor said that would be good enough."

"Did he say where he got these treasures?"

"He only said there was a secret location in the desert, but he didn't talk about the dig site too much. I figured it was in the Valley of the Kings, west of Luxor. That's where most of the ancient treasures are still being dug up."

"What can you tell me about the murder?" I asked. I didn't want to upset Morgan, but I needed to know how it fit in with everything else.

"I got to Egypt maybe six months ago," Morgan said as he sipped his beer. "I hung out with the Professor as he sold off the pieces. He liked to haggle, and it was a slow process."

"How did that go?" I asked.

"At first, things were going okay. But then we started having problems. They were only minor things to start, but a little over a month ago, we had a couple of close calls. The Professor was getting nervous."

"Really? What kind of close calls?" Morgan's story was interesting and was starting to fill in a lot of holes.

"One of the buyers, a guy named Mr. Ahmed, pulled a gun on us and made a lot of threats. Our primary buyer, Raymond Eckart, was also becoming a little too aggressive in his negotiations. I wasn't sure if he would turn violent, but the situation with him was getting uncomfortable. Add to that, one of the dealers we'd sold to turned out to be a government agent."

"What did you do?" I asked. "Did you try to get out of Egypt?"

"The Professor decided to leave the country as soon as possible. His plan was to dump the rest of the pieces for whatever price he could get. Then we'd return to Arizona. He gave me a key and instructions on how to get the remaining figurines from a safety deposit box he'd rented at a bank and sent me out for them."

"That was pretty trusting of him," I said.

"Not really," Morgan said with a chuckle. "Before the Professor told me anything, he made me hand over my passport. Even though we were friends, he wanted to make sure I wouldn't skip the country without him."

"I take it things didn't go smoothly," I said as I got up and grabbed him another beer from the kitchen. I knew getting him drunk probably wasn't the best idea, but it did seem to get him talking.

"When I left for the bank, I noticed two men watching the apartment," Morgan went on. "I called the Professor and told him what was going on. We agreed that after I picked up the pieces from the bank, I would hide out in a hotel on the far side of Cairo for the night."

"What about the Professor?" I asked. "Did he try to leave as well?"

"He was supposed to sneak out the back of the apartment and meet me the next morning for breakfast. From there, we'd go to the dockyards and get on a cargo ship to leave the country."

"I take it he didn't make it the next day?" I asked. "What happened?"

Morgan shook his head, and his face twisted with sadness. "When he didn't show up, I returned to the apartment. Unfortunately, when I arrived, there were half a dozen cop cars out front."

"That couldn't have been pleasant," I said. "What did you do?"

"With the police milling around, I knew I couldn't go back to the apartment," he said, taking another swallow of his beer. "I went back to the hotel. Two days later, I read a story in an English-language newspaper that said I'd been killed and my body would be returned to my sister in Scottsdale."

"How did they mix up the two of you?" I asked, feeling annoyed. "That's caused no end of problems."

"Well, I imagine the Professor still had my passport in his pocket. We looked close enough to be mistaken for each other, and that was it."

"Do you have any idea who killed him? Was it Eckart?"

"No, I think it was the guys staking out my apartment. I'm pretty sure they worked for Mr. Ahmed. As I said, he'd already pulled a gun on us and was a nasty piece of work overall."

"What did you do then?" I asked, leaning closer.

"I waited for a few days until the police guard was pulled. I then returned to the apartment and took Professor Nabil's passport and some cash from a hiding place under a floorboard. I used that to book a passage on a cargo ship going to Mexico. I crossed the U.S. border near Nogales with a group of Hondurans and walked most of the way up here over the past week."

"You know," I said. "Everyone thinks you're dead."

"I figured," he said as his cheeks flushed red. "I probably should have stayed in Cairo and straightened everything out with the police, but I wanted to get out of the country and come home. I had the rest of the Professor's statues, and I knew the killers would be after me next."

"You're going to need to call your sister," I said, giving him the look. "She still thinks you're dead."

He nodded and looked ashamed. "I called her right before coming here to let her know I was okay. She told me about you and that you'd been looking for me. It seemed you'd be someone I could work with on this."

"Did your sister tell you someone had impersonated her to get us to look for your body?"

He nodded as he took a sip of his beer. "She told me. I had a feeling they'd still be coming after me, even though they thought I was dead."

There was a pause while I tried to figure out what to do with the filthy man sitting at my kitchen table.

"Are you getting hungry?" I asked.

"I'm starving," he said, immediately perking up. "Anything you have would be great."

I went into the kitchen, and after searching through my freezer, I pulled out a pizza. As I turned on my oven to pre-heat, I had a thought.

"While this is cooking, why don't you take a shower," I said. "Hand me the dirty clothes from your bag, and I'll wash everything."

Morgan seemed to think this was a brilliant idea and flashed me a grateful smile. But honestly, I wasn't doing this simply to be nice. Even though I'd already opened my windows, Morgan and the clothes in the duffle were starting to stink up the place.

He pulled the heavy canvas bag into the bathroom, and I heard him unzipping it. After two or three minutes, the door opened, and he handed out a dozen disgusting pieces of clothing. I had him put them directly in a laundry basket, so I didn't have to touch anything.

"Hold on," he said as he closed the door. "I'll give you these too."

As he cracked the door open one more time to hand over his current wardrobe, I saw the unzipped bag at his feet. It appeared to contain five or six more wrapped items. Each was larger than the bundle containing the cat he'd already given me.

Chapter Eleven

Morgan came out of the bathroom twenty-five minutes later, wearing nothing but a pair of stained gray sweatpants. Fortunately, the garment seemed to be one of the few pieces that didn't smell like death's grandfather.

Now that Morgan had cleaned up and shaved off the beard, I could see that he was a handsome man with a great body. Even though dozens of tattoos covered his arms, chest, and back, I could see why women would be attracted to him.

He moved to the couch, where I fed him the pizza and several more beers. At first, he ate and drank eagerly. But by the time he reached his sixth or seventh beer, the energy seemed to drain out of him. It seemed like a good time to ask him some questions.

"Do you have any idea why everyone is after you?" I asked. "Is it the pieces of artwork you have with you?"

"Only partially," he admitted. "After our first close call in Cairo, probably five months ago, the Professor became worried that he'd be kidnapped or even killed. During a night of drinking, he gave me a code that was somehow associated with a piece he called the pharaoh's mask and told me to keep it safe."

"Associated with a mask? Like how to retrieve it?"

"I think so, but he wouldn't tell me anything more about

it. He once let it slip that the code was for the Devil's Highway, but I never found out how that was connected to anything."

"The Devil's Highway sounds somewhat metaphorical," I observed. "What did you do once you got the code?"

"I had it tattooed on my stomach," he said, laughing. "I think everyone's after my dead body so they can find out what it is."

I looked at him like he was an idiot. It confirmed what Eckart had already told me, but *jeez.*

"I know," he said with a chuckle and a shake of his head. "But I knew it was important and didn't want to take a chance of losing it."

"But still," I said. "Having it permanently inked on your body rather than writing it on a scrap of paper seems a little extreme."

He laughed again and waved his hand over his chest. "Hey, what's one more tattoo? I thought it would be a nice souvenir of my time in Egypt. Unfortunately, I was drunk at the time, and most of the people at the bar overheard my plan to have a secret code tattooed on me."

"Really? What happened?"

"I got the tattoo and ended up with a beautiful woman who'd been in the bar that night. I'd met her before and thought she was really into me. But I later realized she was only after the Professor's code."

"How did you find that out?" I asked as I leaned closer.

"I could tell by the way she was always fixated on it," he said, sadness and bitterness in his voice. "Mind you, this was after she'd spent six weeks living with me and pretending to care about me. All the time, she was only after the code."

Morgan sipped his Corona and briefly talked about what he had in mind for the next day. But by this point, the beer had taken over, and he wasn't making a lot of sense. Ten minutes later, he laid back and passed out on the couch.

I finished the laundry and folded everything into piles on the coffee table next to the little gold cat. Morgan was lying on his back with his head on a throw pillow and was snoring loudly.

Looking at the many tattoos on his chest and stomach, I started thinking about the story of the secret code. I drank one of my few remaining beers, munched on the last piece of pizza, and pondered if there'd be a way I could see it.

I was about to give up in frustration when I got a horrible idea. Morgan was still only wearing the sweatpants, and I suspected he was going commando underneath. Maybe I could get a picture of the tattoo after all?

I took out my phone and set it to the camera function. Acting quickly, before I lost my nerve, I carefully lifted the waistband of his sweatpants about an inch and slid the camera into the darkness.

Using the flash, I took over a dozen shots. Carefully avoiding Mr. Wiggles, I made sure to move the camera lens around to get any tattoos he had down there.

Even in his drunken and exhausted state, Morgan must have felt the movement in his nether regions. He let out a lewd chuckle and smiled.

He sleepily moved his hand down to investigate the tugging and pulling sensations. As he was scratching and rearranging himself, I used the opportunity to pull the phone out and slowly lower the waistband.

Even as Morgan grunted with contentment and rolled to his side, I went into the bedroom and closed the door.

Flipping back through the pictures I'd taken, I saw nothing that looked like a code.

I'd reached the last photo and had almost given up. But then I saw a small black tattoo of several numbers. I breathed a sigh of relief as I grabbed a pen and wrote down the code.

32.4012 -114.11

As I looked at it, I realized that if the code was symmetrical, it might be incomplete. It was hard to tell, but I might have missed something at the end.

I went back through the pictures and studied each of them. Now that I knew what I was looking for, I could barely make out the last two numbers, a nine and an eight, on an earlier image. I added it to my code.

32.4012 -114.1198

I looked at what I had written and shook my head. It seemed like there'd been a lot of pain and misery over such a simple thing, whatever it was.

When I woke up the following day, I wasn't surprised that Marlowe had spent his Friday night at Grandma Henderson's. He can usually tolerate visitors if they simply come and then leave, but a strange man spending the night was too much for him.

I made a pot of coffee and got ready for the day. I wanted to get to the Tropical Paradise early enough to get the lay of the land before everyone showed up for the baking contest.

I was in the kitchen cooking bacon and eggs when Morgan woke up. Even though he looked much better than when I'd first met him the previous afternoon, I could tell he'd been through a rough couple of weeks.

"What are you going to do next?" I asked as I handed him a coffee in my Doctor Who mug. I was using an oversized coffee cup I'd picked up from a souvenir shop during my brief vacation in Vail.

"That's a good question," he said as he sipped the coffee. "With everyone looking for me, I can't stay in my apartment. I also don't want to endanger my sister by going to her place. I explained that when I called her yesterday."

"I'm pretty sure Eckart will search your place soon, if he hasn't done so already," I said. "At the very least, he'll have someone monitoring it."

Morgan nodded as if he thought that as well. "I'm not sure how connected the people looking for me are. But I probably shouldn't use my credit cards or the ATM."

"That's even if they're still working," I observed. "With you declared dead, the bank might have already placed a hold on your accounts."

"Yeah," he said, getting a frown and nodding in frustration. "You're probably right. I'll have my sister go down and check things out with the bank."

We stood in my kitchen, sipping coffee, neither of us saying a word. After almost a minute, the silence became uncomfortable.

I'll probably regret this.

"Um, you can stay here until things are straightened out," I said, going to the stove and dishing up some eggs and bacon for him.

"Thank you," he said, sounding sincere. "I appreciate it, and I'll try not to cause any problems."

As I stood in front of my bathroom mirror and prepared to leave for my day of looking at cupcakes, I thought about Morgan staying alone in my apartment. He seemed like a nice enough guy, but in reality, he was a stranger to me.

I went into my bedroom closet and pulled down the shoebox containing my jewelry from the top shelf. With all the people I'd had in and out of my apartment over the past few months, I knew I'd been lucky that nothing had been stolen.

I also got the feeling that when Gabriella called me, I wouldn't have a lot of time before I needed to head to the airport. I pulled out my daypack and filled it with everything I would need for a week on the road. Well, that was assuming I wore minimal makeup, only had one pair of shoes, and could get away with wearing the same clothing two or three days in a row.

I then went to the drawer in my bedroom nightstand, where I kept my personal paperwork. I dug around until I found my U.S. passport and put it in my bag. After pulling out my ski coat and tossing it on the daypack, I felt as ready as possible.

I decided to see if Grandma Henderson would keep my shoebox until I could go to my bank and rent a safety deposit box. Even though it would be inconvenient to stop by the bank whenever I wanted to wear a piece of jewelry, I'd feel better knowing everything was safe.

"I'll be out for a while, maybe all day," I said, digging out a business card, then going through my junk drawer and handing Morgan the spare key. "This will let you back into the apartment, and here's my card. You can call me anytime, and I'll answer if I can."

Morgan got up and slopped more coffee into his mug. "I'll probably stay here most of the day," he said with a sleepy yawn. "It's been a long couple of weeks. I'll probably lie on the couch and take a nap or two."

I went into the hallway and turned to lock my door. As if she'd been listening for me to leave, Grandma's door opened, and she stuck her head out.

"Hello, Laura," she said. "Is everything alright? Marlowe seemed a little upset when he came over last night."

"Everything's fine," I said. "I have a man staying in my apartment, and I think it spooked him."

"A man?" Grandma asked. "You mean Max?"

"Not Max," I said as I shook my head. "He might be here for a few days and will probably go in and out several times. But him being here is a secret, so don't let anyone know about it."

Grandma's eyes twinkled, and she got a faraway look. "Oh, I understand, dear," she said, patting me on the arm. "If Max comes over, I won't say a word about the new man you have hidden in your apartment."

"It's not like that," I said, a little frustrated. "If Max comes over, you can tell him about it."

Grandma smiled. "Oh really? I wouldn't have guessed Max was into any of that kinky stuff."

I shook my head again, now becoming exasperated. "No, it's not like that either. I only meant I didn't want everyone to know I have a man in my apartment."

"It's okay," she said as she again patted my arm. "I know how you young kids are nowadays. I'm not judging."

I again shook my head in frustration but then thought

better of trying to explain. "Um, would you do me a favor?" I asked.

"What can I do for you, dear?" she asked.

"Would you keep this somewhere safe for a couple of days?" I asked as I handed her the shoebox. "It's my jewelry, and I don't want to leave it in the apartment while I'm out. I'll get a safety deposit box at my bank in a few days, but until then, would you keep it with you?"

Grandma gave me a look that was sort of hard to read. "Of course," she said. "I'll put it in the drawer with my nightgowns. I don't think anyone will bother it there."

"Have you and Bob figured out what you're going to do with all the extra furniture and knickknacks yet?"

Grandma gave me a look that could have curdled milk. "Not yet. We've only decided to get rid of one piece so far, and that was only because one of the legs was halfway broken off already."

I walked down to the parking lot and glanced over at the dumpster. Sure enough, one of the overstuffed chairs that had been in the corner of Grandma's apartment was now visible, poking out of the top.

I hoped Grandma and Bob could come to an understanding. They'd only been married for a couple of months, and I'd hate to see something like this spoil things for them.

I made it to the Camelback Ballroom at the Tropical Paradise a little after eleven. Even though the show wasn't starting until noon, the ballroom was starting to fill up, and a buzz of excitement was in the air.

A dozen long tables with white linens had been set up in the middle of the room. People were bringing in their baked goods and carefully setting up their displays.

I was amazed at the variety of food on display. Since this was an open competition, some categories seemed to have upwards of thirty or forty entries.

This was especially true of the cookie group. From the program, there were fifteen sub-categories. This translated to two long tables being completely filled with plates of six cookies each.

I drifted over to the cupcake table and found Beatrice's entry of six cakes near the front. Per the rules, the cupcakes were on a plain paper plate.

Each of her entries was perfect. The icing was beautifully applied, and each cake was identical. The only difference was where the dark chocolate shavings had landed on the top of each cupcake. Still, even that gave a pleasant feeling of spontaneous creativity.

I then found Kaitlin's entries, the green icing with the blue sugar sprinkles. Her cupcakes didn't have the same look of uniformity that shone out in some of the other groups. Instead, they looked like something I could have whipped up in my kitchen.

Once the show started, Adam went to the small stage at the front and made a speech welcoming the bakers and introduced the officers of the club, including a woman named Linda Romero as the vice president.

Linda then went over the schedule for the day. She announced that the judging of each category would begin immediately, and the top six finalists from each group would be announced at four o'clock.

These top six finalists would then compete at the

championship bake-off, which would be held in the ballroom Tuesday evening, starting at five o'clock. The individual category winners, the Best of Group, and the Best of Show winners would then be announced Tuesday at eight.

I found Beatrice standing with a group of fellow bakers. She introduced me as a friend and new club member, and we eventually broke away to talk.

"Your cupcakes look great," I told her. "I'm sure you'll make it to the final round."

"Probably," she said with a shrug. "Making it to the championship is never problem. Winning is another matter. When I am competing against young skinny blonde girl and the judge has his eye on her, it will make it difficult to win."

"Are you sure Adam's interested in Kaitlin?" I asked. "His wife is stunning, and he seems pretty happy with her."

"I also have been investigating devil woman and the judge," Beatrice said with a scowl, lowering her voice. "According to people who have known them both for a long time, Adam and Kaitlin dated for over a year when they went to ASU."

"Wow," I said. "That does put a new spin on things."

"Not only that," Beatrice said, now getting excited. "But he also dated Shirley, the younger sister, back in college. He only stop dating them when he started seeing Naomi."

"Adam has known both sisters for fifteen or twenty years?" I asked, nodding my head as the pieces started falling into place. "That likely makes what's happening here more than a simple coincidence."

Chapter Twelve

The next several hours consisted of groups of judges going from table to table, eating the baked goods, and making notes on their clipboards. The judges were loosely followed by the bakers, who wanted to watch the judging but not be overly obvious about it.

A DJ had set up his equipment on the stage and began playing music. Popular dance tunes mixed in with disco came flooding out of the speakers. A large group of younger bakers had gathered on the dance floor and seemed to be having a great time.

On the far side of the ballroom, the resort had rolled in some portable ovens, and people were giving live cooking classes on cakes, pies, and cookies. The baking food gave off some enchanting aromas that quickly made me hungry.

Fortunately, a table had been set up to sell baked items made by the club members. I didn't find any of Beatrice's cupcakes, but I did find some dark chocolate fudge brownies to die for.

After the delicious dessert, I went to the bar to get a soda. To my surprise, Kaitlin walked up and asked the bartender for two glasses of chardonnay. I knew I wouldn't get a better chance than this to learn more about her.

"Hi," I said as I turned to face her. "My name's Laura.

I'm new here."

"Oh, hi, Laura," she said, flashing a pretty smile. "It's good to meet you. I'm Kaitlin Kingston."

"You won the cupcake competition last year, didn't you?" I asked.

"And the four years before that," she laughed as she rolled her eyes.

"Wow," I said, trying to sound surprised. "You must have some sort of wonderful cupcake recipe."

"Honestly, I don't know why I keep winning," she said with a shrug and a dismissive shake of her head. "I'm not that great of a baker. I mainly do it for fun. Most of the ladies here have been baking all their lives, and they make some amazing things."

"You don't think you should've won?" I asked. I knew some skepticism was in my voice.

"Not really," she said with a shrug. "I honestly don't know what the judges see in my baking. But I'm hoping to make the top six again this year so I can get to the bake-off on Tuesday."

"If you don't think you can win, why worry about making it to the championships?" I asked.

"Oh, because it's exciting," she said, again giving me a broad, friendly smile. "I've had so much fun doing this over the last few years. My niece has started competing, and spending time with her and my sister is great." As she said this, she lifted the second glass of chardonnay to show it was destined for her sibling.

"Shirley, my sister, has been a club member for years. She's the one who started me baking in the first place. Beth, my niece, is a pie maker. She's entered her cherry crumble recipe in the junior pie category this year, and I hope she gets in the top six."

Kaitlin took off to give her sister the wine, and I tried to figure out what had just happened. Rather than being a manipulating bitch, Kaitlin seemed like a nice person. None of this was making sense.

An hour into the judging, I went out to the main lobby to find a bathroom. Returning towards the ballroom, I saw Shirley going down a side hallway leading to some of the smaller conference rooms.

Thinking this was odd, I parked myself on a couch against a far wall and pretended to look at my phone. Less than three minutes later, Adam entered the lobby and casually walked down the same hallway.

Wondering what was up, I followed, only stopping when I heard voices. They'd ended up inside one of the unused conference rooms, but the door was open, and I could more or less hear the conversation.

"You need to be a good boy with this," I heard Shirley say. Her tone was stern yet affectionate.

Adam said something back. He seemed upset, but his words were too quiet to make out.

"If you behave yourself, everything will be fine," Shirley said in a motherly tone. "I know you think your reputation is damaged, but things could be so much worse."

Adam said something else, but it was again too quiet to hear the words. Frustrated, I listened a few moments longer until the voices stopped.

I knew this was my cue to leave before I got caught. I

returned to the lobby and again sat on the couch.

Adam strolled back into view less than thirty seconds later. He then made a beeline back to the Camelback Ballroom.

Shirley returned about a minute after that. She had a happy smile and seemed to be in a great mood.

The last hour of the baking show consisted of Adam standing on the stage, announcing the top six contestants who had made it to the finals in each category. As the winners in each group were announced, there were shouts and squeals of happiness from the finalists. I also saw more than one angry baker storm out of the ballroom when they didn't make the cut.

The cake group was the last to be announced. As Adam went through the individual categories, I found myself getting caught up in the excitement.

When Adam read off the names of the six cupcake qualifiers, I felt a surge of relief when Beatrice's name was called. I also wasn't overly surprised when Kaitlin was announced as a finalist.

As the meeting broke up, I found Beatrice gathering three of her cupcakes that had remained after the judging. "Would you like these?" she asked. "Max seldom eats cake, and I can put them in box to keep fresh."

That would be great," I said. "I haven't had one of your cupcakes yet. I'm glad you made it into the finals."

"On Tuesday, I will make six perfect cupcakes," Beatrice said. "Then we'll see if devil woman wins again or not."

I took the box of cupcakes out to the car and called Max. "Hey," I said. "Are you still in the office? Would you like some company?"

"Your timing's perfect," he said. "I was in the process of finishing for the day. Why don't you come up? If you're done with the baking contest, we can figure out what to do for dinner."

I walked up the curving stairs in the lobby to the mezzanine level, then down the balcony to the big glass doors of Scottsdale Land and Resort Management, Inc. This was the organization that owned all of the resorts controlled by Max.

Since this was late on a Saturday afternoon, the outer doors to the offices were locked. Fortunately, I had a badge that gave me access whenever I wanted to enter.

I dug the card from my bag and pressed it against a black plastic square next to the entrance. There was a buzz, and the doors unlocked.

I walked through the mostly empty halls until I got to the executive offices. Since no one was at the admin desk, I called Max on the phone.

"I'm here," I said when he answered.

The door to the office buzzed, and I walked in. As I expected, Max was sitting behind what I still thought of as Tony's desk. He had several stacks of papers in front of him and was flipping through a multi-page document.

Max stood, came around the desk, and met me in the middle of the office for a warm hug. I used the opportunity to kiss him several times while keeping my arms wrapped tightly around his firm body.

"How'd the contest go?" he asked, leading me to the couch against the wall. "Did Beatrice make it to the finals next week?"

"Yes," I said as I leaned against him. "But the devil woman also made the top six."

"Were you able to learn anything?" Max asked. "Do you think she's manipulating the head judge? Beatrice thinks she might be trading sex for wins."

"I don't think so," I said, sounding skeptical. "I've met the woman. Her name's Kaitlin and she seems rather nice. I haven't seen anything that would lead me to believe she's influencing the judge. I think it's more her sister, Shirley. I heard her in a private conversation with the judge, and it seems like they have something going on."

"Well," he said as he leaned over to kiss me. "I hope you can figure out what's happening. Beatrice has been seriously stressing over her cupcakes for the past month. It's sweet of you to offer to help."

"Oh, I expect to be compensated," I said, looking at him with my best bedroom eyes. I then thought of the other thing that had been on my mind. "Have you heard anything from Gabriella yet?"

At the mention of Gabriella, Max's face fell. "No, I haven't heard a thing," he said quietly. "I've tried all of the back-channel ways I have to get word on her, but there hasn't been anything so far."

I knew I should tell Max about my phone call and Gabriella's package. But I wasn't sure the best way I should do it. "Um, if it turned out there was a way I could help her, would it upset you if I tried?"

Max paused and gave me a long look. He seemed to read

my mind. "She's made contact with you?"

I nodded my head. "Gabriella called yesterday from Sevastopol. She said she'd been shot and blown up but was otherwise okay. She thought she had a good escape plan but said if she got stuck, she might need me to pretend to be her step-sister and come get her."

Max paused, and I could see him mulling over the situation. "If she calls on you to help, I know you'll do whatever you can," he finally said. "But I ask that you keep me in the loop. I'll give you whatever advice I can. Plus, I don't want to wonder what happened to you if you suddenly disappear."

I nodded again, and we both sat in silence for several moments. "Hey," I said, wanting to talk about anything else. "Are you still interested in dinner?"

"Why don't we go over to my place?" Max asked as he leaned over to kiss me softly. "We don't have a cook tonight, but I can pick up some take-out Thai."

"That sounds perfect," I said, envisioning how lovely a quiet evening with Max would be.

"Alright," he said as he kissed me again. "Give me an hour and come over. Maybe we can find a good movie on TV."

I made it over to Max's house a little before seven. He'd apparently only beaten me by a few minutes. After he let me in, he busied himself by arranging boxes of Thai food on the kitchen table.

When it came to my pedestrian taste in wine, Max had given up on trying to pair the right wine with the food. I saw he'd opened a bottle of my favorite cabernet and had it sitting next to my plate.

"Other than chasing around cupcake bakers and rogue judges, what have you been up to all week?" Max asked as we munched on our green curry chicken, ginger beef, and pad Thai.

"Well, you know I've been looking for a dead body," I said, waiting for Max to start laughing again.

When he kept a straight face, I continued. "I actually found him last night, or I should say *he* found *me*." This time, Max raised a questioning eyebrow.

"It turns out he's not dead. There was a mix-up in Egypt, and a man named Professor Nabil died instead. Morgan West is still alive, and he made his way back into Scottsdale yesterday."

"I take it you ran into him?" Max asked.

I nodded my head. "He called his sister to tell her that he was still alive. After the shock of hearing her brother wasn't dead, she told him about my efforts to track down his body. There are other people here actively looking for anything they can find on Morgan, so he can't go back to his place. Instead, he came to mine. I think he was mainly looking for someplace safe to stay for a few days."

"Is this your way of telling me you have a man staying at your apartment with you?" Max asked as he snorted out a laugh.

"Yes," I said as I glowered at him. "It's not funny. Grandma already thinks you'll be over soon for some sort of weird three-way."

"Sorry," Max said, smiling as he held up his hand. "If it makes you uncomfortable, I could get him a room at one of the resorts. We could check him in anonymously if you think someone may be monitoring his movements."

"If this stretches out more than a few days, I'll probably take you up on that," I said. "But something's going on, and it all seems to revolve around Morgan. Having him nearby seems like the best way for me to get to the bottom of things."

Max again released a short chuckle and shook his head. "Let me know if I can do anything else with this one. I can't have a strange man living with my girlfriend for too long. You might start to get ideas."

I got a warm shiver that made me feel great all over. "I love the sound of that," I cooed, reaching over to hold his hand.

"What?" Max asked. "Living with a strange man?"

"No, jerk," I teased. "Being your girlfriend. It's a wonderful feeling."

"I'm glad you still like it," he teased back as he leaned over to kiss me. "It took you long enough to decide to do it."

"Speaking of strange men staying in my place," I said. "I've decided to rent a safety deposit box for my jewelry. I seem to have a lot of people in and out of my apartment, and I worry that someone will find everything eventually."

"It's probably a good idea," Max said. "I've been a little surprised that you haven't gotten yourself a more secure location for your things. Some of your jewelry is rather valuable."

"I know," I admitted. "But wearing a piece is usually a spur-of-the-moment decision. I'm not sure how well I'll handle only being able to get at the jewelry during banking hours. It means I'll need to pre-plan things, and you know how bad I am at doing that."

"If that's your main concern, why don't you get a box at

Casino Scottsdale?" Max asked. "The casino vault is as secure as any bank, and you can access your items whenever you'd like."

"I know your group manages some of the gambling houses around here. Is Casino Scottsdale one of yours?"

"Well, we don't own it, of course, but we have a long-term contract to handle portions of the management and security."

"Is it on your side or Johnny's?" I asked.

"The casinos fell on my side but could have gone either way. In the end, Tony felt that with the scrutiny the casinos get from the government bureaucrats, it would be best if they were seen as another legitimate side to our resorts."

"I'm a little surprised you can rent a safety deposit box at the casino," I said. "I've never heard of that before."

"We get a lot of high rollers who stay at the hotel and like to carry cash. Plus, you'd be surprised at how many people living in Scottsdale have things they'd like to have safely stashed away."

"And you can get items out of it twenty-four hours a day?"

"That's right. We found that guests of the hotel would often run short of cash in the middle of the night, especially if they were having a run of bad luck at the tables."

"And you didn't want them to stop playing if they still had a wad of cash in their safety deposit box," I said with a touch of snark.

"Well, we *are* running a casino," he said, giving me a knowing nod. "After getting several requests from VIP guests to access the vault late at night, we opened it up for any time availability."

"Thanks for telling me about this," I said. "I love the idea of getting my things whenever I want. You know all about my crazy schedule."

Max took out a business card and wrote some information on the back. "Take this to Vicky Harper at VIP Guest Services at the casino," Max said. "I think she's working tomorrow. I'll drop her a note in the morning and let her know you'll be stopping by."

As Max was writing, I'd gently reached up and touched my head where Owen had hit me. It was still sore but seemed to be getting better. I briefly thought about telling Max about my adventure in the morgue locker but then thought better of it. That was a tale that could be kept for another day.

After finishing most of the Thai food, we cuddled on Max's couch and watched an action movie that seemed to be one long car chase. Unfortunately, I didn't make it over halfway through before I started to yawn.

"I'm sorry," I said. "It's been a long week, and I'm still a little behind on my sleep."

"That's not a problem," he said, pulling me against his chest. "Rather than go home tonight, why don't you stay here? I'll let you sleep, and you can take off whenever you need to tomorrow."

"I'd love that," I said, even as I yawned again. "But I hadn't planned on staying here tonight. I didn't bring a nightgown or clothes for tomorrow."

"I guess you'll have to sleep naked," Max said with a grin. "I know I've suggested this before, but maybe you should think about bringing over a few things so you don't have this problem in the future."

I smiled and nodded as Max talked about bringing over clothes. He'd brought up the idea a few times before, and I'd always deflected it. Max didn't realize it, but he'd hit on a delicate subject.

Until now, I'd been careful about not bringing over too many things to leave at his house. I had a toothbrush and a designated towel rack in the bathroom, but I'd so far drawn the line at filling the closets with my clothes.

I knew from experience that bringing over clothes was the first step to moving in together. Although part of me was thrilled at the idea of living with Max, part of me was terrified.

It wasn't Max's prior criminal history, although Gina still thought that could cause problems down the line. It was more the potential loss of freedom and my independence.

I knew my lifestyle would change once I was living with a man, even if that wasn't the original plan. I knew I wouldn't be able to come and go as I pleased, at least not without some questions.

Having my decisions and lifestyle constantly examined was the main reason I had broken up with Reno, my previous boyfriend, a detective with the Scottsdale police department. I worried my relationship with Max might also turn that way if we became roommates.

I ended up falling asleep against Max as the movie played on. He kissed me awake when it ended, and I staggered into the bedroom. He helped me pull off my clothes, and we crawled into bed.

The last thing I remembered was the texture of his bedding. Max seemed to have the world's softest sheets, and feeling them against my bare skin was always a sensual treat.

Chapter Thirteen

I made it back to my apartment around ten on Sunday morning. I wanted to head to the casino to stash my jewelry while I had some free time. I also needed to figure out what to do with Morgan.

I got off the elevator as Grandpa Bob came out of his apartment. I caught up with him as he turned to lock the door.

"Good morning," I said.

"Hey, cookie," Bob said. "What's shakin', bacon?"

"Nothing much, stay in touch," I said, laughing. "Is Grandma in today? I need to get something from her."

"She's there," he said with a note of discomfort.

"Have you and Grandma decided what to do with all the new furniture, the vases, and the pictures?"

"Not yet," he said with a touch of regret. "Honestly, I don't care so much about the stuff, but the kids flipped their wigs when I said I was going to give everything to a thrift store. I guess they'd all chipped in to buy the furniture, back when I first moved into my old place, and they didn't want to see it tossed."

"I can see that," I said. "But I'm not sure if there's enough room in your apartment for all the new pieces."

"Yeah, I know," he admitted, sounding like this had been

a discussion topic for the last several days. "We'll need to figure out what to do with everything. I don't want to live with someone who's always mad at me. I got a full ration of that in my last marriage."

"Well, let me know how I can help," I said. "Even if it's only to cart some things down to the dumpster."

When I walked into my place, Morgan was watching TV on the couch, looking like he'd just woken up. He'd made a pot of coffee, filling the apartment with its wonderful morning aroma.

I poured a mug and sat at my kitchen table. The news was on the TV at a low volume, and we spent a few minutes sipping coffee and watching the local headlines.

"Now that you're in town, have you considered doing something with the figurines?" I asked, eyeing the duffle on the floor next to the couch. "I'm sure we could find somewhere safe to store everything while you figure out what you want to do with them."

Morgan looked down at his bag. He sighed and shook his head slowly. "I've been dragging the Professor's trinkets around for over a month, and they're a pain in the ass. But I know how valuable they are, so I didn't want to simply toss them."

"I'm not suggesting you throw them away," I said. "But my apartment isn't exactly known for being a secure fortress. I'm going to store some things of mine in a safety deposit box at Casino Scottsdale later this morning. Maybe you could keep your things there as well."

He let out a small groan of frustration. I could see this was a question that had been bugging him.

"You're right," he admitted. "I do need to get rid of everything. I'm getting tired of babysitting these things. They seem to attract danger, and I don't want to end up like the Professor."

"Are you going to try to sell them?"

"Sure, if I could get some cash out of the deal, then great. The Professor had been dealing with Raymond Eckart, and you said he's in town. The guy's a crook, but he does have decent connections. I could probably dump everything on him and come out of it okay."

"Or there's always a pawnshop," I observed. "If all the pieces are gold, that's worth something in itself."

"No," Morgan said, shaking his head. "Not a pawnshop. I'd rather give them to someone who knew what they had. I'm not all that big into ancient Egypt, but the Professor did his best to teach me about the artifacts. There's a lot of history behind them."

"What about a museum?" I asked. "I have an acquaintance who works at the Phoenix Art Museum. She'd probably be glad to get a collection like yours."

"It might come down to that," he admitted. "But since I don't have any paperwork, a museum wouldn't pay me anything for them. They'd probably assume I stole them from someone and maybe even try to turn me in as a tomb robber."

"It sounds like you're stuck dealing with Eckart," I said, feeling uneasy. "I know how dangerous he is, but he'd at least handle the pieces respectfully."

"There was another guy we were working with in Egypt who was okay," Morgan said, sounding thoughtful. "Maybe we could get ahold of him. He was associated with the Egyptian Museum in Cairo."

"I've never heard of that museum," I said.

"It's supposedly the world's largest in terms of ancient Egyptian artifacts. The Professor took me there a couple of times so I could learn about the different kingdoms and dynasties. It was a fascinating place."

"This museum guy sounds interesting," I said. "Tell me about him."

"His job was to travel around and buy antiquities from tomb robbers and people like us who sold things on the black market. He didn't offer nearly as much as Eckart, but his heart seemed to be in the right place. The Professor ended up selling him several of his statues."

"What was his name?" I asked. "Do you have any idea how we could contact him?"

"No, I never knew a lot about him," Morgan said with a shake of his head. "He always went through the Professor whenever we dealt with him. But he called himself Mustafa Yousef."

I'll be damned.

"Mustafa?" I asked, surprised. "I've met him. He's in Scottsdale and is one of the people who hired us to look for your body."

Morgan's eyes lit up. "Interesting," he said as he seemed to think about the implications. "Do you think you could arrange a meeting? If I could sell, or even give, the figurines to him, that would save me a world of hassle. I hate trying to keep these things safe while I drag them around."

Morgan paused and seemed to think of something. His tone and posture softened. "Mustafa didn't happen to have anyone traveling with him, did he?"

"Like who?" I asked, confused.

"A woman," Morgan confessed with a chuckle and a shake of his head. "I know she dated Mustafa for a while back in Egypt. She then pretended to care about me, but I later figured out she was only looking for the Professor's code."

"No, but I think that's why Mustafa is looking for your corpse. I'm pretty sure he's after the information on your tattoo."

"And you said Eckart also knows about it?"

"Um, honestly?" I asked. "I think everyone even casually involved with this knows about the code. From what I've gathered, you were rather loud the night in the bar when you decided to get it inked on your stomach."

Morgan laughed and again shook his head. "And I thought I was at least a little subtle about getting the tattoo."

"I've talked with Eckart about it already," I said. "He's interviewed the woman who did the tattoo back in Cairo."

"You're serious?" Morgan asked. "What did she tell him?"

"She gave him some of the numbers and described how long the code was. It was apparently enough to provide Eckart with a general idea of how to find the rest of the pieces. It's why so many people are here in Scottsdale, looking for your corpse."

As Morgan thought about it, he nodded. All the pieces of what had been happening to him seemed to come together to form a clear picture.

"See if you can arrange a meeting with Mustafa Yousef," Morgan said with resolve. "I'll see if he wants to take these things off my hands. Hopefully, he'll give me something for the effort. But even if he doesn't, I know they'll end up somewhere legitimate. The Professor would want that."

"I'll give him a call and see how soon he can make it," I said. "With any luck, we'll be able to wrap this up later today."

I called Mustafa, but he didn't answer. I then left a message for him to call me back and disconnected.

"I'll try again later this afternoon and again in the morning," I said. "I'll let you know if I can set something up for tomorrow."

I let Morgan know I was leaving, went into the hallway, and knocked on Grandma's door.

"Why, Laura," she said as she invited me into her apartment. "Come on in. How are things going with your secret new man?"

"Things are going fine," I said, not wanting to explain the situation again.

"And you said that Max knows about him?" Grandma asked, concerned. "I wouldn't want to see the men arguing over you."

"It's okay," I said, my temple starting to pound with the start of a headache. "Max knows all about him. Would I be able to get the shoebox back?"

"Of course, dear. I'll go back to the bedroom and get it for you."

Of all the casinos I've been to in Arizona, Casino Scottsdale was one of the nicest. It had a massive gambling floor and featured a luxury hotel with a vast tropical pool and an enormous poolside bar.

By design, they offered few services for children and families. As a result, you could spend the afternoon at the pool without the screaming kids you'll find at many of the resorts. I'd been here a few times over the years when prices during the summer months dropped to something approaching reasonable.

As I arrived, I was a little shocked at how many cars filled the parking lot for a Sunday afternoon. I'd always considered casinos as places you went for entertainment on a Friday or Saturday night. There was apparently a culture of day gambling I'd known nothing about.

I went to the gaming floor and made my way over to VIP Guest Services. It was in a separate room near the resort check-in desk and was quite posh.

As I entered, I asked the woman who greeted me for Vicky Harper. She directed me to a glamorous-looking woman wearing heels, a turquoise blue dress, and several pieces of expensive-looking jewelry. Her make-up was nicely applied, and her short brunette hair had a modern artistic style.

"I'm Victoria Harper," she said as she extended her hand. "How can I help you?"

"My name's Laura Black," I said as I showed her the card Max had given me the previous night. "I've heard the casino rents out safety deposit boxes."

"We do indeed," she said as she led me to her desk. "Mr. Bettencourt sent me an email saying you'd be over today. You have a year's comp on whatever size box you need."

"I only have a few pieces," I said, holding up my shoebox. "It doesn't need to be too large."

She typed into her computer briefly, then picked up the phone on her desk and made a call. "Pull box 318 for a new account."

While we waited, Victoria had me fill out a card with my name, address, and driver's license number. She then had me stand against a Casino Scottsdale backdrop hanging on the wall and took my picture.

A beefy security guard in a black polo came into the office from a hallway in the back. He was pushing a stainless steel cart with large black wheels and a thick handle.

The guard then opened the lid of the cart and pulled out a long metal box with a hinged lid. Vicky took the box and led me into a smaller private room off to the side.

The two of them waited outside while I transferred my jewelry into their new home. I let them know I was finished, and the guard locked the box into the cart and handed me a key.

"That's all there is to it," Victoria said as the guard wheeled the cart to the back of the office. "Here is a card for a year's comp at VIP valet. Stop by guest services, day or night, if we can do anything for you."

Chapter Fourteen

On the way to the office the following morning, I stopped by the doughnut shop and got a dozen fresh pastries. When I walked up to Sophie's cubicle, she looked at the box like a hungry dog eyeing a steak.

"What'd you do all weekend?" Sophie asked as she pulled out a Boston cream. "Just the cupcakes, or did you do anything fun? Have you heard from Gabriella yet?"

"Nothing from Gabriella," I said as I put the doughnuts on the breakroom table and pulled a Diet Pepsi from the fridge. "I mainly worked on the cupcake thing. You'd be amazed how seriously those ladies take their baking."

"No," she said, laughing, her mouth full of doughnut. "I get it. My mom takes that sort of stuff to heart, especially for some of her special recipes. I honestly don't think I'll learn the secret ingredients for her famous *Chilaquiles en salsa verde* until she passes them down in her will."

"Oh, there's one more thing," I said, almost not wanting to bring it up. "Last Friday, when I got home from work, Morgan West met me in the parking lot of my apartment."

"What?" Sophie asked, her face going pale. "Morgan West is dead. He's been dead for a month. We have confirmation on that from the government of Egypt and the state of Arizona. What exactly did you see in your parking lot?"

"At first, I thought he was a homeless guy," I said. "But it turns out that Morgan's been alive the entire time."

"No," Sophie said as she shook her head and frowned. "Dead people don't suddenly spring back to life. I don't know what you think you saw in your parking lot, but it sounds like you're dealing with either a vampire or a poltergeist situation. Were its feet touching the ground when it came toward you? Or was it sort of, floating?"

I shook my head and might have given her an eye roll. "I'm pretty sure it was actually Morgan. He explained there'd been a mix-up in Egypt."

"What kind of mix-up?" Sophie asked, her eyes narrowed with suspicion.

"It turns out that Professor Nabil was the man murdered in the apartment. The Professor had Morgan's passport in his pocket at the time. When the police came to investigate, the local detectives listed Morgan as being the murder victim, and the story sort of grew from there."

"When it comes to dealing with the undead, I wouldn't take any chances," Sophie said, shaking her head. "Next time you get a chance, poke him in the arm with a fork or something. See if he bleeds."

"Well, I'm not sure I'll stick a fork in him, but I'll let you know if anything like that happens. Morgan will be staying at my place until this is resolved."

Sophie gave me a look that seemed to say I was nuts. "Did you ever find out why so many people are looking for him?" she asked.

"Yeah, it turns out that before he died, Professor Nabil gave Morgan a secret code that would let him get something called the funeral mask of an ancient Egyptian pharaoh named Men-her Ra. Morgan then had the code tattooed on his lower stomach."

"Funeral mask?" Sophie asked, a look of confusion on her face. "What the hell is that?"

"I looked it up," I said. "It's a gold covering that goes directly over the head and shoulders of the mummy. It has an exact likeness of the pharaoh so everyone would know what he looked like when he got to the afterlife."

Sophie swallowed a couple of times and grew pale again. "You're looking for a mask that spent a couple of thousand years touching the face of a dead Egyptian mummy?"

"Um, yeah," I said. "I guess we are."

"Why do you keep doing these things?" she asked, waving her arms and sounding frustrated. "Is there a curse on this thing too?"

"I don't know," I shrugged. "Maybe."

"From everything I've seen in movies, no ancient magic is stronger than an Egyptian mummy's curse. You got away pretty cleanly with the last jinxed thing you were looking for. I seriously don't know how long your luck is going to hold out."

I went to the breakroom table and grabbed a chocolate doughnut. Returning to my cubicle, I could see Sophie starting to get over her heebie-jeebies about Morgan.

"Assuming that the entity you have living with you is actually Morgan West," she said. "What's he like?"

"He seems okay," I said. "I get the feeling he didn't know what he was getting into when he went to Egypt. Now he's in over his head."

"Is he as cute as he looked in the picture that the woman pretending to be Kelsey brought over?"

"Yeah, I think you'd approve," I said with a laugh. "But you should see all the tattoos he has. The guy looks like Adam Levine."

"Hey, don't you say mean things about Adam Levine," Sophie said with a touch of annoyance. "You know Maroon 5 is one of my favorite groups of all time."

I made a call to Mustafa Yousef. Again, he didn't answer, so I left a message telling him I needed to speak with him as soon as possible.

Next, I called Dr. Janice Lee at the Phoenix Art Museum. She was an expert on Asian art, and I'd worked with her before when I'd been on an assignment for the movie star Stig Stevens.

"Dr. Lee," I said when she answered. "This is Laura Black. I don't know if you remember me, but we discussed a jade sculpture called *The Child* some time ago."

"I do indeed remember you and our conversation," she said in her silky-smooth voice. "Three months after you asked me about the figurine, the authorities in China announced that *The Child* had been found and that it had been put on permanent display next to *The Mother*. I've often wondered what the connection was between our talk and the piece being recovered."

"Well, it was certainly helpful," I said.

"Let me ask you, assuming this is something you can tell me. Did you get to see or touch the actual sculpture?"

"Um, yes," I said, laughing at the memory. "When I found it, it was in a hotel room in North Scottsdale. It had been given away as a party favor and was being used as an accent piece to give the place a splash of color. Some kids had been playing with it, and the jade was on the floor, mixed in with a pile of pillows and toys."

"Oh my god," she breathed out. "That sculpture was nearly a thousand years old and was literally priceless. It could have easily been damaged."

"That's true," I admitted. "But it eventually made it back to its proper home in China. I felt pretty good about the outcome."

Dr. Lee paused as if having a moment. Finally, she spoke.

"Thank you for the story. It fills in some gaps for me. I'm grateful I was able to contribute, in my own small way, to having the piece recovered. But what can I do for you today?"

"I'm looking for someone knowledgeable about the artwork of ancient Egypt."

"Really?" she asked, curiosity in her voice. "Are you on the trail of something notable?"

"Maybe," I said. "But I don't know anything about this, and I was hoping to talk with an expert."

"Unfortunately, there isn't anyone here at the museum with that as an area of specialization. We have many European art pieces in the collection, but only a few from ancient Egypt."

"Alright," I said. "I knew it was a long shot. But thank you anyway."

"Don't be discouraged yet," Dr. Lee said. "I do happen to have a friend who teaches at Arizona State. She's a professor of history, and the ancient Middle East is one of her focus areas."

"That's great," I said. "If you can give me her name, I'll look her up."

"I can do better than that," she said. After a moment, my phone buzzed with a text. "Her name is Professor Mariam Salah, and I sent her contact information to you. When you talk with her, tell her I said hello."

"I will," I said. "And thank you."

I next called Mariam Salah at ASU. "Professor," I said when she answered. "My name's Laura Black, and I got your number from Dr. Lee at the Phoenix Art Museum."

"Oh, of course," she said with a bright and cheerful voice. "How's Janice doing?"

"She's doing well," I said. "She thought you might be able to help me. I have some questions about a piece of ancient Egyptian artwork."

"Well, I'm not an expert," she confessed. "But I do know a thing or two on the subject. If you'd like to talk about ancient art, why don't you come to my office?"

"That would be perfect," I said.

"I have open hours this morning from ten until noon. I'm in Coor Hall on the main ASU campus, room 501."

"Thanks," I said. "I'll see you there."

I drove down to the main campus of ASU in Tempe. As I looked for an open visitor's space, I realized I hadn't been here since I'd worked with Professor Mindy.

I eventually gave up on finding a space on the street and ended up at a parking garage on Myrtle Avenue. From there,

I made my way to Coor Hall, a six-story building that seemed to house the offices for most of the departments on the west side of campus.

I took the elevator up to the fifth floor and made my way to room 501. As I walked in, there were several offices for the Professors who worked there, and the space was a low buzz of people talking.

I found Professor Salah's office and knocked on the doorframe. She looked up from her desk and invited me in.

"Hi, Professor," I said. "I'm Laura Black. We talked on the phone a few minutes ago."

The Professor was a small woman in her late forties with short dark hair and large black glasses. She stood up and walked to me, smiling. After shaking my hand, she waved me to a chair in front of her desk and took a seat herself.

"You mentioned that you wanted to discuss a piece of Egyptian artwork?" she asked.

"Yeah," I said. "I wanted to get your impressions on this."

I reached into my bag and pulled out the cat statue. I'd wrapped it in a soft winter scarf to keep it from getting scratched. I carefully removed the protective layers and set the small figurine on her desk.

The Professor's eyes opened wide with surprise as she leaned forward, gazing at the cat for several moments without saying anything. She then absentmindedly opened a drawer, pulled out a pair of white gloves, and slipped them on. Picking up the cat, she slowly turned the figurine.

"What can you tell me about this?" she asked, reaching into her drawer again and pulling out a sizable magnifying glass. Using the lens, she closely examined the little gold sculpture.

"I got it as part of an investigation I'm working on," I said. "I'm mainly interested in learning what this is and where it could have come from."

She handed me the magnifying glass and let me look as she pointed to some markings on the cat.

"Do you see the scarab beetles on the cat's head and chest? Those symbolize rebirth. It's not unusual to find these in Egyptian tombs. From the design of the scarabs, the figurine appears to be from the late first kingdom, probably somewhere between the sixth and tenth dynasties."

"Really?" I asked, a little flabbergasted. "How long ago was that?"

She sat back in her chair. "About four thousand years ago."

"What do you know about an Egyptian Pharaoh called Men-her Ra?" I asked.

"I know of the name, but I don't know a lot about him. He was a pharaoh in the eighth dynasty."

"Did he build a big pyramid or anything like that?"

She shook her head. "No, the pyramids were built much earlier."

"But there was a pharaoh called Men-her Ra?" I pushed.

"As far as we know. Do you have information that this piece came from his tomb? The more we can piece together about that time, the better our understanding of ancient Egypt will be."

I shrugged. "That's what I was told. If it's true, do you know what it's worth, assuming it's real?"

A small digital scale sat on a cabinet next to her desk with a piece of black felt on it. She turned on the scale and carefully set the cat on the cloth.

"The figurine weighs a little over sixty-three troy ounces," she said. "Keep in mind, the Egyptians seldom used pure gold. Twenty-five percent or so of their gold was typically silver."

She took out a calculator from her desk and started pushing buttons. "If we use fifteen hundred dollars per ounce for the eighteen-carat gold, that puts the figurine at just under a hundred thousand dollars. But that's not counting the historical significance of the piece."

"And if you add that in?" I asked as I leaned forward.

She blew out a breath. "Again, you'd need an expert to know for sure. But I saw a similar sculpture that went up for auction last year. It brought in a little over a million dollars."

Wow!

She must have seen the look in my eyes because she held up her hand. "Before you get too excited, the piece at the auction house was fully documented and had a guaranteed clear title. An object like this likely has no paperwork, and there might be a legal fight over who has the rights to it. That would knock down the cash value of the figurine, probably by half."

"One more question," I said. "What can you tell me about funeral masks?"

"It's the object most people think of when they talk about the treasures of King Tut," she said. "It's a gold mask with an exact likeness of the king's face. It sits directly on the head and shoulders of the mummy."

"Okay," I said, nodding. "That fits in with what I've been reading. Did all the pharaohs have a funeral mask?"

She shrugged. "All of them we know of. Of course, most of the tombs were looted long before anyone thought to preserve anything in a museum."

"If someone were to find the funeral mask of Pharaoh Men-her Ra, any idea what that would be worth?"

She gave me a look that was sort of hard to read. I'm not sure if she thought I was serious or not. "Well, if you could find that and it could be authenticated, you'd probably be talking fifty to eighty million dollars, give or take."

"Thanks," I said. "I appreciate the information."

I was about to get up when a thought struck me. According to what Morgan had said, Professor Nabil had found the pieces in the desert. I'd assumed he meant the deserts of Egypt, but now I wondered if he could have been referring to the deserts around here.

I looked at Professor Salah. "Have you ever heard of ancient Egyptian pieces like this being buried or hidden in Arizona?"

The question seemed to make her pause, and she sat back to think about it. "There's only one legend about that," she finally said. "At least only one that I know about. This came from an old diary a colleague found at an estate sale a few years ago in California."

"How does the story go?" I asked, leaning forward.

"Well, the tale's about a wealthy Spanish governor from Mexico who was moving part of his fortune, including several gold figurines, to an estate he'd been granted in California."

"How long ago was this?" I asked.

"This was sometime in the 1780s. Like most people back then, they were forced to take the *El Camino del Diablo*, the Devil's Road."

"What's that?" I asked. "I think I've heard the term before."

"Oh, it's a very famous trail. Before the railroads were built, the only way to get from northern Mexico to California was a path the indigenous peoples had used for hundreds of years. It passed by the only two semi-reliable sources of water in the region. The Tule Tanks and the *Tinajas Altos*."

"Semi-reliable water? I asked.

"The trail passes through a desolate portion of the Sonoran Desert along the Arizona-Mexico border. Depending on the year and how many people had been to the basins before, many travelers found themselves in the furnace-like conditions without any water."

"I can only imagine what a nasty death that would be," I said, recalling a couple of close calls I'd had from being stranded in the desert.

"There are records of over two thousand people dying along the trail," Professor Salah said. "And that's only the more modern ones they bothered to document."

"That sounds brutal," I said. "I've traveled through that part of the state a few times in the summer. I always felt a little uneasy about the conditions outside, even in an air-conditioned car."

"Anyway," Professor Salah continued. "The story goes that several members of the governor's household staff, along with his personal guards, were transporting his fortune across the desert. Unfortunately, when they arrived at the *Tinajas Altos*, they found the water basins to be completely dry."

"Wow," I said with a shake of my head. "What happened to them?"

"According to the account in the diary, the group attempted to continue, but the horse pulling the wagon holding the crates died from dehydration. They apparently decided they'd have better luck traveling without the heavy treasure."

"That's so dreadful," I said as I visualized their terrible situation. "What did they do?"

"They went up one of the canyons and hid everything in a rock formation called The Thousand Caves. They then tried to reach the Gila River, the next water source, another fifteen or twenty miles to the north."

"Did they make it?" I asked. I knew I was stressing about something that had happened two hundred and fifty years ago, but I couldn't help it.

The Professor shook her head. "Unfortunately, all but one of them died along the way. The lone survivor was a woman from the household staff. The details of the story came from her diary."

"Did they ever go back to get everything they'd hidden in the cave?"

"After the woman recovered from the ordeal, she tried to lead the governor back to where they'd hidden the treasure, but nothing looked familiar to her. The recovery party searched the area for over a month but never found anything."

"Wow," I said. "You'd think people would still be looking for it."

"They *have* been," she said with a laugh. "But at this point, it's merely a colorful legend." The Professor then picked up the cat figurine sitting on her desk. "Or maybe it's not only a legend?"

"Thanks for the story," I said. "It's helpful."

"If you want to know more about it, I'd talk with Omar Nabil. He's another professor in the department and the one who found the diary. He tells the story much better than I do. Although, I think he's currently on some sort of extended sabbatical."

"I'll look into that," I said, feeling sort of crappy. I didn't think I should be the one to tell her about the Professor.

She then paused and looked at me. "I'm not sure how you acquired this," she said, slowly turning the cat over. "But pieces like this have a long history of being cursed. Death often surrounds the artifacts of ancient Egypt. I would be extremely vigilant. Plus, if you picked it up during an investigation, I imagine someone will be looking to get it back."

Jeez, I can't tell Sophie about a curse.

"Thanks, Professor," I said. "And, um, if you could keep this between us, I'd appreciate it."

Chapter Fifteen

I returned to the office and plopped down in my cubicle. Sophie was working on a report, and Gina's cube was empty.

I opened my bag and took out the gold cat figurine. As I unwrapped it, Sophie's eyes opened wide.

"Where'd you get that?" she asked. "Is it real gold?"

"I got it from Morgan. He gave it to me in exchange for helping him out with his problems."

"Well," Sophie said with a laugh. "If it's made of gold, I think you got the better end of that deal."

"I was over at ASU this morning, talking with a professor of art history. She didn't think it was a forgery."

"Don't show it to Gina," Sophie said with an eye roll. "She'd make you hand it over to the authorities."

"Hey," I said. "I got it as payment for helping out Morgan."

"I don't think it matters when it sounds like he stole it from someone else. You know you'd at least get a lecture from her."

Knowing Sophie was probably right, I took the ancient cat figurine, re-wrapped it in my scarf, and put it in the bottom drawer in my cubicle.

I still hadn't heard from Mustafa, so I called and left him another message. I was hoping to get him together with Morgan as soon as possible. I knew having so much gold in my place was a recipe for disaster, and I wanted to get the figurines out of my apartment.

I stayed at my desk for the next half an hour, looking at the paper containing the code. It still didn't make any sense to me. I even used the computer to run searches on the numbers. As I continued to puzzle out the code, my phone rang with Phony Kelsey's ID.

I'd planned on calling her today to ask what was going on. I guess this way, she'd saved me the trouble.

"Laura," the woman said. "It's Kelsey Dawson. I was curious about how the investigation was going. Have you had any luck in tracking down Morgan's body yet?"

"You can drop the act," I said, annoyed. "We had the real Kelsey Dawson in here. She told us that someone had broken into her house. They stole her wallet and the papers concerning Morgan. Was that you?"

There was a pause as the phone went silent for a moment.

"Fine," she said. "I'll drop the pretense. You're right. I'm involved in this. But I need to know if you've found Morgan's body yet. I specifically need to know if you've gotten the secret code everyone's so excited about."

I was annoyed at this woman to the point where I was too upset even to lie. I tried to compose myself, but unfortunately, she gathered the truth from my silence.

"Ahh," she exclaimed. "So, you did get it. I knew you

were a clever girl. I'll need to meet with you, right away."

"And why should I have anything to do with you?" I asked. "All you've done is lie to me."

"You're right," she admitted. "I'm not exactly sure of the legalities, but I'm still kind of a client of your law office. That must carry some weight. Plus, I'll personally pay you another ten thousand dollars in cash for the code."

"Where do you want to meet?" I asked.

"Let's go to the McCormick-Stillman Railroad Park," she said. "I drove by there yesterday, and it looks interesting."

"I take it you aren't from around here," I observed. "If you grew up in Scottsdale, you'd have gone to about a dozen birthday parties there as a kid."

"No," she admitted. "I grew up in Colorado Springs. This is my first time in Arizona."

"When do you want to meet?" I asked. "I'll be free for the next couple of hours."

"Why don't we do it now," she said. "I'll be there in about half an hour."

"Fine," I said, still not thrilled about seeing the woman again. But I knew it would be a chance to see how she fit in with everything else. "I'll be there."

Sophie had been following the conversation, and she looked at me questioningly.

"I'm heading over to the railroad park to meet with Phony Kelsey," I said. "I'll let you know if anything comes out of it."

As I stood to leave, I opened my desk drawer and tossed in the paper with the code. I knew it was still a mystery that needed to be solved.

I drove up Scottsdale Road until I got to Indian Bend, then pulled into the lot for the railroad park. After I found a space, I got out and glanced around but didn't see Phony Kelsey anywhere.

The park covered thirty or forty acres, with lots of relatively quiet places to have a conversation. I scolded myself for not being more specific about where to meet.

Pulling out my phone, I called my former client, but she didn't pick up. After leaving her a message to contact me with her location, I disconnected.

The first stop was the park's two playgrounds. There were tons of squealing kids and many mothers watching them, but Phony Kelsey wasn't anywhere.

Next, I entered the model railroad building, where half a dozen toy trains were chugging around on scaled tracks through carefully crafted scenery. I again saw tons of kids, mostly with their dads, but my target wasn't there.

I went back outside and ended up at the station for the Paradise and Pacific steam locomotive. Not finding her there either, I returned to the parking lot and ended up back at my car.

Instead of Phony Kelsey, Owen was standing next to my Miata. He wasn't wearing his jacket, and I didn't see a gun. Seeing him immediately pissed me off.

"Eckart wants to talk with you," the kid said, trying to act tough. "He wants to see you, right away."

"I'm waiting for someone," I said, trying to hold down my anger at seeing the man who had tried to kill me. "Tell him I can meet later today."

Owen shook his head. "She ain't coming. So, if you want to know what's going on and still want that ten thousand she promised, you'd better come to the meeting."

"And if I don't come?" I asked.

"I couldn't care less," he sneered. "But if you don't show up, you learn nothing and don't get the money. It's that simple."

Owen took off in his rental, and I followed. We went east on Indian Bend, then south on Hayden, ending up at the same apartment complex as before.

Going up to the room, Owen took out a key and opened the door. The apartment appeared to be empty except for the bulk of Raymond Eckart.

He sat on the overstuffed chair, watching an old black-and-white *film noir* on the television. In front of him, on the coffee table, was a large snifter containing a brown liquid.

"Ah, Miss Black," Raymond said as he stood. "It is truly a pleasure to see you again. I understand that you were successful in locating the body of Morgan West."

"Why do you expect me to tell you anything?" I blurted out. "I was willing to deal with you when we first met. Instead, I was bashed in the head and stuffed into a mortuary vault, left to die."

"Surely, Miss Black, I never meant for you to be injured," Raymond said, chuckling. "I merely had Owen place you in the storage locker to keep you out of harm's way while we removed the body of Professor Nabil from the Coroner's laboratory."

"You didn't mean to hurt me?" I asked, my voice rising. "Those mortuary vaults are airtight, not to mention freezing. I almost suffocated in there."

"Maybe you shouldn't have stuck your nose into our business," Owen snapped at me. "Did you ever think of that?"

"Owen, behave yourself," Eckart said kindly. "We're all good friends here."

"Why did you steal the body of that man from the Medical Examiner?" I asked. "Without the tattoo, it wasn't going to do you any good."

"That's true," Eckart admitted with a nod. "We'd been prepared to take Morgan's body. I was as surprised as anyone to see the body of Professor Nabil in the vault. I took him back with us to learn if there were any clues on his corpse that could help us out."

"Did you think the Professor might have also tattooed the code on his body?"

"I will admit, the thought had crossed my mind," Eckart nodded. "The odds were against it, but since the body was there, I wanted to confirm it for myself."

"What about the lab tech who let you into the building?" I asked. "Nobody's seen Brian McCoy since that night."

Eckart paused, picked up the snifter, swirled it twice, and then took a deep drink. "Well, I paid the man handsomely for his services," he chuckled. "I would assume he's on a beach somewhere having a bit of a holiday."

There was a knock at the door of the apartment. Raymond absentmindedly waved for Owen to answer it.

As the boy swung open the door, I was surprised to see Phony Kelsey Dawson walk in. As with the two other times I'd seen her, she was dressed in a low-cut, form-fitting outfit that showed off her fit body.

"Hello, Laura," she said as she strolled to the center of the room.

"You," I blurted out. "Are you going to tell me who you are and what you want? It's obvious you aren't Kelsey Dawson."

"Laura Black," Raymond boomed out with his deep voice. "Let me introduce you to Miss Sabrina Lambert. She's been on my payroll since I lured her away from Mustafa Yousef some six months ago."

"Thank you for coming out to meet with us," Sabrina said, making herself comfortable on one end of the couch. "I'm sorry for the further deception, but Raymond wanted to talk with you, and I wasn't sure you would've come here otherwise."

"Why do you want to see me?" I asked.

"I thought it would have been obvious by now," Sabrina said. "You told me you were able to get the code from Morgan's body. We'll need you to hand it over to us."

"And why would I want to do that?" I fumed. "You used lies and deception to get me to look for Morgan. I did it because I thought you cared about him. But all this time, you were only looking for the code."

"Laura," she said, a touch of pleading in her voice. "Please don't be this way. You'll need to tell Raymond everything you know. I don't want to see you getting hurt."

"What? You're going to try to hurt me?" I asked, mentally gearing up for a fight.

"No, of course not," she said, shaking her head. "You don't need to worry about me."

I heard movement and looked to the back of the

apartment. Owen was now alert, his face flushed with excitement.

"Yes, Miss Black," Raymond said with a serious tone. "Unfortunately, what Sabrina says is true. If you don't hand over the code you retrieved from Morgan's body, I'll have Owen beat the information out of you. However, I feel I must warn you. He has a pair of brass knuckles and enjoys hitting women in the face. I've tried to get him to stop the practice, but he apparently harbors some ill feelings toward the fairer sex. It's quite possible you'll be disfigured for life."

"Fine," I said, pulling my phone from my back pocket. I opened the pictures and flipped through them until I got to the one of the tattoo.

"Here it is," I said as I forwarded the photo to Sabrina's phone. "Don't ask how I got it."

Sabrina opened the message and stared at the image as if it was a hot naked man. "That's it," she said, half to herself. "I recognize the surrounding tattoos."

She forwarded the photo, and I heard Eckhart's phone ping with the incoming message.

"Ahh," Raymond said as he studied the picture. "I've been searching for this for quite some time. It is indeed satisfying to have finally obtained it."

After another thirty seconds, he lifted his head. He had a somewhat puzzled look on his face. "Is this the entire code?" he asked. "It doesn't appear to be quite right."

"You have the picture of the tattoo," I said. "That's what I got."

"Very well," Raymond said with a nod. "I'm a man of his word, and I believe payment is due."

Eckart opened a drawer in an end table and pulled out a stack of new hundred-dollar bills. Like the bundle Sabrina had given Sophie, the yellow-gold treasury band was still tightly wrapped around the currency.

"Miss Black, it's been a pleasure doing business with you," he said as he handed me the stack of bills. "Now then, since this is most likely the last time our paths will cross, let's end it with a toast. Would you do the honors and pour the drinks?"

At this point, I only wanted to be gone. I went to the wet bar and poured myself a glass of scotch, pausing only to drop in an ice cube.

I held up the bottle of Macallan for Eckart and gave him a questioning look. "Another Hennessy XO for me," he said, holding up his empty snifter. "If you don't mind."

I took his glass and found the sculptured bottle he'd indicated. I then poured out three fingers of the cognac.

Sabrina walked to the wet bar and made herself a Bacardi rum and Coke. She seemed to know where the soda was stored, underneath the counter, confirming this wasn't her first time in the apartment.

"Thanks for giving us the picture," she said quietly as she poured the Coke into her glass. "I didn't want to see you get hurt."

Before Sabrina returned to the couch, she looked at Owen and motioned to the bottles on the counter. He was again standing against the back wall, watching over the group.

"You know I don't drink," he said with an angry scowl.

"That's quite true," Eckhart said with a slight chuckle. "Owen likes to maintain his wits at all times. As a bonus, it will help him maintain his smooth skin for years."

Walking across the room, I handed the glass to Eckart. He lifted the snifter and spent a moment swirling the

Hennessy and taking in the aroma.

"To Pharaoh Men-her Ra," he said as he lifted his glass. "He's been dead for four thousand years, but we may still profit from his legacy."

I lifted my glass, as did Sabrina. Eckhart brought the snifter to his lips and slurped half of it down in a long noisy swallow.

After maybe two or three minutes, we'd finished our drinks. I set my glass on the wet bar counter and turned toward the door.

"One last thing before you go," Raymond said. "It's been quite beneficial doing business with you over the past few days. However, I fear this is where our roads will diverge. I trust that you won't feel the need to seek out my company again."

"No," I said. "I don't think we'll seee eash other agggain."

As I said this, I knew I had slurred some of the words. It was like this had been my fifth scotch, not my first.

What the hell?

Sabrina looked at me with concern while Eckart snorted out a small laugh as he sipped his Hennessy. His eyes peered at me over the top of the snifter. Owen took a step forward, now interested in whatever was happening with me.

I glanced at my empty glass sitting on the wet bar counter. The single ice cube was still visible, slowly melting in the room's warm air.

How could I have been so stupid?

I turned to go out the door. I needed to leave before whatever drug was in the scotch took effect.

I took three unsteady steps and made it to the door. I

reached out for the handle but couldn't seem to get a grip on it.

Sabrina got up from the couch and hurried towards me. "Laura, what's wrong?" she asked. Her hand was on my arm, and her voice sounded distant and worried. "Are you okay?"

I began to feel giddy, and the room started to spin. I knew I had to leave, but I was quickly losing focus. I tried again to open the door, but everything went dark.

Chapter Sixteen

I was standing on the deck of a luxury cruise ship somewhere that seemed tropical. I looked out over an azure-blue ocean and could feel the warm, humid sea air on my face as the boat traveled to parts unknown.

Cruise Director Julie McCoy and Captain Stubing were standing next to me, having a discussion about a passenger on the ship who was causing trouble. Not wanting to get involved, I turned and walked to the bar where Isaac Washington was talking with Gopher Smith.

As I approached, Isaac handed me a colorful drink in a tall hurricane glass with a pink umbrella sticking out of the top. I was going to take the drink when I saw Max standing at the end of the bar.

Something about seeing Max told me I wasn't on a ship in the middle of the ocean. As the vision of Gopher and Isaac faded, I found myself lying on a king-sized bed in what appeared to be Eckart's apartment.

From the brightness outside and the sun's position, it must have been nine or nine-thirty in the morning. From my bag, the theme to *The Love Boat* softly played.

I sat up slowly and swung my feet off the side of the bed. I still felt groggy and had a pounding headache.

Looking around the room, I found my shoes neatly

placed on the floor beside a dresser. My purse was hanging over a chair by its strap.

The phone had stopped ringing, but I pulled it out of my bag and hit the button to return Max's call. He answered right away.

"Hey," I said, knowing I must sound like crap.

"Laura?" Max asked. "Are you alright? It sounds like I woke you."

"No, it's okay," I said, trying to get my eyes to focus. "I had a weird night, and I appreciate you checking on me."

"Sure," he said with a slight chuckle. "As long as everything's okay."

"Yeah, I'm getting some movement on my assignment at work, and the finals for the cupcakes are tonight. I'll call you as soon as it's over."

"I hope you can do something for Beatrice," Max said. "I know she's counting on you."

After disconnecting the phone, I picked up my bag and looked through it. Everything, including my Glock, was still there.

The only thing missing was the money Eckart had given me. But honestly, I would have been more surprised if it had still been there.

I pulled out the pistol and checked that it was still loaded. I then carefully searched the apartment.

It was apparent that Eckart and Owen had cleared out while I was unconscious. The bedroom was completely empty, as was the living room.

After ensuring I was alone and the door to the hallway was locked, I searched the drawers and closets of the bedroom. Nothing remained, not even a stray sock.

I returned to the living room and did a quick search. The booze from the wet bar had been removed.

The only exception was the scotch bottle, which remained on the counter next to some dirty glassware. Somebody had poured all of it out, presumably down the wet bar sink.

I picked up the Macallan, opened it, and carefully sniffed. Unfortunately, I couldn't identify what the scotch had been laced with. All I could do was shake my head at the waste of a good bottle.

Also on the counter was a note, written in a delicate hand.

Laura, I want you to know I had nothing to do with them drugging you. I only found out that Raymond had placed a sedative in the scotch bottle after you had collapsed onto the floor. Please don't follow us. I persuaded them against doing anything physical to you this time, but I can't be certain you won't get hurt if they see you again. Sorry for the deception in your office the other day. It's been a crappy couple of months for me as well. ~Sabrina~

I searched through my bag, found my bottle of Advil, and shook out a couple of tablets. I opened the cabinet under the wet bar and came up with a can of Coke. I popped the top, then tossed back the pills.

As I stood against the counter, getting my equilibrium back, I looked down at my phone and saw I had three voicemails. The first was from Max. He'd called about ten the previous evening, wishing me a good night.

The second was from Sophie. She'd called an hour before I'd woken up, asking if I wanted to go to lunch.

The last one was from Mustafa Yousef. He said he was returning my call and wanted to know if I'd been able to come up with any leads on finding Morgan's body.

I was glad Gabriella hadn't tried to reach me while I was unconscious. I knew if she had called, she'd be counting on me to help her. I'd try my best not to let her down.

I drove to the office and went in through the back door. Sophie was in her cubicle, and Gina was again out.

I went to the fridge and pulled out a bottle of Diet Pepsi. Opening the soda with a prolonged hissing noise, I plopped down in my chair and let out a long breath.

"Is it me, or is that the same outfit you wore yesterday?" Sophie asked. "Did you get locked in a mortuary vault again?"

I shook my head slowly. "No, I drank a scotch with a knockout drug in it yesterday afternoon. I only woke up about an hour ago. I still sort of feel like crap."

"Really?" Sophie asked, now alert. "Were you at a party or something? That once happened to me. I learned never to accept a drink from a guy with a man-bun."

"Not really," I said with a slow shake of my head. "I was at the apartment with Eckart, Owen, and Phony Kelsey. I handed over part of a secret code I got from Morgan, and they drugged me."

"You know," she observed. "If you keep wearing the same clothes, think of how much time you'll save doing the laundry each week."

I knew she was only trying to be funny, but I wasn't in the mood. I looked back at her with my Death Stare.

"Well," Sophie said, ignoring my look. "Remember the

dead body your friend Eckart stole from the Medical Examiner's office?"

"Sure," I said as I leaned back in the chair and rubbed my eyes. "That was Professor Nabil."

"Well," she said, pointing to the newspaper sitting on her desk. "It looks like they fished him out of the Salt River in Tempe last night. Some joggers found him in the marshy part of the river just before it gets to Tempe Town Lake."

"What happened?" I asked. "Does it say?"

"The paper only had three paragraphs on it. It said they found a body with a bullet wound in the chest, but police on the scene said it appeared that the man had been dead for some time."

"Anything else?"

"According to the paper, the detective in charge of the case thought there might be a connection between the dead body and a recent break-in at the Scottsdale Medical Examiner's lab."

"Well, that clears up the mystery of what happened to Professor Nabil," I observed. "Once Eckart figured out he couldn't learn anything new from the corpse, he must have had Owen dump him in the river. The paper didn't say anything about finding another dead body, did it?"

"Who's body are you looking for now?" Sophie asked, sounding concerned.

"The lab tech, Brian McCoy. Eckart was supposedly going to pay him a couple of thousand to let them into the lab so they could steal the body. Eckart got a little upset when he found out it was the wrong corpse."

"Do you know for sure if something happened to your Brian guy?" she asked. "Or is he simply a no-show?"

"Nobody's seen him since that night in the lab. Brian didn't seem all that bright, but he didn't strike me as evil or anything. Honestly, I'm worried about what might have happened to him."

I next called Mustafa back. This time I was able to get ahold of him.

I let him know I had some new information on Morgan. I didn't want to meet at the office, so I arranged to meet him at three o'clock at Duke's, a local sports bar on McDowell Road and the Scottsdale Greenbelt.

By eleven thirty, I was feeling much better. The headache had receded, and I was starting to get hungry.

I'd pulled out the paper with the code from where I'd left it in my desk. I was staring at it again, trying to figure out how it fit in with everything else. It was a little frustrating that nothing obvious came to mind.

Is that the secret code you were talking about?" Sophie asked. "Let me look at it. Maybe I'll have some brilliant idea what it's for."

I handed over the paper. Sophie looked at the numbers for several minutes without coming up with anything that made sense.

"Did you try Googling it?" she asked.

"Yes," I said with a nod. "It took it as an equation and said the answer was negative eighty-one."

"Well, that's not very helpful," she observed. "Maybe it's like the page of a book he had in his place. You know, if you open to a specific page and read the first line of a specific paragraph, the answer is written there."

"Maybe," I said. "But then the book would be in an apartment in Cairo. I don't think I could ever get to it."

"Are you ready for lunch?" I asked after Sophie had made a half-dozen guesses, none of them good. "Do you mind if we do tacos down the street again?"

"I was only waiting for you to get hungry," she said. "Gina won't be back until later this afternoon, but do you want to invite Debbie?"

"Are you getting along with her better now?" I asked.

"Yeah, she's alright," Sophie said, sounding a little sad. "I talked with her, and it wasn't like she was actively trying to steal my job or anything. It was only one of Lenny's good deeds going amuck."

We walked up to the front with Sophie still holding the paper with the code.

"Maybe it's for a safety deposit box," she said as she looked at the paper. "If you know which bank it's in, you give them these numbers, and they give you the loot."

"If that's true, we'd need to find the right place," I said. "But I haven't heard anything about a bank being involved. At least not one in Arizona."

"What are you trying to figure out?" Debbie asked as we got to her desk.

"We've got a code that's supposed to lead us to a secret treasure," I said.

"Mind if I take a crack at it?" she asked. "I used to be pretty good at codes as a kid."

"Be my guest," I said as I handed over the numbers. "I could really use some help."

"Oh," she said after glancing at the paper. "That's not a code. Those are GPS coordinates. And map positions thirty-two and negative one hundred fourteen are for somewhere in southwest Arizona."

"Wait a minute," Sophie said, sounding slightly annoyed that Debbie had come up with an answer so quickly. "How do you know that?"

"I had a husband who liked to geocache," Debbie said, reminiscing. "It's a boring game where everyone drives around in a Jeep for the weekend, and you find things using map coordinates. You become familiar with the local numbers after you do it a few times."

"I'm confused," I said. "I thought longitude and latitude coordinates were in degrees, hours, and minutes. At least, that's what I learned back in sixth grade. These numbers aren't arranged anything like that."

"Well, sure," Debbie said. "You can display map coordinates like that. But this is the format most people use if you have a modern GPS device."

Sophie looked at me, and I shrugged. "Okay," I said. "If the code numbers are map coordinates, the next step is to find out where they're located."

Debbie turned to her computer, brought up Google Earth, and typed in the numbers. When she did, it brought up a picture of a rock-strewn side of a barren mountain somewhere in the desert.

We gathered around to look, but it wasn't anything we were familiar with. It was only a massive mound of rocks and desert scrub, seemingly in the middle of nowhere.

"Zoom out a little," I said. "We'll need to figure out where this is."

As Debbie pulled out, we could see a dirt road about two

miles east of the mountain going north and south. "According to the map," Debbie said as she pointed, "this road is called *El Camino del Diablo.*"

"The Devil's Highway?" Sophie asked, her eyes growing slightly larger.

"Zoom out some more," I said. "I still can't tell where it is."

"It looks like those coordinates are on the side of a mountain in the middle of the desert," Debbie said. "Maybe fifteen or twenty miles south of Welton."

"Welton?" Sophie asked, confused. "Where's that? Is it somewhere near Donkey Dump?"

"Oh, that sounds totally made up," I said. "There isn't a town in Arizona called Donkey Dump, is there?"

Sophie only shrugged.

"Welton is about thirty miles east of Yuma," Debbie said. "From Scottsdale, you can get to the start of the *El Camino del Diablo* in two and a half or three hours. From there, it looks like it would take another hour or so to drive down to the spot marked by the coordinates."

A thought struck me. "Um, what if you only typed in part of the code? Where does that put you?"

"Give me what you've got," Debbie said. "We'll find out."

I told her the numbers I had read from the first picture I'd taken of Morgan's tattoo. I knew that the last two digits were missing. This was the image I'd given to Sabrina and Raymond Eckart.

"If that's all you had to work with," Debbie said. "That would put you about half a mile east of the actual location." She then snickered and tapped her computer monitor.

"What's so funny?" I asked.

"Those coordinates would put you on the top of this black-rock mesa called Raven Butte."

"If the bad guys use that as their target location, they won't even be close," Sophie said, smiling. "I bet they'll miss it altogether."

"Trust me," Debbie said. "In my experience with geocaching, if your coordinates are off by more than a couple hundred feet, it's almost impossible to find something by randomly wandering around."

"Nice," I said, knowing I'd made it difficult for Eckart.

"One other thing," Debbie said as she stared at her monitor. "That mountain is in the middle of the Barry Goldwater Bombing Range. The military actively uses that area for live bombing practice. The coordinates are on the side of the range controlled by the Marines."

"That really doesn't sound all that safe," Sophie said.

"Do they let civilians go in there?" I asked.

"Oh sure, they'll let you enter," Debbie nodded. "There's not a gate or anything. But if you plan on driving around down there, you'll need a four-wheel-drive vehicle and a bombing range permit."

"Do you have to jump through hoops to get a permit?" I asked.

Debbie shook her head. "No. Permits are free. All you do is fill out an online form. But you do need to get them in advance. Let me know if you decide to go, and I'll print one up for you."

We locked up the office and headed down the street for tacos. As we waited for our lunch to arrive, Sophie asked me where I was with the cupcake contest. This piqued Debbie's interest, so I gave her a quick recap.

"My boyfriend's cook, Beatrice, makes delicious cupcakes, and she enters them each year in a baking contest at the Scottsdale Cookie and Cake Club. Unfortunately, a woman named Kaitlin has won the cupcake category every year for the last five years."

"How are Kaitlin's cupcakes?" Debbie asked. "They must be delicious."

"Not really," Sophie said as she scrunched up her nose. "I tried one the other night, and it wasn't so good."

"The contest judge for the entire time has been Adam Jordan. As it turns out, Adam dated both Kaitlin and her sister Shirley back in college before meeting his current wife, Naomi. The other day, I listened as Adam and Shirley snuck away to meet in a conference room."

"Did they spill any secrets?" Sophie asked.

"Not really. Adam seemed to be worried about his reputation. Shirley then told him there were worse things that could happen."

"Was that it?" Sophie asked.

"Yeah," I admitted. "It's not much to go on."

"So, you have a judge who seems to be involved with the sister of a contestant, and this contestant always wins?" Debbie asked.

"Yup," I said. "The finals are tonight, and I have nothing."

"Can you apply any pressure on the judge not to have the sister win this time?" Debbie asked.

"I don't know what I could do," I admitted. "I don't have any solid evidence he's throwing the contest."

"Can't you sway him with lies, rumors, and innuendo?" Sophie asked. "You're pretty good at that."

"Hey," I said, trying to figure out if I should take that as a compliment or an insult.

"Those are great qualities to have as an investigator," Debbie quickly added as she saw the look on my face. "I'm sure they've helped you in your career."

"Fine," I said. "Maybe I can call Adam Jordan and imply that people know all about his little scheme, even if we don't have any proof. Who knows, maybe he'll do the right thing this year?"

When we returned from lunch, I went back to my cubicle and called Adam Jordan at the number Sophie had gotten from the secret software. When he answered, he had a polished and professional phone voice.

"Mr. Jordan," I said. "My name is Laura Black. I'm an investigator here in Scottsdale, and I've been asked to look into some odd things that seem to be happening at your cake club competition."

"What are you talking about?" he asked, his voice rising slightly.

"It's been noticed that one of the contestants has won the frosted cupcake category for the last five years, even though the general consensus is that she's not the strongest baker. It's also been rumored that you previously dated this contestant when you both attended ASU."

"Look," he said, now definitely angry. "The same people enter the bake-off every year, and it's not unusual to have the same person win multiple times. I don't know where you're getting your information, but whenever there's a contest, you'll have grateful winners, and you'll have sore losers. They'll need to get over it."

"You're saying no one is holding something over your head to sway your decisions?" I asked.

"This is only a baking contest," he said, now calmer and trying to sound reasonable. "Except for the Best of Group and Best of Show awards, there isn't anything on the line except for pride and the color of the ribbon. It all comes down to opinion, and everybody has one. If somebody doesn't like my opinions on who makes the best cupcakes, they can quit the club and go to a different one. Good day, Miss Black."

As Adam disconnected, I thought about the call. Maybe it was because he was a professional politician, but his answer seemed to be a little too smooth and polished to be from the heart.

I drove back to my place and told Morgan about the meeting I'd set up with Mustafa. He still seemed eager to get rid of everything, so we wheeled the duffle out to my car.

When we arrived at Duke's, there was a Diamondbacks spring training game on most of the displays in the bar. Since the inside was too noisy for conversation, I led us outside to one of the tables against the low wrought-iron fence overlooking the Greenbelt.

As we sat, Morgan took the bag containing the ancient relics and propped it against the fence. I got comfortable and studied the menu.

I realized that the last time I'd been here was with Jerry

Phifer, the manager for the movie star Stig Stevens. It seemed like a long time ago.

A waitress stopped by, and I ordered a pitcher of Dos Equis Amber and some appetizers. I aimed to make this meeting more of a social event rather than strictly about business. Fortunately, the server was efficient, and we had the beer within minutes.

It was a beautiful spring day, sunny with a light breeze and temperatures in the upper seventies. Morgan and I spent several moments in silence, sipping our beers and watching the rollerbladers and joggers on the trail through the park.

Moments after the waitress delivered the food, Mustafa appeared at our table. His gaze slid from me to Morgan.

There was a moment of hesitation, then a look of shock and disbelief washed across Mustafa's face. This was followed by something that seemed to be anger or maybe annoyance.

"Morgan West," Mustafa said with some bitterness after he recovered. "You're supposed to be dead."

"Yeah," Morgan said. "I get that a lot."

"You were looking for Morgan's body, and here it is," I said. "I think I've fulfilled my part of your contract with Lenny."

"Yes, I guess you did," Mustafa said, nodding slowly.

I was expecting him to be impressed. But for some reason, I got the feeling Mustafa was disappointed that Morgan was still alive.

Wanting to keep the mood light, I poured Mustafa a Dos Equis and had him load up a plate of nachos. He stared at Morgan, still very much alive, and quickly downed half of his beer.

"With the death of Professor Nabil, I had assumed you were dead as well," Mustafa said to Morgan, still with a trace of hostility. "However, it seems the reports in the Cairo paper were inaccurate."

"The Professor had my passport in his pocket when the police found him," Morgan said, repeating the story he had already told me. "The detective on scene made the easy assumption, which turned out to be incorrect."

"Since you are alive, why did you want to contact me?" Mustafa asked, now with a touch of confusion.

"Back in Cairo, you expressed an interest in the Professor's remaining figurines. Do you still want to buy them?"

"What? You have them?" Mustafa asked, now fully alert.

Morgan glanced at the duffle bag at his feet, then back to Mustafa. "I have them right here."

"Yes," Mustafa breathed out, all traces of resentment now gone. "I'm very much interested, in all of them."

We spent the next half hour unwrapping each piece and handing them to Mustafa for inspection. He'd slipped on a pair of white gloves he'd pulled from his pocket and handled each statue with reverence.

As he examined the third statue, I became curious about him. "What is it you do for a living?" I asked.

"As Morgan might have told you," Mustafa said absentmindedly as he studied the underside of a small bird statue that looked like a falcon. "I'm with the Ministry of Tourism and Antiquities and work for the Egyptian Museum in Cairo. My job is hunting down and purchasing certain unique pieces that come onto the open market. They are then returned to the museum to be preserved for the people of Egypt and scholars worldwide."

"Okay," I said. "I get that you want to preserve your country's heritage. But traveling around the world and buying expensive items has to be a major drain on your museum."

"My department generates a profit each year," Mustafa said as he turned the statue over and studied some markings on the bird's chest using a small magnifying glass he'd pulled from his pocket.

"Once the museum catalogs and verifies the items, they'll be loaned to other museums throughout the world. You'd be surprised how much we make from these traveling exhibits. It's what enables me to come out and look for more artifacts."

"Do you think you'll be able to have a traveling exhibit of Pharaoh Men-her Ra?"

"In time," he said, sounding somewhat disappointed. "Unfortunately, the pieces from his tomb have become greatly scattered over the centuries."

Chapter Seventeen

Mustafa carefully examined the remaining two figurines and was thrilled by what he saw. By the time he was done, we had a collection of six gold sculptures sitting on the table, nestled between the hot wings, the nachos, and the beer.

"Each item appears to be genuine," Mustafa said. "How do you wish to proceed?"

"What would you give me if I handed over these statues to you?" Morgan asked.

"I'll make the same deal with you as I offered the Professor," Mustafa said. "Give me what you have, and I'll wire you a finder's fee of one hundred thousand U.S. dollars. The pieces will go to The Egyptian Museum in Cairo, and you'll be done with them."

"And if I don't?" Morgan asked.

Mustafa shrugged. "I'd be disappointed, of course. But you'd have no further trouble from me. Truth be told, any of the black-market dealers, such as our friend Eckart, would give you a far better price for them. But then the figurines would disappear into private collections and be lost to the world. Plus, when dealing with those types of dealers, you're as likely to get a bullet to the head as payment."

"I appreciate that," Morgan said, sounding thoughtful. "I think it's why the Professor spent so much time dealing directly with you."

"There is something else to keep in mind," Mustafa said. "I would urge you to rid yourself of these things quickly, in any case. Influential people will always desire antiquities such as these. I tried to warn the Professor that there would always be a violent element after them. He didn't listen, and it cost him his life."

Morgan thought about it and nodded his head in acknowledgment. "Toward the end, when the walls were closing in, the Professor talked about selling everything to you and being done with it. I think he was probably on the right track."

"Let me toss in something to sweeten the deal," Mustafa said. "Give me the artifacts, and I'll work with the government in Egypt to bring you back from the dead. I can't imagine the paperwork you'll need to complete to prove you're alive. We could help with that by admitting we made a mistake in declaring you dead."

There was a moment of silence while Morgan thought about his situation. "Alright," he finally said. "Let's do it your way. But since I'm listed as dead, they've already shut me down at my bank. You'll need to wire the money to my sister's account. I'll get you the numbers."

The two men shook hands, and the deal was done. We placed everything back in the duffle, and Morgan handed it to Mustafa.

"Very good," the Egyptian said. "I'll contact the embassy in San Francisco and arrange to have these picked up. I'll need to fill out a stack of forms, but I'll make sure you get your fee in two or three weeks."

"You said you're working to put together a traveling exhibit of the treasures of Men-her Ra?" I asked.

"It's a goal," Mustafa said with a shrug. "Over the past two years, I've purchased five pieces from the Professor. These additional six will greatly help, but I'd still need several more to make the collection worthwhile."

"How many are you looking for?" I asked.

"The excepted standard is twenty to thirty pieces for a traveling exhibition," Mustafa said, looking slightly discouraged. Although, we could get away with fewer pieces if we had something special as the centerpiece."

"You're thinking you'd have a better collection if you had the pharaoh's funeral mask?" I asked.

"Yes," Mustafa said with a grin. "The Professor hinted that he knew the location of the mask of Men-her Ra. If I could acquire that, it would make a substantial exhibit."

"Well," Morgan said. "I'd like to help you with that, but the Professor didn't tell me where it is."

"According to the rumors I've heard," Mustafa said, a gleam in his eye, "you possess a code that will lead you to it."

"Well, I have a code," Morgan admitted. "The Professor gave it to me back in Cairo. But I'm not sure how it will lead us to the Pharaoh's mask."

Jeez, what do I tell him now?

"If you give us the code," I said, "I bet we can come up with something."

"I might as well," Morgan said with a shrug. "The Professor is dead, and the sooner this is over, the better." He then rattled off a string of familiar numbers, and I dutifully typed them into my phone. I saw that Mustafa was doing the same."

"Um," I said as I tried to determine the best way to tell

him what I knew. "These appear to be GPS coordinates."

"Yeah, I thought they could be something like that," Morgan admitted. "But I looked them up, and they're nowhere near Egypt."

"Here," I said as I opened the map function on my phone and typed in the numbers. "This is where the coordinates point to."

I handed him the phone, and he looked puzzled. "Okay," he said. "I've seen this before. It's what I brought up when I punched the numbers into my computer. It's a hill in the middle of nowhere, but it's not in Egypt. It's here in the U.S."

"Yes," I said. "But look at the dirt road about two miles to the east. Can you read the name?"

"*El Camino del Diablo*," he said, half to himself. "The Devil's Highway. I'll be damned. Where exactly is this?"

"It's here in Arizona," I said, taking back the phone and zooming out to show him. "It's near the border of Mexico, about thirty miles southeast of Yuma."

"You believe the mask is here, not in Egypt?" Mustafa asked. He then leaned back, and I could see him thinking. "That is possible, given the reported history of the piece. But what is the significance of the Devil's Road?"

"It's something the Professor once told me when I asked him about the artifacts," Morgan said. "He said he got them by going down the Devil's Highway. I never knew what he meant, but this can't be a coincidence."

"What do you want to do?" I asked.

"We need to go out and look for the mask," Morgan said.

"Don't forget, Eckhart's been in town all week," I reminded him, trying to skim over my involvement. "He likely has a good idea where the mask is, and I wouldn't be surprised if he's also heading out to the desert. If you want to have a chance of getting to the treasure before him, we should probably go soon, at least in the next day or two."

"We'll need several things if we're going to go exploring in that part of the state," Morgan said. "It's only March, and it won't be overly hot, but I've lived here all my life. The Sonoran Desert isn't something to mess around with, no matter the time of year."

"I'd like to go with you," Mustafa said. "I have a budget for such things and will be willing to finance the expedition. In exchange, I would ask for first right of refusal on the mask if we were to find it."

Morgan thought about it and nodded his head. "Alright. I seriously don't care a lot about the pharaoh's mask. Getting another finder's fee for it would be great, but I mainly don't want Eckhart to get it. The guy's a jerk."

"Very well," Mustafa said. "Let us come up with a list of supplies. We can get everything today and leave in the morning."

We quickly made plans to meet at my apartment parking lot at five the following morning. Mustafa seemed to have put aside whatever ill feelings he had towards Morgan, and together they made plans to go to a mining supply store and purchase the items.

I returned to the office and told Debbie about my trip to the Goldwater Bombing Range we had planned for the following morning. She pulled up the government website for the range and quickly filled in the needed information for the permit.

The site confirmed that there was no active bombing scheduled for the part of the range we'd be heading through, and it gave us a permit. Debbie printed it and handed it to me.

"Good luck," she said. "Make sure to be careful down there. You might run into some people wandering through the desert so close to the border. Not all of them are friendly."

My phone rang, and I pulled it out of my back pocket. I tensed, thinking it might be Gabriella. I relaxed when I saw it was Cricket.

"Laura, it's Cricket," her friendly voice said when I answered.

"Hi, Cricket," I said. "It's good to hear from you. Thanks again for pulling me out of the locker the other day. I still get the heebie-jeebies when I think about what could have happened."

"I'm glad I was there," she said. "Have you gotten any word about what happened to Brian yet? No one's seen him since last Thursday, and I suppose you heard about them finding the body in the river.

"Yeah, I did hear about that."

"I'm starting to get a bad feeling about Brian," she said. "I told you before I sort of feel responsible for him, and he's not the kind to blow off work, at least not without a good reason."

"There's an outside chance I might be able to pick up some more information on him," I said. "I'm going to be in the same area as the two guys who were with him when they broke into the lab last Thursday night."

"You mean the creeper from the parking lot?" she asked.

"Yeah, him and his boss. They're out in the desert, a little southeast of Yuma."

"What are they doing out there?" she asked, sounding confused. "That's a brutal part of the state to wander around in."

"They're looking for hidden treasure," I laughed.

"Bring me along with you?" Cricket asked. From her tone, I could tell she was serious.

"Um, I usually don't take people with me," I said. "Those two guys are a little unstable. It could be dangerous."

"I don't care," she insisted. "I need to help. I'll want to know I did everything possible in case the worst happens to Brian. I've been to that part of the state several times before, exploring ghost towns and old mining sites in the Goldwater Bombing Range. Besides, I've been deflecting the police's questions about your involvement the other night, not to mention I did let you out of the vault. You do sorta owe me."

I'll probably regret this.

"Fine," I said, giving her my address. "We're meeting at my apartment tomorrow morning at five. We might be out for a couple of days. But seriously, if you've been there before, you know it's a remote part of the deep desert. No Starbucks and no cell phone service."

"I get it," she said with a laugh. "I'll let Dr. Wilson know I'll be out for a day or two. Besides, I could use an adventure."

I made it back to the Camelback Ballroom at the Tropical Paradise a few minutes before five. It was filling up fast with bakers and their families. I was surprised by how many people were already there.

I drifted over to the wedding cake table, where all six bakers were busily adding finishing touches to their colorful multi-tiered creations. I was amazed at the cakes they'd put on display. Each was a beautiful work of art, nicer than anything I'd ever seen at an actual wedding.

I then went to the table with the frosted cupcakes. Six groupings of six cupcakes each had been arranged. Most of the groups were on some sort of acrylic display that showed off each cake from multiple angles.

The mood of the ballroom was slightly more formal than it had been for the open competition. Instead of the lively dance tunes from the previous Saturday, classic jazz played from the speakers on stage at a subdued level.

Adam went up to the stage as the event began and made some opening remarks. He thanked everyone for coming and went over the format of the evening.

He explained there were a total of seventy-two sub-categories spread across eight groups. Each group would have two assistant judges, specialists in the baking style, and Adam would serve as head judge.

The winners in each category would be announced at eight o'clock, followed by prizes for Best of Group for each baking style and the overall Best of Show.

The assistant judges for each group went to their tables and started their evaluations. Each made notes as they carefully examined, smelled, and tasted the cookies, pies, muffins, breads, pastries, and cakes. As the head judge, Adam went from table to table and seemed to take in everything at once.

The cash bar had again been set up, along with tables of

baked goods for sale. I found Beatrice talking with a group of friends. She broke away, and we had a few moments together.

"How are you doing?" I asked. "This is a lot more exciting than I thought it would be. You can feel the tension and excitement in the air."

"I've always liked baking contests," she said. "Even as a girl, I would enter my cookies and pies in my village's spring festival and would often do well. Were you able to find out why Kaitlin always wins?"

"The story hasn't changed a lot from what you already know. Adam dated Kaitlin and her sister Shirley in college, and now he declares Kaitlin the winner each year. Unfortunately, I didn't find the smoking gun of bribery or blackmail. For whatever reason, Adam apparently believes her cupcakes are the best, and there isn't a lot we can do about it."

Beatrice's face fell slightly. "That is okay," she said. "I knew it was a difficult task. I think that next year, I enter different category. Maybe then I have chance of winning."

The music slowly faded at eight o'clock, and Adam went to the stage to announce the winners. As he read from his clipboard, it was a slow process, taking nearly twenty-five minutes to get to the cupcake category.

As she waited for the results, Beatrice stood in a circle of fellow bakers directly in front of Adam. Kaitlin stood on the far side of the stage with Shirley and Beth.

I knew Shirley didn't have anything entered in the contest, but she seemed excited for her sister and daughter.

As usual, Beth stood beside her mother, typing on her phone, a slightly bored look on her face.

When Adam got to the cupcake category, Beatrice's eyes sparkled, and she leaned forward to hear the results.

"And the winner of the frosted cupcake category is…" Adam began, pausing for effect. "Beatrice Albescu for her trois chocolate mousse *prăjitură* cupcakes."

There was a collective gasp from several of the ladies, who started clapping for their friend. Beatrice looked stunned, then flashed a beautiful smile.

"Don't you think you've made a mistake, Adam?" Shirley loudly spat out as she took a step toward the head judge. Adam's face paled as his eyes darted between Shirley and Beth.

Adam's wife, Naomi, had been standing on the stage near the back. She drifted across the stage to join her husband when she heard the commotion. She looked worried and confused as Shirley stared daggers at her spouse.

Although Adam was clearly going through some emotional distress, his voice seemed firm with resolve. "No," he said, looking directly at Shirley. "Kaitlin didn't win this year. The other contestants were clearly better."

After staring at Adam and Naomi for several heartbeats, Shirley seemed to come to a decision. Her face puckered into a vindictive sneer.

"Fine," Shirley hissed out as she marched her daughter towards the stage. "In that case, Naomi, I want you to meet Beth, Adam's lovechild."

"Mom, stop it," Beth cried out as she pushed Shirley's hand away from her shoulder. It was apparent she had no idea what her mother was talking about.

There was a moment of shocked silence from everyone

listening to the conversation. Adam's jaw muscles visibly clenched, and he stared back at Shirley, loathing in his eyes.

"What are you talking about?" Kaitlin asked as she looked between Shirley and Adam. It seemed clear that she was as confused as anyone.

"Oh, sure," Shirley snarled out at her older sister. "You got to date Adam first, but he fell in love with me. We'd started planning our life together. Then he met *Na-o-mi* and dumped me like I was yesterday's garbage."

"My god, Shirley," Kaitlin moaned out. "What are you doing?"

"I knew I couldn't lose the man I loved to a slutty bimbo like Naomi," Shirley implored as she stepped closer to her sister. Her eyes had gone a little crazy, and it was apparent she was intent on spilling her dirty laundry as publicly as possible.

"Even though he'd started dating Naomi, I told Adam I wanted one more roll in the hay, you know, so I could have a final pleasant memory of our time together. He went for it, of course, and I made sure to time it so I'd get pregnant. Men are so stupid."

There was murmuring in the crowd as everyone caught onto what was happening. I noticed that most of the cupcake contestants had gathered close to hear the argument better.

Adam's face had turned crimson, and I could feel his anger rising. Naomi was shaking, and tears had begun to run down her face.

"Adam only seemed disgusted when I told him about the baby I had growing inside me," Shirley loudly continued, still looking at her older sister. "But I've been holding it over his head ever since. If he doesn't do whatever I say, I'll drag him to family court and sue him for fifteen years of back child support. Naomi would divorce him faster than snapping my fingers. Trust me, he does whatever I say, money, jewelry, anything I want, including making you the winner each year."

"Mom, you're a psycho," Beth yelled at her mother before running out of the ballroom.

Kaitlin's face paled as she realized the implications of what Shirley had revealed. She stepped back from her sister and looked around at the other cupcake contestants, most of whom were now staring daggers at her.

"I'm so sorry," Kaitlin said as she looked at her fellow bakers. "I knew something was off with this. I never should have won."

Naomi began to sob openly and hurried out of the room. Adam asked the other cake judges to the stage, and they had a brief conference. He then went to the microphone to make an announcement.

"In light of recent events, I have disqualified myself as a judge for this competition," he said. His voice was surprisingly steady. I got the feeling he'd been waiting for something like this to happen.

"In addition, I'm resigning my position as club president, effective immediately. The remaining judges have declared Beatrice's cupcakes as Best of Group for cakes."

There were some gasps from the crowd but also a round of applause. Many of the bakers seemed to know what had been happening with the judging over the years and nodded in agreement.

Adam walked off the stage and handed the clipboard containing the winner's names to Linda Romero, the woman he had introduced as the club's vice president. He then quickly left the ballroom. Linda walked up to the stage to announce the remaining winners.

After talking with her friends for several minutes, Beatrice came up to me, her eyes sparkling with tears. "Thank you so much," she said. "I was wrong about Kaitlin. It turned out that her sister was the devil woman."

"You won the Best Cake ribbon," I said. "That's pretty exciting. I'm sorry you didn't win Best of Show as well."

"No," Beatrice said, a touch of anger flaring in her eyes. "I lose that to a woman who makes blueberry muffins. She also wins every year, but her muffins are no good. They are dry and tasteless. She probably has blackmail material on the muffin judge as well. We can look into her next year."

Great.

Chapter Eighteen

I woke to the alarm the following morning and forced myself awake. I'd set it for three-thirty, which had seemed reasonable when I'd gone to bed. But now that I was sitting up in the dark room, it seemed much too early.

Marlowe briefly woke up and looked at me. I thought he would get up and run to the kitchen for an early breakfast. Instead, he lowered his head and was back asleep within seconds.

Morgan and Mustafa had taken off the previous afternoon to get the supplies, and Morgan hadn't returned until almost midnight. I'd heard him come in, but I'd quickly gone back to sleep.

By the time I got out of the shower and dressed for a trip in the desert, Morgan had already made us a pot of coffee. While he got ready, I scurried around and finished loading a small duffle with everything I could think of, including a change of clothes, a wide-brimmed hat, and some SPF-50 sunscreen.

Once Morgan had dressed, I followed him down to the parking lot, where a giant white Chevy Suburban four-wheel-drive SUV was parked. The eastern horizon was beginning to glow with the upcoming sunrise, and the birds had already started their morning chorus.

Morgan got into the driver's seat and began to organize things for the trip. I climbed into the back and relaxed on the sofa-sized bench seat while waiting for the others to arrive.

Mustafa pulled into the lot a few minutes before five in his maroon rental sedan. He parked beside the Suburban and removed a daypack and a large camera bag from the trunk. He also took out Morgan's old duffle bag. It appeared to be empty.

"In case we get lucky and find an artifact, I'll be able to carry it back in this," he said.

When we opened the back of the big SUV to toss everything in, I saw that Morgan had come well-supplied. In addition to four cases of bottled water, there were picks, shovels, gloves, flashlights, coils of rope, and several long metal pry bars. There were also two sacks full of groceries.

"Why are you bringing all of that along?" I asked, somewhat confused. "It looks like you're going excavating."

"I once heard the Professor say he could have had the mask if he'd brought a crowbar. It didn't make much sense then, but now I think it does."

Cricket drove up in her black BMW convertible, and I had her park next to my Miata. As she climbed out of the car, she was again dressed in black, this time in a *Siouxsie and the Banshees* concert T-shirt, cargo pants, spiked dog collar, and combat boots.

She'd toned down the makeup a bit, as had I. This seemed practical since we'd probably all be sweating before the day was over.

Cricket then pulled out a well-used backpack that was almost as big as she was. Judging by how she hefted it, the pack must have been heavy.

"You did come ready for an adventure," I laughed.

"I brought everything I'd possibly need for a trip in the desert," she said, shoving the pack into the back of the Suburban. "I see you already have plenty of water, so I'll leave most of mine in the trunk."

I made introductions. I'd already told both men that Cricket would be coming along to look for information on her coworker, Brian, and neither had objected.

Cricket shook Mustafa's hand, but when I told her who Morgan was, she stopped and stared, clearly spooked.

"Um, Morgan West?" she stammered. "You're supposed to be dead. I filled out a bunch of forms on you last week. There was even a corpse with your name on his toe tag."

"I know," he said, somewhat embarrassed. "There was a bit of a mix-up. I'm sure I'll need to spend several months straightening out the paperwork on this."

Cricket and I took the back bench seat, leaving the front for Morgan and Mustafa. I caught Cricket glancing at Morgan as we went down the highway. I couldn't tell if she was checking out his body or if she wanted to make sure he hadn't come back from the dead.

We drove west on Interstate 10, heading for the deep desert, and I started to pepper Mustafa with questions about the treasure. Fortunately, he took my inquiries in stride and seemed to go into lecture mode when I asked about the Pharaoh's mask.

"When we learned the mask could be in Arizona, you said it made sense," I said. "What did you mean by that?"

"As to where the remaining treasures of Men-her Ra are located, there are two main theories," Mustafa said in a tone that implied he'd made the same speech many times before.

"The first hypothesis is that the mask was part of the lost treasure of Antonio María de Bucareli, the Viceroy of New Spain, as they called Mexico at the time. The treasure was supposedly lost while being transported to the territories of California in the 1780s."

"Okay, that's the trail we're on now," I said. "What's the other theory?"

"The more popular speculation is that the mask, along with the bulk of the pharaoh's treasure, was captured by Muhammad I, the Sultan of Morocco, in about 1640 and moved to the royal palace in Marrakesh. Pieces from the tomb of Men-her Ra have appeared there several times over the last three hundred years."

After going west on Interstate 10 for half an hour, we turned south on Arizona Route 85 and drove to the desert town of Gila Bend. Once we arrived, we stopped for a bathroom and snack break at the Gila Bend Food Mart.

As we walked through the store, it seemed like it was more of a Mexican souvenir shop than anything else. Leaving the town, we again turned west, this time on Interstate 8.

As we drove, I chatted with Cricket and learned a little about her. She told me she'd come from a wealthy Paradise Valley family but was in the middle of a rebellious streak that had started in high school.

She'd fallen in with a group of goth friends and had discovered she loved the lifestyle. Halfway through college, Cricket also learned that she was fascinated by death. This led her to get a job at the Medical Examiner's lab.

"Of course, it sorta makes it hard to date," she admitted with a giggle. "Not many guys want to get serious with a tiny goth girl who's into dead bodies."

We made it to the western Arizona town of Welton at seven forty-five. It had been an unusually wet spring, and vistas of blooming desert plants had highlighted the drive down. Typical of March, the wind was almost non-existent, and there wasn't a cloud from horizon to horizon.

The sun had already climbed a good way into the eastern sky, but fortunately, the high for the day would only be in the mid-eighties. This was in contrast to July when daytime temperatures were regularly over a hundred and fifteen.

After exiting the highway, we stopped at a Chevron station to fill the tank. We then went across the street to a Jack in the Box for a quick breakfast.

Feeling refreshed after the long car ride, we climbed back in. Morgan maneuvered the big SUV south of the town along an irrigation canal. He then turned onto the dirt road that was the Devil's Highway.

It felt a little strange starting on the road at the place people for centuries had considered the end of the trail. The Gila River was only a mile north of here, and I could get a sense of the grateful feeling the people must have felt as they emerged from the desert to see the green riverbanks in the distance.

After calling the number listed on the permit to check in, we crossed into the Goldwater Bombing Range. I then gave Morgan the visitor's pass to put on the dash.

The range had several marked keep-out areas they used for live bombing practice. Fortunately, we weren't planning on going near any of them.

Cricket had her phone out and started reading out loud

from the Goldwater Range website. "Access to the bombing range presents the danger of permanent, painful, disabling, and disfiguring injury or death due to high explosive detonations from falling objects such as aircraft, aerial targets, live ammunition, missiles, bombs, and other similar dangerous situations."

After she finished reading, she looked at me with a wicked gleam. "Pretty cool, huh?" she asked.

Cell phone service stopped after about ten miles of traveling down the road. Morgan pulled out a topography map and handed Mustafa a handheld satellite GPS receiver.

As we got further into the desert, the landscaping became noticeably drier and more desolate. After twenty minutes of traveling down the *El Camino del Diablo*, there was nothing but dirt, sand, clumps of desert grass, and a few low bushes.

The hour-long drive south toward the *Tinajas Altos* and the Thousand Caves wasn't as bad as I feared it would be. Although the Devil's Highway was indeed terrifying in years past, today, it was a wide dirt road that seemed well maintained.

I got the feeling that this was less for the occasional tourist who might wander down it and more for the military and border patrol who likely used the road regularly. Every few miles, we'd pass a sign reminding us that we were on a Marine Corps bombing range and to stay on the road.

As we drove south along the *El Camino del Diablo*, we gradually drew closer to a range of mountains to the west. After skirting the hills for half an hour, a large black mesa came into view.

"That's Raven Butte," Morgan said as he pointed. "The place we're going is behind the hill and a little to the west. This is where we get off the main road."

After stopping for a few moments to consult the map and the GPS, Morgan pulled the Suburban onto an old set of tire tracks. We drove slowly down the bumpy and rutted trail, and after maybe five minutes, a roadrunner appeared.

He was maybe fifteen feet from the passenger side of the SUV, running between the scrub. He seemed interested in what we were doing and kept pace with us for almost fifteen minutes.

Mustafa had never seen a live roadrunner before, and he laughed because it didn't look anything like the cartoon version. We continued our slow ride, bouncing down the trail for another two or three miles, eventually coming to the ridge of mountains.

The GPS led us to the mouth of a small valley directly west of Raven Butte. Morgan veered into the canyon, and we soon found ourselves driving along a small dry river arroyo.

After creeping along the riverbed for maybe a hundred yards, Morgan stopped. He and Mustafa consulted the map and the GPS for almost a minute.

"The coordinates appear to be a little way up that hill," Morgan said, pointing to the rocky slope of the low mountain that formed the canyon's north side. "We'll need to climb forty or fifty feet up to reach the spot."

Morgan parked the SUV, and we all piled out. Standing up and stretching after bouncing around in the back seat felt great.

"I don't see any other tire tracks or footprints on the road," Morgan said. "You told me Eckart had part of the code and might be out here. Do you know where he'll be looking?"

"I think he'll be searching the top of that mesa," I said, pointing to Raven Butte, towering over us to the east. "I don't know if he can see us from up there, but it's probably best to do this as quickly as possible."

We started climbing the side of the hill at the point Morgan had indicated. Several rocks and giant boulders were strewn over the mountain, making ascending difficult.

After two or three minutes, Morgan indicated we should stop. I was glad since the short scramble had left me winded.

"Okay," Morgan said as he looked down at his GPS. "We're dead center here. Everybody look around."

"What are we searching for?" Cricket asked.

"I don't exactly know," Morgan admitted. "A cave or a pit, something that could hide wooden crates. It could even be a marker that tells us where to dig."

The four of us spread out and started to search. Not knowing what we were looking for made it somewhat more difficult, but I figured we'd know it when we saw it.

When we didn't find anything that looked promising where we were, we spread out and started to search randomly. Morgan and Mustafa drifted up to a large rock formation further up the hill, and Cricket went deeper into the valley. I started exploring more toward the mouth of the canyon.

We looked for almost an hour without finding a thing. After searching to the mouth of the canyon, I went a little lower on the hill and started to go back in.

I tried to place myself as a person in the 1780s who was dying of thirst. If they had come into the canyon with heavy boxes of treasure, they wouldn't have gone far up the hill. They likely would've shoved everything into the first cave or good-sized hole they could locate.

"I think I found it," Cricket called out. She'd gone about forty yards to the west and was slightly lower down the hill. She was standing in front of a large boulder, waving her arms.

We made our way over to her, seeing nothing unusual the entire time.

"What is it?" I asked as I walked up to the small goth woman.

"Here," she said, pointing downward, a broad smile on her face. Sure enough, at the base of the rock was a cave opening.

The entrance was relatively large, a little over five feet high and at least three feet across. Due to the arrangement of the rocks around the boulder, you had to be directly over the opening to see it.

"Huh," I said. "I can see why no one but the Professor found this place. It wouldn't be visible from below or even from above if you happened to climb any of the mountains around here.

Now that we had a possible location, we returned to the SUV. Morgan backed it up along the dry riverbed until it was even with the entrance to the cave.

We then loaded up with supplies. Cricket collected four flashlights, Mustafa grabbed two shovels, and Morgan took the pry bars.

I gathered four bottles of water and handed them out. Climbing around the hill had made me thirsty, and I imagined the others felt the same.

Scrambling back up the hill, we again stood at the opening under the boulder. There was a growing sense of excitement and a little nervousness as we prepared to see what lay in the darkness beyond the mouth of the cave.

"I'll let one of you go in first," Cricket said, looking around the group, sounding slightly uneasy. "I've lived in Arizona all my life and know that caverns in the desert usually aren't empty. I brought along a snakebite kit, but I don't want to use it on myself."

Morgan took one of the flashlights and carefully went in through the man-sized opening. Mustafa went next.

I hung out with Cricket until Morgan stuck his head back out. "We didn't see any snakes or animals," he said, "but they seem to use this as a den. You'll have to watch where you step."

Cricket and I turned on our flashlights and entered. After a short passageway where I constantly had to duck, the ceiling and walls opened to form a wide chamber with a roof a dozen feet above our heads.

The floor was covered in dirt and was more or less flat, giving everyone enough room to spread out. As Morgan had noted, the ground was littered with gnawed bones and tufts of fur.

We each had a flashlight that lit up portions of the room as we took in our surroundings. The ceiling and floor seemed to come together as the back of the cavern disappeared into the darkness, beyond where our lights reached.

While Morgan and Mustafa began exploring the back of the cave, my first task was to use the flashlight to go over every square inch of the cavern. I noticed Cricket was doing the same thing.

Although Morgan had said the area was empty, I knew from experience how a rattlesnake could coil itself into the smallest of cracks to sleep off the heat of the day and didn't want to startle one awake. Even under the best circumstances, the nearest hospital was in Yuma, a two-hour drive from here.

As we searched, it was apparent that if anything treasure-related had been stashed in this part of the cave, it was long gone, either carried away by Professor Nabil or others over the years. This didn't surprise me, but it was still somewhat disappointing.

We went to the back of the cave, and the ceiling gradually descended. Within about thirty feet, the passageway had been reduced to a low opening, about four feet high and five feet across.

After crawling along this narrow passageway for maybe fifteen or twenty feet, the cave roof dropped further. Mustafa and Morgan stopped, but fortunately, Cricket was small enough to keep going.

I watched as Cricket's flashlight slowly disappeared into the tiny opening. I told myself that if she needed help, I'd go in after her. But the memories of being trapped in the mortuary vault were still too fresh for me to purposefully dive into such a tight space.

"I see it," Cricket called back excitedly after crawling maybe fifteen feet into the narrow space. "There's a wooden crate all the way in the back."

"How big is it?" Morgan asked.

"Maybe three feet by four," she replied. "It's a little over a foot and a half high."

"That's about the right size to hold the mask," Mustafa said, nodding. I could see he was grinning, and his face was flushed with excitement.

"Can you pull it out?" I shouted to her.

"Hold on," Cricket called back. "Let me see what I can do."

Chapter Nineteen

The three of us huddled together in the darkness, our flashlights trained on the narrow opening. After maybe three or four minutes, Cricket crawled back out. Judging by the wide smile on her face, she seemed to be enjoying herself.

"The crate's jammed against the back wall where the cave ends," Cricket said, slightly out of breath. "But it's blocked by a big rock that must have fallen from the ceiling."

"Do you think we can move the stone out of the way?" I asked.

"Well, it doesn't look like it's hung up on anything," she said as she thought about it. "But I'm sure the rock weighs more than I do."

"What's the best way to move the boulder?" Morgan asked. "Could you use a pry bar to move the rock far enough away to get the crate out?"

"I don't think so," she said with a shake of her head. "It's pretty narrow back there. Even with a pry bar, I doubt I could do more than wiggle it a few inches.

"If we fed a rope in, do you think you could wrap it around the bolder?" I asked Cricket.

"Probably," she said. "But, like I told you, that rock is pretty big. Even with all of us, I'm not sure we'd be able to pull it out."

"The cave isn't too far from the Suburban," I reminded her. "And we have plenty of rope. If you can loop a line around the rock, we could use the vehicle to pull it out of the way."

Like most good ideas, it seemed to be the obvious solution once it had been voiced. I climbed out of the cave with Mustafa, and we scrambled down to the big SUV.

We pulled out what looked like the longest and thickest coil of rope from the back. I then made a loop on one end and wrapped it around the ball on the trailer hitch.

While Mustafa stayed in the vehicle, I climbed back up the hill, letting the coil of rope play out as I ascended. I'd also brought a blanket and placed it over the rock at the cave's entrance. With all of the pulling that was about to happen, I didn't want the rough stone to fray or cut the line.

I dragged the remaining rope into the cavern and gave the end to Cricket. She smiled and scampered into the narrow space at the back of the cave to loop the line around the boulder.

When Cricket returned, everyone climbed out of the cavern. Morgan signaled Mustafa to pull forward slowly. We heard the Suburban fire up and saw the rope go tight as he crept along the dry riverbed, toward the mouth of the canyon.

After he'd gone maybe twenty or twenty-five yards, he stopped. When we returned to the cave, the rock had been dragged to the middle of the central chamber. Morgan then went outside to signal Mustafa to back up and give us some slack on the rope.

With a feeling of growing excitement in our group, Cricket untied her line and got ready to return for the crate. Once the rope was loose, she scrambled to the back of the cave, eager to tie the line around the two-hundred-and-fifty-year-old wooden chest.

"Okay," she said when she returned to the main chamber. "We should be able to pull it out ourselves. It doesn't look that heavy, and if we use the SUV, it might get damaged."

Morgan went out to wave Mustafa in. Once he arrived, now carrying his camera bag, everyone grabbed the rope and pulled.

As the rope went taught, we realized Cricket was right. The crate was light enough to be moved by hand.

The box seemed to pull forward about ten feet but then got hung up on something. Cricket again went back through the narrow opening, this time with the smaller pry bar, and worked to free it.

"Try it now," she called out. "I'll stay back here to make sure it doesn't get stuck again."

We again pulled, and this time the line drew smoothly. Within a minute, the wooden box slid into the central chamber.

Cricket returned to the group, and we pointed our flashlights down at the treasure chest. We paused for a full minute, examining the crate and admiring the antique wood.

The tiny goth girl ran her hand along the top of the crate, and after a moment, everyone else did the same. There was something thrilling about touching an object that so many others had searched for throughout the centuries.

The box had bulky iron hinges and a substantial clasp. All the metal pieces were covered with a thick layer of smooth dark patina.

Holding the box shut was a large iron lock. It reminded me of the old Spanish lock on the chest containing the Lost Sister.

"Wow," Cricket said. "Look at that old lock. I don't know how we'll get it off, even assuming we had the key. It looks like it's been rusted over for at least a hundred years."

Mustafa removed a professional-looking camera from his bag and attached a large flash. He then asked us to pose for pictures with the treasure chest. I reminded him that after crawling around the insides of a filthy cave, none of us looked our best, but he seemed to think our disarray would make for better photos.

After taking pictures of the group, Mustafa took several images of Cricket with her hand on the crate next to the old lock. He seemed to think her hair, makeup, T-shirt, and even the dog collar would make for compelling photos.

Mustafa then gave his camera to me, and I took several images of him beside the crate and some with his hands on the lock. I could see him visualizing his picture on the cover of some archeological journal.

"We'll take some more photos inside the cave and then some outside in the light," Mustafa said to our group, sounding like he'd previously documented this sort of thing. "It's important that we have images of the mask being held in the hands of the discoverers. It usually becomes a highlight of the exhibition."

"Before we get to the mask, we'll need to remove the lock," Morgan observed.

"Wait a minute," I said, remembering the steps Professor Mindy had gone through. "There are proper ways to remove these old locks. We might need to take the chest back to Tempe to get some chemicals and skeleton keys from a friend of mine."

Ignoring me, Morgan took the pry bar, jammed it under the lock, and pushed. The antique lock popped away from the ancient wood of the box and landed in pieces on the cave's dirt floor.

"I guess that works as well," I said. I looked at Mustafa, who shrugged and gave me a sympathetic look.

As the men forced up the lid of the wooden chest, Cricket and I reached in and pulled out several yellowed bundles of a coarse cloth they'd used as packing material. There were a lot of fabric pieces, most of which tore and crumbled as we removed them.

"Nobody move," barked out a harsh voice from the mouth of the cave. "I'll shoot the first one who tries anything. Hell, I'll shoot the first one who flinches."

Crap.

I didn't need to look. I already knew who it was. I turned to see the tall skinny figure of Owen.

He stood slightly inside the opening, his obscenely large pistol pointing at the group. His other hand held a flashlight that he shone in our eyes.

"Everyone back away from the box, nice and slow," he said in a youthful voice meant to sound tough.

I silently cursed myself for leaving my bag with my pistol in the Suburban. I hadn't thought I'd need it while digging through a cave.

As we moved to the far side of the chamber, Raymond Eckart stepped into the opening. He also had a flashlight, and his beam immediately fixated on the crate.

"Ahh," Eckart said, glee in his voice. "I see you were able to extract the mask from its resting place, brilliant."

His flashlight then landed on the pile of pry bars and shovels. "I also see you had the foresight to bring the proper equipment. Very clever of you. But how did you know to do this, I wonder?"

Eckart then took the time to look over our group. His

flashlight went from Cricket to me, and he seemed unconcerned. He then turned the light toward Mustafa.

"I see our representative from the Egyptian government is here," Eckart said with a chuckle. "Dr. Yousef, I would have thought you'd have given up on your quest to recover the mask once you realized you would need to leave Egypt. This is a bit outside of your jurisdiction. Is it not?"

"I follow the items, wherever they are," Mustafa said with a shrug.

Eckhart then turned his light toward Morgan, and it took him a moment to process what he was seeing.

"You, sir, are supposed to be dead," Eckart said with a touch of humor.

"Yeah," Morgan replied sarcastically. "I know. Sorry to disappoint you."

"Seeing you alive is something I didn't expect to witness," Eckart admitted. "However, it clarifies how the group knew to come here and what equipment to bring. Very good. I commend your ingenuity. You'd convinced the world that you were deceased, allowing you to look for the treasure unhindered, as it were."

"Yes, and so far, all it's accomplished is to get my bank accounts closed," Morgan said.

"Lesson learned," Eckart said with a nod and a snort of laughter. He pointed his flashlight back at Cricket, who was still holding a bundle of the cloth padding.

"Young lady," he said. "It appears as if you were about to uncover the funeral mask of Pharaoh Men-her Ra. Please proceed."

"The rest of you keep back," Owen yelled out, his flashlight dancing back and forth between everyone in the cavern. "Any sudden movements, and I'll shoot."

"Where's Brian?" Cricket asked Eckart. "The last time anyone saw him, he let you into the Medical Examiner's lab. Did you kill him?"

Eckart gave her a puzzled and somewhat hurt look. "I honestly have no idea where the young man is," he said. "After I paid him his fee, he seemed happy enough. He drove out of the parking lot as if he had somewhere urgent to go."

"Get on with it," Owen barked out to Cricket. "I have no problem shooting you and letting someone else get the mask."

Cricket returned to the crate and pulled out more of the fabric pieces. Once she had a sizeable pile of cloth on the floor of the cave, I took a step forward, eager to see the large, wrapped bundle containing the Pharaoh's mask.

I was somewhat confused when it became apparent that the crate contained ten or twelve smaller items instead of one large piece. The objects were each about the size of a football and were wrapped in the same yellowed linen that had been around the gold cat.

"I can pretty much see to the bottom of the crate," Cricket said as she looked between the men. "I'm sorry, but unless it's really small, I don't think your mask is in here."

"What?" Mustafa and Eckhart said in unison. Disbelief was evident in their voices.

The three men crowded up and quickly searched through the chest. As it sank in that the mask wasn't in the box, there was a collective groan of frustration from the men.

"Is there perhaps another chest located here in the cave?" Eckart asked.

"No," Cricket said. "This one was trapped in the back. We had to yank out a big rock to free it. You can look around, but this was it."

As Eckhart saw the disappointment on Mustafa's face, he realized Cricket was telling the truth. He thought about it and nodded.

"Yes, then the mask must be in Morocco," Eckart said, half to himself. "Baaka Salam, the black-market dealer in Casablanca, told me he had a tenuous lead on it several months ago. I refused to listen, thinking the Professor's code was the better trail to follow."

Eckart again paused. When he looked up, there was a renewed fire in his eyes. "Owen, I see the truth now. We were fools to come to America. We should have gone to Morocco first."

"Let's unwrap one of these things," Cricket said. "I'd like to see what we have here."

We turned to Eckart, and he shrugged. Now that it was clear that he wouldn't get the Pharaoh's mask, he seemed a little less concerned than he had been.

Cricket reached out for the nearest bundle, but Mustafa stopped her.

"It's obvious the mask isn't in there," he said with a touch of sadness. "But we possibly have some four-thousand-year-old artifacts here. I must insist that from this point on, any direct contact with whatever is inside this crate be handled appropriately."

Keeping an eye on Owen, Mustafa produced a pair of white gloves and gave them to Cricket. She slid them on, and he handed her one of the smaller wrapped bundles.

"It's heavy," she said as she cradled the object.

Mustafa looked over at Eckart. "I need to document the find," he said. "You know the importance of having pictures taken at the moment of discovery."

"By all means," Eckart said with a slight wave.

"However, do not include images of either Owen or myself."

Mustafa had us gather around the open crate for several more pictures. He directed us to look at Cricket as she held the first object. Eckart even helped out by taking several group pictures with Mustafa's camera.

There was an air of expectancy as Cricket started to unwind the linen. Mustafa hovered in front of her, taking maybe a dozen photos as she worked.

At first, Cricket tried to be careful, but the cloth crumbled to pieces in her hands as she tried to unwind it. Finally, she began pulling off the fabric in chunks, not bothering to unwrap it.

The beams of our flashlights reflected over the piece as the last of the cloth came off. I was expecting a brilliant flash of gold. But as I looked closer, the metal wasn't bright. It was more of a dull-looking brown.

I was confused and turned to Mustafa when the Egyptian started laughing. "Hand me the artifact," he asked Cricket, his white gloves already on.

As he took the little figurine, we could see it was a bird, similar to the gold falcon from the other day. He closely examined the object using the light of his flashlight, and he laughed again.

"Please document this," he said, handing his camera to me. I took a dozen pictures of him holding the bird, some in close-up and some with the open crate in the background.

Eckart walked up, and Mustafa handed him the sculpture. I noticed that the big man had already donned a pair of white gloves.

"It's not the Pharaoh's mask," Eckart said as he examined the artifact under the light of his flashlight. "But it definitely could have come from his tomb. The statue is made of brass, of course, which was a common artist's material back then. But the piece is in excellent condition. You can see that the inlaid pieces of lapis lazuli are intact and still tightly embedded in the metal."

Mustafa gave the brass falcon to Cricket and had her hold the piece over the open crate, the other wrapped artifacts visible in the background. His camera again flashed as he captured fifteen or twenty images.

He then asked her to hold the ancient bird statue next to her face and took several close-ups. I noticed he framed the photos to ensure he got Cricket's partially shaved head, multiple piercings, and spiked dog collar.

"So, no gold?" I asked.

"It doesn't appear so," Mustafa said with a touch of melancholy. "The crate appears to contain secondary brass statuettes. But to be sure, we should unwrap the other items and ensure nothing priceless is mixed in with these pieces."

"Let us take the crate down to our vehicles," Eckart said. "Then we can examine each of the artifacts in the light of the sun."

After closing the lid, Morgan and Mustafa each grabbed an end. Working together, they manhandled the crate out through the cave's opening. Owen followed behind them, his pistol still trained on the two men.

Cricket and I followed the chest out of the cavern and trailed behind the men as they carried it down the rocky slope toward the dry riverbed. I made sure to grab the blanket I had left at the lip of the cave.

A blue Ford Bronco was parked next to the Suburban. I had been curious about how Eckart had found us in the cave so quickly. My question was answered when I saw that the rope from the back bumper of our SUV was still going directly to the opening on the side of the hill.

I sighed at how stupid we'd been. Even a blind person would have been able to follow that.

In the back seat of the Ford was a brunette woman with her face in the open window. Even from this distance, I could see that it was Sabrina. Eckhart must have told her to stay in the vehicle.

Suddenly, the back door of the Bronco flew open, and Sabrina ran up the hill in a sprint, her chestnut hair trailing behind her. She wasn't exactly dressed for the desert, in a low-cut red T-shirt and dark short-shorts, but she had at least changed into sensible shoes.

Mustafa lowered his end of the crate, and a look of joy spread over his face. He then drifted down the mountain, his arms open to greet her.

Sabrina ran past Mustafa and instead flung herself against Morgan. She briefly paused to look at his face, then wrapped her arms around him and burst into tears.

"I thought you were dead," she sobbed. "Oh, my god. I thought you were dead." Her voice was then lost in hysterical weeping.

Morgan looked down at her with a look of annoyance or even anger on his face. However, acceptance gradually replaced this, and he wrapped his arms around her. After another moment, they were desperately kissing, and Morgan seemed to be also on the verge of crying.

Mustafa's face fell as he looked at Sabrina with longing and despair. It was as if his world had suddenly crashed down around him. After a moment, he lowered his head and drifted back up the hill to get his end of the crate.

What kind of weird love triangle did they have going on?

Chapter Twenty

After another few moments of kissing and crying, Sabrina untangled herself from Morgan, letting him get his end of the crate. Morgan and Mustafa then carried the ancient treasure chest down to the SUVs, Sabrina never leaving Morgan's side.

Mustafa absentmindedly looked around the area and sat the crate on a flat rocky outcrop on the banks of the dry riverbed. I could see he had chosen the spot for the exciting pictures he could take with several blooming desert plants as a background.

Mustafa then had Cricket go through the chest and unwrap each item. He took several pictures, but I could see that his heart was no longer in it. He kept glancing at Sabrina, standing against Morgan, her arms tightly wrapped around him.

As each piece was unwrapped, Eckart and Mustafa took several minutes examining the artifact. I had guessed that the pieces were valuable. Still, I learned from the conversations between the two men that they thought the many items that had been extracted from the cave were the most significant Egyptian archeological find in over twenty years.

There were two statues that I especially liked. Each was about a foot and a half high.

The first was a man with the head of a bird. Eckart identified this as Horus. Mustafa then explained that Horus was the ancient Egyptian god of kingship, healing, protection, the sun, and the sky.

The other statue I found interesting was a man with the head of a dog. Mustafa said this was Anubis, the god of funerals, protector of graves, and guide to the underworld.

"When anyone of importance was buried," Mustafa said. "They often had Anubis placed with them to help lead them to the afterlife."

By the time Cricket was done unwrapping, eleven brass statues had been lined up on a flat rock. The pieces sat on the blanket I had pulled from the Suburban, and the desert flowers gave some color to the background.

Mustafa seemed to recover his equilibrium as he handled the ancient artifacts. By the time the eleventh piece had been unwrapped, he appeared to be in a relatively good mood. He took videos and pictures of the items for several minutes, using the branches of a mesquite tree to help frame the pieces.

For his part, Eckart paid close attention to what Cricket was doing as she uncovered the first several pieces. But he seemed to gradually lose interest when it was apparent that the artifacts were all made of brass, not gold.

"What's next?" Mustafa asked Eckart as he finished taking the pictures. "You have the gun. Are you going to take these?"

"That, sir, is a question I have been pondering since the young lady unwrapped the falcon up in the cave," Eckart admitted.

"And?" Mustafa asked.

"These pieces are of excellent quality," Eckart mused.

"Suppose you can establish they came from the tomb of Men-her Ra. In that case, I imagine you could get upwards of six to eight million for the lot, assuming you properly structured the sales."

"I would estimate more than that," Mustafa said. "But these would go into the permanent collection of the Egyptian Museum."

"Of course," Eckart said with a wave of dismissal. "But as you know, my usual clientele only deals in gold antiquities, no matter the history or quality of the piece. Since I'd need to sell these pieces to an entirely new set of clients, smuggling fifty pounds of brass isn't worth the risk, even considering the possible reward these could bring."

"What do you propose?" Mustafa asked.

"Dr. Yousef, in exchange for your promise to wire me an appropriate finder's fee, I will leave these artifacts in your capable hands. In addition, I ask that you look the other way the next time we meet in Egypt, professionally speaking."

"I could do that," Mustafa said with a nod. "But there is nothing wrong with these artifacts. With a little effort, you could make a substantial profit from them. You're willing to give them to me in exchange for a fee and a future favor?"

Eckart looked like he was about to say something but paused and seemed to think better of it. "This one time," he said, "I'll be completely candid with you."

"I'd appreciate that," Mustafa said.

"I've been in the business for many years," Eckart admitted. "I've made money and spent time in prison over artifacts such as these. I've learned my limitations and have grown to appreciate these items for what they represent. I'm spending the remaining years of my career searching for the truly remarkable, something that will cap off my legacy. So yes, take these now, and don't get in my way if I come across something unique."

"Thank you," Mustafa said. "With these artifacts, I'll have enough to create a traveling exhibition of the treasures of Men-her Ra. As you know, I've wanted to do this since I acquired the first piece from Cartier, the Frenchman, some fifteen years ago."

"Now then," Eckart said, looking at Morgan. "Before we depart, I have one last piece of business. Where are the remaining gold statuettes the Professor had? If you still possess them, I'll offer you a most generous price for the lot."

"Sorry," Morgan said as he shook his head. "They're on their way back to Cairo and the Egyptian Museum."

"That, sir, is a pity," Eckart said, disappointed. "I could have turned a nice profit on those items. Museums are the single most disruptive factor I have in my business. They are vast black holes that suck the best antiquities out of the market."

He then looked at Mustafa and dipped his head, acknowledging defeat. The Egyptian, in turn, bowed to the black-market dealer.

Eckart reached over to the group of statues, plucked up the Horus figurine, and examined it briefly. "With your permission, I will keep this trinket as a memento. It will remind me of my folly and as a souvenir of my trip to America. You can, of course, adjust my fee appropriately."

Mustafa briefly hesitated, then nodded, and the deal was done.

"Come, Owen," Eckart said. "We're off to follow the real clue. We can be in San Diego in time for dinner. We'll then take the first plane to Morocco. With a little luck, we'll have the mask of Men-her Ra by this time next month."

Mustafa drifted over to the remaining figurines and began rewrapping them, stowing them in the crate. He worked quickly, and within minutes, he had everything ready to go.

I untied the rope from the back bumper and pulled it down from the mountain, coiling it as I gathered it in. It was stowed in the back of the big SUV in five minutes.

Eckart wrapped the Horus statue and placed it in a piece of luggage. He spent a few minutes watching us work, then drifted over to where Sabrina and Morgan were packing items into the Suburban.

"My dear," Eckart said kindly to Sabrina. "We're leaving momentarily. Are you coming with us? I've found our partnership to be quite profitable these last several months and would no doubt be able to use your considerable talents in the future."

"No, you go," she said. "I'm not leaving Morgan, not after everything that's happened."

"Very well," Eckart said, nodding. "I assumed that would be your answer. I'll be sorry to see you go, but I understand love. Perhaps we can work together again, sometime in the future."

Sabrina walked to the Bronco and pulled out a purse and a suitcase.

"Is there room in there for my things?" she asked Morgan.

"I think so," he said with a broad smile as he placed the bags in the back of the SUV with everything else.

Raymond barked out several orders to Owen, and within two minutes, he seemed ready to go. Eckart then walked up to Mustafa.

As the black-market dealer approached the Egyptian, I felt a sudden tingle of fear. There was a cold gleam in Eckart's eyes. Morgan and Owen must have also sensed something amiss, and I saw them become alert.

"Now, Dr. Yousef," Eckart said, "please understand that I do trust you, but only to a point. You must forgive me, but I can't have you following us, at least not for a day or two. Owen, shoot out their tires."

With a smirk of satisfaction, Owen yanked the big pistol from his shoulder holster, aimed at the Suburban, and squeezed the trigger. There was a deafening explosion as the gun kicked, and the back tire of the SUV collapsed with a rapid woosh of air.

Owen then took aim at the front tire and was about to fire when Morgan lunged at him. The boy was knocked off his feet, and the pistol flew out of his hand.

Owen quickly got up, his arms wildly swinging as he shouted angry obscenities. Then, both men began to punch each other.

At first, they seemed to trade blows evenly. However, it was soon apparent that Morgan was a much better fighter.

After twenty-five or thirty seconds of sparring, Morgan threw a hard right punch that landed on Owen's jaw with a sickening crack. Owen staggered, and his eyes lost focus. Morgan then lifted Owen and slammed him to the ground, knocking the wind out of him.

Unfortunately, Owen had landed with his hand next to his pistol. The two men seemed to realize this at the same time, and there was a scramble.

Morgan lunged for the gun, and there was an explosion of a gunshot. Morgan dropped to the ground, yelling in pain and clutching his inner thigh.

Mustafa jumped on Owen, and I pulled the gun from his hand. Cricket screamed, and Sabrina rushed to protect Morgan.

Owen shoved Mustafa out of the way and quickly got up. His eyes were wild, and it looked like he would go after Morgan again.

"Owen, enough," Eckart bellowed at the boy. "This is not how business is transacted."

Owen seemed to deflate, and he staggered toward Eckart, anger and hurt in his eyes. The big man looked at the boy's face, which was already starting to swell, and shook his head with surprising sympathy.

"It appears your jaw is broken," Eckart said quietly as he brushed a tear from the boy's eye. "Get into the vehicle, and I'll get you medical attention."

Without another word, Owen climbed into the passenger seat of the Bronco and closed the door. Eckart became grim as he slowly walked to Morgan, who lay on his back, bleeding in the dirt.

"That was a foolish thing you did, and now you've paid the price," Eckart told Morgan, who had grown pale and was grimacing in pain. "Assuming you survive, I trust you won't try to follow us. If I see you again, I won't guarantee your safety. In fact, I imagine you won't come out so lucky next time."

Sabrina collapsed next to Morgan, crying and holding his hand. Eckart turned and walked back to the Bronco. He climbed in, the engine fired up, and the two men drove away.

"Mustafa," I yelled. "Change the tire on the Suburban. We need to get to a hospital as soon as possible. Cricket and I will take care of Morgan."

Mustafa thought about what I had said, nodded, and then

hurried away to work on the tire.

Morgan was still flat on his back, moaning in pain. It was apparent the bullet had severely damaged his inner right thigh.

"I need to see what we're working with," Cricket said. The tone of her voice made it clear she knew what she was doing. "Help me rip away the pant leg."

Morgan was wearing khaki cargo pants, and we worked to tear away the material from the area around the wound. Once we could see the leg, we could tell it was bad.

"Oh my god," Sabrina moaned. "He's bleeding to death."

Cricket pulled the belt from her shorts and started to wrap it around the upper part of Morgan's leg as a tourniquet.

"There's a medical bag in my backpack," Cricket said calmly. "I'll need it, right away."

"I'll get it," I said, getting up and hurrying to the Suburban.

I was glad to be able to help and thankful to be away from Morgan. I don't generally consider myself squeamish, but I felt a little woozy after seeing the wound.

Mustafa already had the back of the SUV open, and he was pulling everything out to get at the jack and the spare tire. I rooted around in Cricket's backpack until I found a sizeable canvas bag with a red cross printed in a white circle.

"Here," I said as I set the medical kit beside Cricket.

"Thanks," she said. "Would you open it?"

When I unzipped the bag, it unfolded to reveal it was full of medical tools and vials of drugs. Cricket saw me looking at the equipment.

"As part of my training at the M.E. lab, I'm a fully

certified paramedic," she said as she pulled out a hospital tourniquet and quickly used it to replace her belt on Morgan's leg.

"Okay," she said, seeming to relax. "Now we should be able to find out what we're dealing with."

With the bleeding slowed to a trickle, Cricket took a pair of blue gloves from a package, then used a bottle of clear liquid to rinse out the gash in Morgan's leg.

Cricket opened a bundle of gauze and pressed it against the wound. She sighed and shook her head when she looked at the damage.

"The bullet nicked the artery," she told Morgan. "The hole isn't huge, but that's what's causing the bleeding. Unfortunately, it's not going to stop on its own."

Cricket looked up at Morgan's face. He'd lost almost all color and was in obvious pain, but he was alert and seemed to understand the situation.

"This goes beyond what I'm certified to do," she said, looking into his eyes. "But with your permission, I'll close the hole in your artery."

"Do it," he said through gritted teeth. "I've seen things like this in the Marines. We're at least two hours out from Yuma. The tourniquet will cause as much damage as it fixes."

Cricket nodded, then started to arrange her medical tools.

"I'll have to tell Sophie that I saw you bleeding," I said to Morgan to help lighten the mood. "She still thinks you may be a vampire or a poltergeist."

"I wish I *was* a vampire," Morgan said with a weak laugh. "This hurts like a bitch."

With the bleeding temporarily stopped, Cricket asked

Morgan about drug allergies and other medical conditions he had. She then pulled out a drug ampule and filled a syringe halfway.

"This will take the edge off," she said as she injected the sedative. Morgan seemed to relax almost immediately, and some of his color returned.

Cricket then took out another syringe and gave him a local anesthetic. "I could use some extra light," she said as she removed a tiny, curved needle, threaded with a thin black filament, from a plastic package.

I took out the flashlight I still had in my pocket and turned it on. I then did my best to hold the light steady, even though looking at the wound made me a little queasy.

Working quickly and with skill, Cricket started to close the artery. After placing four or five tiny stitches, she took out a larger needle and sewed up the gash in his leg.

"You'll still need to go to the hospital and have this looked at," Cricket said to Morgan when she'd finished. "They may want to redo everything I did. They'll probably want to clean the wound, if nothing else. But this will stop the bleeding until you get to a proper emergency room."

I went back to the Suburban to help Mustafa with the tire. I had assumed it would be a simple procedure, but he had the owner's manual out and seemed puzzled by the instructions.

After reading the needed steps, we opened a small access hatch on the back bumper. We then shoved in the jack handle to lower the tire from a cable underneath the SUV.

Once we had the spare free from the cable, it was a relatively simple process to jack up the vehicle and change the tire. Within about fifteen minutes, we'd lowered the Suburban onto the spare.

I next helped Mustafa load the wooden crate into the SUV. As we placed it in the back, I knew it contained around six to eight million dollars worth of ancient Egyptian artifacts. Still, for some reason, that hadn't sunk in yet. We then quickly crammed in most of the other items.

Morgan was still conscious, but the drugs had made him dopey. It took all four of us to get him into the back seat of the SUV without reopening the wound.

Sabrina climbed in next to Morgan. Cricket climbed in on the other side of him to help monitor the injury.

I took the driver's seat while Mustafa gathered the GPS and topography map. He said he'd navigate us back to the interstate, some twenty miles to the north.

The drive to Yuma took us almost three hours. After hitting the first hard bump as we came out of the canyon along the dry riverbed, Cricket warned us that knocks like that could open up the wound again.

After her warning, I was forced to drive much slower than I liked. The four-mile drive to get back to *El Camino del Diablo* took over an hour.

It was early evening by the time we reached the Yuma Regional Medical Center, a large hospital in the middle of town. After arriving at the entrance to the emergency department, Morgan was hurried to an examination room.

The four of us collapsed into the chairs in the waiting area. It had been an extremely long day for everyone and wouldn't be over anytime soon.

Two hours later, we'd filled up on candy and snacks from a vending machine and were milling around the waiting room. My phone began to vibrate, and I had a weird premonition it was Gabriella. Fortunately, when I looked at the readout, it was Max.

"I hadn't heard from you all day," he said with a boyfriend's tone of concern. "How did your trip to the desert go? Were you able to find the artifact you were looking for?"

"Well, it didn't go exactly to plan. But the assignment is winding down. I'll probably stay in Yuma tonight with Morgan, Sabrina, and Cricket. But I imagine I'll be back in town tomorrow night."

"If you're free on Friday night, Tony is putting together a dinner. I understand it will be a small group."

"I should be available," I said. "Any idea what's going on?"

"No, Tony wants to keep it as a surprise. But I've been assured it's good news. It's going to be a champagne and caviar kind of event, so if you're able to come, be sure to wear a long dress."

Ten minutes later, we were greeted by a doctor in green surgical scrubs who came out to the waiting room.

"Are you the group who treated Morgan West in the field?" he asked.

"I did," Cricket said timidly as she raised her hand about halfway.

The doctor nodded and looked down at the woman in the dusty black outfit. "We opened the wound and re-cleaned everything. Fortunately, we didn't need to touch the artery. You did a nice job of closing it."

"Thanks," Cricket said, a wide grin on her face. "I've had a lot of practice over the past couple of years."

The doctor looked sideways at the tiny goth woman but otherwise didn't respond. We then stood for a moment in uncomfortable silence.

"Um, we'll keep him here overnight," the surgeon continued. "But there's no reason he can't go home tomorrow. He'll need to stay off his feet for a week or so, but he should fully recover."

"When can we see him?" Sabrina asked.

"He's being admitted now. You can go up as soon as we get a room number."

"You three get some sleep," Sabrina said. "I'll see if I can stay with Morgan tonight. I'll sleep on a chair in his room if nothing else."

After going out to the car and giving Sabrina her suitcase, we ended up at a budget motel a few blocks from the hospital. Only two rooms were available, so Mustafa took one while Cricket and I took the other.

I was happy that in the rush to repack the SUV, we had managed to include our overnight bags and Cricket's backpack. After briefly discussing what to do with the treasure, we carried the crate to Mustafa's room, which was fortunately on the ground floor.

We agreed to meet at eight the following day for breakfast and then went to the rooms. I kicked off my shoes, yanked off my pants, and pulled my shirt over my head, all but collapsing onto the bed. It had been a long day, and I was exhausted.

As I began to drift off to sleep, I noticed that Cricket had done the same thing. Only in her case, she'd removed the spiked dog collar first.

Chapter Twenty-One

We met for breakfast at a Denny's down the street. Mustafa brought Morgan's old duffle bag, which he said now contained the brass figurines. It looked a little odd, but I could understand him not wanting to leave them in a motel room.

As we ate, Mustafa let us know he'd be staying behind in Yuma while he arranged for transportation to Egypt with the embassy in San Francisco. He vowed the treasures wouldn't leave his sight until he personally delivered them to the Egyptian Museum in Cairo.

"I'd like to thank both of you for your help with this," he said as he sipped his breakfast coffee. "If it hadn't been for your assistance, I'm sure the figurines would be on their way to the black market, destined to go to the highest bidder. I doubt I would've ever been able to gather the complete collection."

Cricket blushed, and I nodded in acknowledgment. "Let Leonard know that my museum will write him an official note of thanks," Mustafa said as he looked at me. "He can close the case and forward any remaining funds from the retainer."

Remaining funds? I thought. *He doesn't know Lenny very well.*

"I'll send a photo release form to your law office email address," Mustafa continued, looking at me. "Please have everyone sign one and return them to me. I'm not saying anyone will be famous or anything. Still, I can see both of you, along with Morgan, figuring prominently in the program when I put together the traveling exhibit."

After breakfast, we returned to the room to pack up for the trip back to Scottsdale. From the next room, we heard Mustafa on the phone, presumably to his embassy.

Cricket and I drove back to the hospital. After checking with the front desk, we found Morgan and Sabrina in a private room overlooking a nearby park.

Now that he had been patched up and was no longer responsible for the figurines, Morgan seemed to be in a much better mood. The fact that Sabrina had pulled her chair next to the bed and was holding his hand also seemed to help.

"With Eckart gone, it will be nice to return to my apartment," Morgan said, looking at me. "Thanks for letting me stay at your place for the past couple of days. It turned out to be very helpful."

"I'm glad it worked out," I said. "Well, other than you being shot and all."

"When I can walk again," Morgan said, "I'll need to grab the things I left in your living room. Then I'll be out of your hair for good."

"It's no problem," I said. "Give me a day or two, and I'll gather everything up and drop them off at your apartment."

"I appreciate that," he said, looking down at his leg. "I won't be driving anywhere for a while."

"What about you?" I asked Sabrina. "What are you going to be doing?"

She looked over at Morgan and hesitated. "I don't know

what I'll be doing," she said. "I've been too busy to even think about it."

There was an awkward pause while everybody waited for Morgan to say something.

"Would you mind staying with me?" Morgan asked. "At least for a couple of days? With this leg, I won't be good for much, and I could use some help."

Sabrina beamed. "That sounds like a wonderful idea," she cooed. "I remember what you like to eat, and I'll be glad to cook for you."

Doctors and nurses came and went from the room all morning. No one seemed overly concerned about Morgan's condition, which I took as a good sign.

Morgan was discharged a little after three o'clock, and a nurse helped us load him into the backseat of the Suburban. Sabrina climbed in next to him, and Cricket was riding shotgun.

"Unfortunately, I'm going to need to go back to the dig site as soon as I can walk again," Morgan said as we drove back to Scottsdale. "We left a lot of equipment in the cave and the riverbed. The story of what we did up there will likely come out soon, and I don't want the Marines to come looking for me for littering their bombing range."

"Yeah," I laughed. "I guess we had other things on our minds when we left. Let me know when you're ready to do it. If you rent us another four-wheeled drive, I imagine I could talk my friend Sophie into coming with us."

"I'll come too," Cricket said, flashing her smile. "Mustafa already asked if I could go back and take some high-resolution images of the cave and the area around it. It's all for his documentation of the find."

Luckily for us, the drive back to Scottsdale was

uneventful. Whenever I glanced in the mirror, Morgan and Sabrina were holding hands. Cricket spent most of the time on her phone, texting with friends and uploading the story on social media.

We made it to Scottsdale a little after six thirty. Morgan asked if we could stop by his sister's house to pick up his apartment key.

When we pulled up to Kelsey's house, I said I'd bring her out to the car. I knew that seeing her brother and the woman who had stolen her identity at the same time might be a little jarring.

Fortunately, Kelsey was so excited to see her brother alive that she didn't seem to care when I introduced Sabrina as the woman who had impersonated her at the law office. Surprisingly, she thanked Sabrina for helping to bring her brother back to Scottsdale, alive and well.

After seeing the bandages around Morgan's leg, Kelsey brought out a pair of crutches. "You'll probably want to rent a wheelchair for the next few days," she said to Sabrina. "But these should help you at least get him back and forth from the couch to the bathroom tonight."

After the tearful reunion at Kelsey's house, we dropped Morgan and Sabrina off at their apartment. Fortunately, it was on the ground floor, and we could move him in relatively quickly using the crutches.

I next drove Cricket back to my apartment so she could pick up her car. We speculated on what could have happened with Brian, but we still had no idea. I told Cricket I'd keep an ear open and let her know if I learned anything.

"Thanks for letting me tag along," she beamed as we pulled into my apartment parking lot. "That was the most fun I've had in a long time."

"But you were threatened at gunpoint, and Morgan was shot," I reminded her. "He had a horrible wound, and if you hadn't been with us, he likely would have bled to death."

"Well, sure," Cricket said, a wicked gleam in her eye. "That's what made it fun."

I woke up the following day feeling fantastic. It was Friday, and I didn't have an assignment to work on.

I had the mystery dinner with Tony and Max later in the evening. But if I was lucky, I wouldn't have anything work-related to do all weekend.

I relished the thought that Morgan was gone, and I had the place all to myself again. Marlowe looked at me from where he was sleeping next to my feet. He also seemed happy that Morgan had moved out.

I lounged around the apartment most of the morning, drinking coffee and watching TV. I'd promised the girls I'd go out to lunch with everyone, so I took off at a quarter to eleven.

I walked out to the hall and turned to lock my apartment. As I did, the door to Grandma's opened. Once again, I got the feeling she'd been listening for me to go out.

"Hi, Grandma," I said. "How are you doing?"

"Well," she said. "That's what I wanted to tell you. We had dinner with Bob's family last night. His youngest daughter and her husband recently bought a cabin outside of

Payson. They mentioned they would need some furniture for it. Bob offered them the extra furniture we had to help furnish the place."

"What about his other kids?" I asked. "Were they okay with that?"

"The other kids didn't object at all," Grandma beamed. "They were mainly concerned that the pieces they bought would be discarded. As long as the furniture is still in the family, everyone's happy."

"So, are things still okay with you and Bob?"

"I suppose so," she said. "I'm still trying to figure out if I like living with a man again or not. I don't remember it being this much work."

"Hey, Laura?" Sophie asked when I walked into the back offices. "When you were getting suffocated to death in the Medical Examiner's office the other day, did you run into a guy named Brian McCoy?"

"Yeah, I told you about him. He's a technician there. Brian was at the lab that night, arguing with Raymond Eckart about Morgan's body. He's been missing ever since. Eckart was supposedly going to pay him two thousand dollars to let him into the lab. Honestly, knowing how violent Owen is, I've been fearing the worst."

"Well, I just read a story about him."

"Oh no," I said, a feeling of dread washing over me. "What happened? They didn't find him in the river as well. Did they?"

"Well, not exactly..."

"Brian didn't seem like a bad guy," I said as I shook my head. "Maybe he wasn't too bright. But he got greedy and started doing business with the wrong people."

"Are you going to let me finish?" Sophie asked, sounding annoyed.

"Sorry," I said. "What about him?"

"I read a story that said Brian McCoy, who works in the Scottsdale Medical Examiner's office, has been vacationing in Las Vegas for the past week. Two nights ago, he hit on one of the progressive slots and won a little over three million dollars."

"You're serious?" I asked.

"Yup. According to the paper, he won it on an *All-American Patriot* slot machine with a three-dollar bet."

"It figures," I said, suddenly feeling grumpy. "I get knocked in the head and almost die, and he gets to retire."

"Sorry," Sophie said with a sad smile and a shake of her head. "Life's an unfair bitch. But if it'll make you feel better about things, I'll buy your lunch today."

"Thanks," I said. "I appreciate it. But after everything that's happened over the last week and a half, I think I'm doing okay."

After lunch with Sophie, Gina, and Debbie, I hung out in the back cubicles. Gina took off after a few minutes, still deep in the J. Barrett Knight assignment.

My best friend wasn't in the mood to work, so after a while, we slipped out the back and went across the street to the coffee shop. We each got a creamy dessert drink and returned to the office to sip them.

By three o'clock, I was thinking about taking off. I knew from experience that Lenny would give me one of the old assignments from the inactive files to work on if he thought I looked too happy.

On the way home, I stopped by Casino Scottsdale, parked using my valet card, then went directly to VIP Guest Services. I wanted to get a couple of pieces of jewelry for Tony's dinner tonight. I also wanted to test how easy it was to get something out of my safety deposit box.

I went to the reception desk and gave the woman my driver's license and my key. She called a number and said a guest needed their box.

Five minutes later, two security men came to the office from the back hallway. One was again pushing a metal trolley.

The security guard in the black polo removed my box and led me into the small private room. I pulled out my diamond pendant necklace, the earrings Max had given me, and Jackie's ruby tennis bracelet.

I told them I was finished, and the security man locked the box back in the trolley. The receptionist asked for my valet token and called for my car.

A new security guard entered the office and told me my car was ready. He then escorted me out to the curb, where my car was waiting.

All in all, getting my jewelry from the casino wasn't nearly as bad as I feared it would be. True, I didn't need to tip the people at the bank. But with my schedule, I knew this was probably the best way to go.

Chapter Twenty-Two

I made it to the Tropical Paradise a little before eight o'clock. As I'd previously agreed with Max, I used valet since I had on some of my jewelry.

I was supposed to meet everybody on the small rooftop terrace that Tony and now Max used as their private retreat within the resort. I went up the curving stairs to the mezzanine level, then entered the Scottsdale Land and Resort Management offices.

I wound through the hallways, eventually ending up at an unremarkable elevator. A familiar-looking Tropical Paradise security guard was standing next to the open door. As I entered the car, he reached in and tapped a keycard against a sensor to let the elevator access the top floor.

After a quick ride by myself up to the roof, the elevator opened to a short hallway with a door at the end. I knew it led out to Tony's private terrace. Carson was standing next to a familiar security podium, taking up the position previously held by Gabriella.

As I thought about her, I felt the ever-present worry. It had been over a week since she'd called, and I was expecting my phone to ring at any time. Hopefully, it wouldn't be in the middle of Tony's dinner.

A round table in the center of the terrace had been set up

for an elegant dinner for seven people. A well-stocked portable bar was situated against one of the side walls.

Milo was positioned behind it, smiling enough to expose his gold tooth, ready to serve the drinks. Another table had been laid out with a dozen types of appetizers.

A small sound system had been set up, playing classic jazz at a low volume. It only added to the incredible views of Scottsdale you got from the roof.

Tony had been walking towards the bar, wearing a black tux with a bow tie. With a feeling of happiness, I noticed that he was barely limping.

"Tony," I said as I walked up and gave him a hug. "You're looking great."

"Thank you," he said in his rough gravelly voice. "I feel stronger every day. Not having the complications of leadership seems to have sped up my recovery."

Standing next to Tony was a slender woman about ten years his junior wearing a gorgeous sapphire blue dress. She was slightly taller than Tony and seemed refined.

She only wore a few jewelry pieces, but they were elegant and appeared custom-made. The only thing that looked somewhat odd in this setting was the bottle of Corona in her hand, the lime still floating on the top.

"Laura, I'd like to introduce you to Celeste," Tony said as I shook the woman's hand. "She's been a close friend of mine for many years. Now that I'm retired, I can be somewhat more open about our relationship."

Wow!

"It's so good to meet you," I said, feeling thrilled. "Honestly, I've always secretly hoped Tony had a friend like you."

"I'm glad you were able to come tonight," Celeste said. "Tony speaks highly of you. He says you've managed to pull him out of a couple of close scrapes."

My cheeks got warm, and I hoped it wasn't too apparent in the dim light. "Thank you," I stammered out. "We've had a few adventures along the way."

The door to the terrace opened, and Johnny Scarpazzi walked in. I'd never seen him in a tux before, but it looked good on him.

I was more than a little shocked when Suzie Lu appeared on his arm. She wore a revealing black sequined dress and black heels.

I knew that Johnny had been keeping their relationship a closely guarded secret, but maybe this intimate setting wasn't considered as being public. From the way Tony and Celeste greeted them as they walked up to the bar, this hadn't been their first time meeting Suzie.

Suzie let out a slight sigh of relief and then hugged Celeste and me in turn. "I'm glad you both are here," she said in her silky-smooth voice. "From the way John talked, I thought I might be the only woman at the party."

"Laura," Tony said, looking slightly confused. "I thought I'd need to introduce you to Miss Lu, but I see you two already know each other."

"Thanks, Tony," I said. "But you're right. We do know each other."

I then gave Johnny a hug. "You look good in a tux," I said.

"Thank you," he said. "I'm finding that dressing for occasions like this is necessary for the job. But I'm slowly getting used to it."

We gathered around the bar, and Milo made everyone a

drink. Tony made sure I tried a new scotch he'd recently discovered, and it was delicious. We also started to do a respectable job on the appetizer table.

I was still waiting for Max to arrive and wondering who the seventh place setting was for. As if reading my mind, Tony got a text on his phone and then called everyone to attention.

"Thank you for indulging my sense of suspense for the evening," he said with a slight chuckle. "As you can see, we're still missing two people. But I've received a text that they're coming up the elevator now."

As our eyes drifted toward the door, the handle turned, and it opened. Max stood in the doorway, looking dapper in a black tux. But even as I admired the view of my boyfriend, I was drawn to his companion.

Gabriella stood next to Max, clinging tightly to his arm. As Carson closed the door, I saw a wheelchair behind him in the hallway.

Gabriella's right leg was stiff and heavily wrapped, and her right arm was in a sling. She had a large purple bruise on the right side of her face, along with a black eye.

I also saw that a good chunk of her dark hair was missing, again on the right side. The frayed edges suggested it might have been burned away.

Tony and Johnny began to applaud, and we all joined in. Even Milo, behind the bar, clapped at seeing his friend. I felt a wild surge of happiness and hurried over to hug her gently.

Max led Gabriella to the table and helped her into a chair. Johnny yelled over at Milo to get them each a drink.

Once everyone had a glass in their hands, Tony again called everybody to attention.

"Tonight, we're celebrating the return of our warrior

after she went out to the wilderness to defeat her foe. I'm happy to report that the piece of shit formerly known as Viktor Pyotrovich Glazkov is no more. In addition, we have our friend Gabriella back, more or less in one piece. Congratulations."

Everybody raised their glass and gave Gabriella their best wishes.

"Thank you," she said quietly, looking at the circle of friends. "It is good to be back. I tell Tony not to make big deal out of it, but you know how he is."

"Are you going to tell us what happened?" Johnny asked, a smile on his beefy face. "It looks like you went through hell."

"In time," she said. "I'll tell you all about it. But for the next week, I only want to sleep."

Everyone applauded once more then Tony said there was time for a final drink before dinner.

After everyone had gone to Gabriella to offer her congratulations on taking care of Viktor, I walked over to where she was sitting.

"It's wonderful to see you," I said, and I could feel my eyes tearing up. "I've been waiting all week for your call. I was ready to come get you, but I'm glad your escape plan worked."

"It's okay," she said. "I knew you would come if I needed you. That's why I chose you. But things worked out in our favor. I got the bullet removed and was able to escape with the help of some locals who still remembered me from the old days."

"I'll get the money and passport back to you," I said. "I don't know what you had to do to get the documents made up. They look real."

"They *are* real," she said, slightly indignantly. "They are completely legitimate. You keep the card and passport. You never know when they might come in handy."

The dinner was delicious, and the conversation was lighthearted. Everyone talked like we were all old friends, which I supposed we more or less were.

As dinner was winding down, I walked to the low wall at the edge of the terrace. I then spent a few moments quietly looking at the lights of the city.

"You look great tonight," Max said in my ear as he walked up and slid an arm around my waist. "It's been hard to keep my eyes off of you. Maybe you'd like to take off with me after this is over for some private cuddle time."

"I'd love that," I said. "Maybe you'd like me to go to your house and spend the night?"

"Actually," he said with a slightly flirty tone. "I gave Beatrice the next two days off to celebrate her win. I'll have the house to myself. Why don't you come over and spend the weekend?"

I thought about the bag I had previously packed and placed in my car but tried to sound surprised.

"The weekend?" I asked. "Alone with you? That sounds perfect."

Yes!

Epilogue

Almost a month had passed since Morgan handed over the treasures of Pharaoh Men-her Ra to Mustafa. I'd picked up a couple of new assignments at work, but nothing that had put my life in danger, at least not so far.

Sophie and I had gone out to dinner with Morgan and Sabrina a few nights before. They were now officially living together as a couple and seemed happy with each other.

Morgan's leg had been healing nicely, and he walked with only a trace of a limp. He'd described that between Cricket's care in the field and the work done in the hospital, the leg felt good and was getting stronger every day.

Sophie had been a little hesitant to meet with Morgan. A couple of times, I noticed she'd look down at her fork, then at Morgan's arm. But after a few drinks, she had declared him to be alive and not a vampire or a poltergeist come back from the dead.

Morgan reported that Mustafa had been as good as his word. The Egyptian Museum in Cairo had wired two hundred thousand dollars into his sister's bank account. In addition, the Egyptian government had started working with the U.S. State Department to correct the paperwork that listed Morgan as being dead.

"My bank accounts have already been restored," he told

us. "I'm hoping I can reactivate my credit cards in another week or two."

Sabrina had gotten a part-time job at the Phoenix Art Museum. It turned out that in addition to her experience in the field, she had a doctorate in art history. I'd called my friend Janice Lee to let her know Sabrina was available, and they quickly found a place for her.

The previous week, Cricket had asked Morgan to come down to the Medical Examiner's lab and explain to Dr. Wilson what had happened to cause the mix-up. It seemed that Brian's failure to log the body of Professor Nabil into the computer system had caused no end of trouble for Dr. Wilson. Having Morgan show up in person apparently did a lot to help resolve the issue.

Gabriella was also on her way to a full recovery. According to what Milo had told Sophie, she was back to working full-time and barely had a limp. Apparently, she'd decided not to fix her hair. Instead, she proudly displayed the missing chunk.

Lenny worked with the local authorities and Morgan's sister, Kelsey, to explain the actions of Sabrina, including her role in helping find the artifacts. Since Sabrina was living with her brother, and Morgan had promised her a cut of the finder's fee, Kelsey declined to press any charges.

Overall, Lenny was thrilled at how the case had been resolved. He'd been able to collect retainers from both Sabrina and Mustafa for the same assignment.

Using his usual creative attorney billing system, he managed to keep everything he had collected as retainers. He didn't seem to care that Sabrina had used deception to become a client. It was a good chunk of income for remarkably little work, at least on his part.

I was in the back offices chatting with Sophie. It seemed she was slowly getting used to working in a cubicle next to the breakroom.

She was also starting to take advantage of being so close to the unsupervised exit to the parking lot. She'd begun scooting out to the coffee shop a couple of times a day.

We were reminiscing about our adventures with Morgan and the Egyptian statues when Lenny came to the cubicles to hand out more work.

"It's a shame you had to give back that little cat sculpture," Sophie said. "I thought it was cute."

Oh, crap.

"What's that look for?" she asked.

I reached into my bottom drawer and brought out the gold cat figurine. It was still wrapped in my scarf.

"Jeez," I exclaimed as I unwrapped the cat sculpture and set it on my desk. "With everything that happened that week, I completely forgot I still had this. I'll need to contact Mustafa."

Lenny gave me a sidelong glance and then looked down at the figurine. Finally, he shook his head. "No, I'd advise you not to do that."

"But I can't keep it," I said. "Morgan gave it to me, but it wasn't rightfully his to give."

"Look," Lenny said as if explaining something to a five-year-old. "We've just received a formal document from the Egyptian Ministry of Tourism and Antiquities that says they've received everything pertaining to the case and consider the matter closed. They thanked us for our help and gave us an additional fee to cover our expenses."

"But don't you think they'd be happy to get the cat back?" I asked.

Lenny frowned and shook his head. "If you return additional items after the fact, it will force them to open everything up again. It wouldn't surprise me if they sent someone over to see what else you'd retained. You could find yourself in legal jeopardy if our country or theirs decides you hid the piece deliberately."

"So, what should I do with it?"

"Keep it as a memento or toss it in the trash," he said, sounding annoyed. "The proper title as to who owns the piece is murky, at best. But as long as you don't try to sell it online, I don't care. Give it to a museum anonymously if that'll help you sleep at night."

I shook my head at the situation. "So, it's wrong to keep it, and I can't sell it. But giving it away to a charity or museum might raise some of the same questions when they dig into the piece's history."

"Yeah, maybe," Lenny said with a shrug. "To be completely safe, you should probably melt it down."

"Melt it down?" I asked, a little shocked at the suggestion.

"Sure, once it's melted, it's just gold. It could have come from anywhere. You could sell it and pay off those credit cards you're always complaining about."

"I think you should keep it," Sophie said. "It reminds me a little of Marlowe."

I picked up the beautiful little figurine and looked at it. After everything we now knew, this was a genuine four-thousand-year-old solid gold sculpture from the tomb of

Pharaoh Men-her Ra. It was a piece of history, and I knew I didn't want to see it destroyed.

I thought about it momentarily, cleared a space on the bookshelf next to my cubicle, then placed the cat on the shelf.

Sophie nodded and flashed me her great smile. Lenny only shook his head and turned to walk up to the front.

Perfect.

On the following pages,
please enjoy a special preview of

Hula Homicide:

A Kristy Piper Aloha Lagoon Mystery
by B A Trimmer.

Hula Homicide: A Kristy Piper Aloha Lagoon Mystery

by B A Trimmer

After divorcing her cheating husband, Scottsdale wedding planner Kristy Darby, now Kristy Piper, had finally achieved her lifelong dream of moving to paradise when she took a job in Hawaii as the Aloha Lagoon resort wedding planner on the gorgeous island of Kauai. Sun, surf, sandy beaches, and glowing brides... what could possibly go wrong?

Turns out, everything...

Hula Homicide

A Kristy Piper
Aloha Lagoon Mystery

B A Trimmer

Chapter One

"Kristy, my necklace is missing," Aunt Audrey moaned as she dropped into one of the chairs at our table. "I'm sure it's been stolen."

"Stolen?" I asked, my voice rising. "Are you talking about that gorgeous diamond and ruby necklace you wore last night?"

As the wedding planner for the Aloha Lagoon Resort, I was responsible for the wedding party's happiness as well as ensuring everything went smoothly. Hearing somebody stole a necklace that must have been worth two hundred thousand dollars was a lousy way to start the week.

"I'm afraid so," Aunt Audrey said, anger and disappointment etched on her face.

Audrey Wentworth was a spry-looking seventy-five-year-old with a kind disposition, and dark hair pulled back in a neat bun. She was the aunt of the bride, Carly Clarkson, who would marry Justin Cooper on Saturday, four days from now.

Due to Aunt Audrey's generosity, the ten members of the wedding party were spending the week at the resort. From what I'd been able to gather, she was a wealthy, childless widow who'd always had a soft spot for Carly, her only niece.

"Well, you definitely had it last night at the reception," I said. "When did you discover it was missing?"

Even though the Aloha reception had been for Carly and Justin, the star of the show had been Aunt Audrey. Hanging around her neck had been a stunning diamond and ruby festoon necklace on a shiny gold chain. The pear-shaped center diamond must have been four or five carats, and the dozen side diamonds and rubies appeared to be over two carats each.

I'd been immediately impressed and completely jealous. Several resort guests in the reception lounge had commented on how beautiful it was.

"I think it was taken while we were at breakfast today," Aunt Audrey said, her voice tinged with disgust. "When I was dressing to go down to the beach, I thought to check on my necklace, but it wasn't in the jewelry case I always keep in my suitcase."

"Didn't you have it in the room safe?" I asked, slightly confused. "I'm pretty sure all the Huts have them."

"It's obvious now that I should have. But I've always heard they're easy to break into and are the first place a thief would look."

"Have you alerted the resort?" I asked, although I knew there usually wasn't a lot they could do with a theft.

"I just spent an hour with Jimmy Toki, the head of resort security," Aunt Audrey said, looking depressed. "I showed him my room and the luggage where I kept the necklace. My next stop is the police station to file a report."

"Would you like some company while you do that?" I asked. Taking an Uber to the police station didn't sound like much fun.

Aunt Audrey's eyes softened with gratitude as she looked at me. "No, I'll be fine. Jimmy's arranged everything.

It's just that the piece has a lot of sentimental value for both Carly and me. I'd planned on giving it to her as a wedding present."

After again assuring me that she didn't need me to accompany her, Aunt Audrey left the table.

I looked over at my assistant, Leilani Alana. She'd silently followed the entire exchange.

"Wow," Leilani said. "That really sucks."

Leilani was not only my assistant at work, she was also my best friend. I'd met her the day after I'd arrived in Kauai, almost six months ago, and we'd been inseparable ever since.

Although people had told us we were nearly identical in personality and attitude, Leilani and I looked nothing alike. I was twenty-nine and tall, with long, mostly natural blonde hair. My eyes were green with flecks of gold and blue that seemed to change colors, depending on the day and my mood.

Leilani was twenty-seven and wasn't quite as tall as me. She was graced with the long, luxuriant, dark hair of a native Hawaiian. She had huge brown eyes, a broad smile, and a gorgeous, expressive face. She was as close as I'd ever come to having a little sister.

Our table was one of many scattered around the outside patio of The Lava Pot, the resort's beachside tiki bar. As required by management, we both wore khaki shorts and our official Aloha Lagoon blue polo shirts.

This was our favorite spot to hang out whenever we scheduled a beach day. The location allowed us to keep an eye on the wedding party, and the big table umbrella gave us plenty of shade.

As always, it was a beautiful day in paradise. The temperature was perfect, delightfully warm with a gentle touch of humidity.

A light breeze ruffled the fronds of the coconut palms along the beach. Fluffy white clouds dotted the sky over the emerald blue of the ocean, signaling fantastic weather for the foreseeable future.

Per the bride's request, the first full day of the week was spent on the beach. Leilani and I watched as the members of the wedding party played a friendly game of three-on-three beach volleyball in one of the sandpits next to the tiki bar.

Typical for the middle of the afternoon, The Lava Pot was doing a brisk business. People were wandering up in a steady stream from the beach to order a beer, a Shark Bite, a Mai Tai, or the house's signature cocktail, the Lava Flow. People on the deck were bobbing their heads to the upbeat classic rock pumping out from inside the bar.

We'd barely begun discussing the disappearance of the necklace when we heard a high-pitched scream from a woman on the beach.

"Geez," Leilani moaned. "What now?"

As we looked toward the noise, we saw one of the bridesmaids, Roxanne Grant, kicking and screaming as she was hauled down the beach over the shoulder of Alex Adair. It appeared that the good-looking groomsman was intent upon tossing her into the Pacific.

Somehow, I wasn't surprised. I'd already pegged Roxanne as the troublemaker of the group. Since arriving the previous afternoon, she'd openly flirted with every guy she'd come across, whether they were married or not. It had been only a matter of time before something happened with Roxanne as the center of attention.

Since I meet so many people at these weddings and names are always hard for me to remember, especially during the first few days, I typically give everyone a private nickname. For these two, it had been easy; he was Movie Star Alex, and she was Flirty Roxanne.

Judging by their body language, Roxanne had apparently said something snarky to Alex as they'd stood together on the beach, watching the group volleyball game. In retaliation, he'd snatched her up and was carrying her down the sand to the surf, her long red hair swishing against the back of Alex's legs.

The way she was twisting and struggling had me worried. Her neon-strawberry bikini top was already a size too small, barely covering her oversized, perfectly tanned boobs. It appeared we were about to have a severe wardrobe malfunction.

Some of the other guys in the wedding party, and a few tourists walking along the boardwalk, must have been thinking along the same lines. Many of them were watching the scene with blatant interest.

"Kristy?" Leilani asked nervously as her eyes followed the spectacle on the beach. "He's not really going to toss her in. Is he?"

By now, the rest of the wedding party had paused their volleyball game to watch the scene unfolding on the beach. There was some laughing and a few good-natured shouts of "Do it!"

One of the groomsmen lifted his beer and called out, "Roxanne, you're going to sleep with the fishes." Even a couple of the bridesmaids were smiling at the exhibition, no doubt thinking it was karma for the shameless way she'd been teasing the men.

"Damn," I groaned. "I think he might actually throw her in."

Instead of smiling and laughing as I would have expected if it had been part of a joke, Alex's jaw was clenched, and he looked like he was fuming. What had Flirty Roxanne said to him? Had she insulted his mother? His manhood?

The bridesmaid twisted and struggled to free herself. Unfortunately, Roxanne's arms were pinned to her sides, and she couldn't do more than kick her legs and shout what I had to assume were vile insults.

As Alex marched with his helpless captive down to the waterline, several sunbathing tourists swiveled their heads to see what the commotion was about.

Although I was appalled by his actions, I had to acknowledge that Alex was classically handsome with his boyish face and medium-length blond hair, as well as a decent body. He'd even arrived in Hawaii with a golden tan.

Once Alex was up to his ankles in the water, he paused. Roxanne stopped struggling, likely thinking he'd changed his mind. But it was clear that Alex was only waiting for the next wave to roll up to the beach.

When it did, he easily tossed the bridesmaid a good six feet out into the ocean. With arms waving and another frantic scream, Roxanne landed with a splash we heard all the way up at The Lava Pot.

Although most of the wedding party clapped and thought it was hilarious, the bride and a couple of the other bridesmaids looked at each other, shock and worry on their faces, before rushing down to the surf as a group to help a soggy Roxanne out of the water.

"Should you go down and referee?" Leilani asked, her head tilted and her eyebrows raised.

"Hmm, not yet. Her hair didn't get too wet, and she's got plenty of people there to help her out. When's our new photographer supposed to arrive? A photo of Roxanne screaming as she flew through the air would've made some fun wedding memories."

I was finding it hard to be sympathetic to Roxanne's plight. It wasn't something I was proud of, but women like that rubbed me the wrong way.

"Jake should've been here already," Leilani said with a deep sigh. "I told him the wedding party would have their first group get-together at noon, here at The Lava Pot."

I gave her a look to show what I thought of the friend of her brother we'd hired to shoot photos of the wedding. I tried to make the look somewhere between irritated and thoroughly annoyed.

"I don't know why he's late," Leilani said as she raised her palms and shrugged her shoulders. "Don't give me that look. I'll give him a call."

She pulled out her phone and scrolled through her contacts. "Maybe he's just on island time?"

I shook my head. When you're a wedding planner and have events timed to the minute, *island time* isn't a term you ever want to hear, especially in connection with someone you'd just hired.

Finding a wedding photographer had turned out to be a lot harder than I'd expected. The good ones tended to be artistic souls who'd go wherever the spirit took them. Hawaii has too many beautiful locations to keep any of them tied down in one spot for more than a month or two.

Leilani's older brother, Kai, had recommended his friend, Jake Hunter, insisting he was an incredible artist who had his own photography business. Of course, I'd met Kai several months ago. My impression had been that the only things he seemed to be interested in were girls and surfing. I wasn't sure if his judgment of what made a good wedding photographer would be all that reliable.

I sighed. Truthfully, I was beginning to get desperate. If this new guy didn't work out, I'd have to pull out the ancient digital SLR camera we kept in the office for emergencies and start taking the pictures myself.

* * *

Twenty minutes after the incident on the beach, the ten people who made up the Clarkson-Cooper wedding party seemed to be in a festive mood again, and the celebration itinerary was back on track. The volleyball game had settled into a steady rhythm with plenty of good-natured laughing and gentle teasing.

Members of the group who weren't actively playing were clustered around the sandpits, chatting and sipping colorful drinks. Almost everyone was smiling, laughing, and seeming to be enjoying themselves. For a wedding planner, that was the best possible outcome.

Clearly, Roxanne had recovered from being tossed into the ocean as she was back to chatting with the groomsmen. Her target was now Angry Eddy Martin.

I'd only briefly met Eddy the night before, and I didn't know a lot about him. I found him to be more rugged than handsome, with a square face, short dark hair, and a thick mustache. He was a barrel-chested man with hairy arms that were covered with tattoos. He was a little shorter than the other men in the group, but he appeared to be powerfully built.

From what I could tell, he wasn't a man who liked to smile a lot. In fact, every time I'd seen him, he'd struck me as being aggravated and spoiling for a fight.

Carly Clarkson, the bride, had mentioned that Eddy

worked in trucking and warehousing. However, she hadn't known exactly how he was involved in either.

Like the rest of the wedding party, Eddy had been friends with the bride and groom since college. From what I could tell, everyone in the group still lived scattered throughout the San Francisco Bay Area.

Flirty Roxanne held a Mai Tai in one hand while her other hand rested on Eddy's shoulder. As she talked, she leaned in and rubbed up against him. I watched her "accidentally" press herself against him three or four more times before he narrowed his eyes, cocked his head to the side, and gave her a questioning look.

She flashed a shy little half-smile and shrugged her shoulders to acknowledge he'd caught her. The muscles in his jaw tensed as his gaze quickly flicked over to Alex and the best man, Wealthy Derek Williams. They were both talking near the patio of The Lava Pot, slightly apart from the rest of the group.

Eddy turned his attention back to Roxanne, and they spoke to each other quietly for a moment. Eddy then relaxed, now looking much less irritated, and nodded his head.

Her mission accomplished, Flirty Roxanne sauntered off to talk to other people in the group with a smug smile on her face. Meanwhile, Eddy took a long, thoughtful sip of his drink as he watched her backside sway seductively as she walked away.

I glanced down at my watch, then raised an eyebrow at Leilani. "Well?" I asked. "Where's our photographer?"

"He just sent me a text," she said, breathing a sigh of relief. "He's on his way." Her look implied that none of what happened was her fault.

"Well, he's almost missed group beach day," I said with

a disappointed shake of my head. "Not having beach pictures on top of a missing necklace isn't how I wanted today to go."

* * *

Once the volleyball game finished, everybody took a break to head back into The Lava Pot for drink refills. The best man, Wealthy Derek Williams, detoured by where Leilani and I were sitting.

I'd met Derek the night before at the Aloha reception. He was about the same age as the rest of the group. After college, he'd started a network technology company in Silicon Valley that had made him rich.

With a slightly soft body and short dark hair sticking out at all angles, I got the impression that Derek wasn't the type to take care of himself. Most of the time, there was a hint of a smile on his face, as if the idea of hanging out with his old college friends was mildly amusing.

The Dolce & Gabbana camouflage cargo shorts and Valentino print shirt he wore matched well with his diamond-studded Rolex watch but were a bit over-the-top. After so many years of drooling over luxury fashion on the internet, it was always entertaining to see someone wearing it.

"Hi, Derek," I said. "How's everything going?"

"Kristy," he said in the clipped tones of an employer addressing a subordinate. "I want to talk with you about my bungalow. According to what I was told, I'd have an ocean view."

Everyone in the group was staying in one of several high-end guest villas scattered between the main building and the beach. The resort had labeled these as *The Huts*, but the name really didn't do justice to the beautiful two-story private cottages.

"Oh no," I said. "Did you not get one?"

"Well, technically. If I stand on the corner of the second-story balcony, I can see the ocean. But it's hardly what I'd call a great ocean view. I'd like to have it changed to something more reasonable."

These types of problems and requests frequently came up throughout a typical wedding week. As a result, I always encourage the guests to use me as their personal concierge, travel agent, party host, and all-around problem solver. If I could tell jokes or juggle flaming bowling pins, I'd probably be asked to do that as well.

"No worries," I said. "Check back in a few minutes. We'll make sure to get it changed around."

It was clear Derek had been building up for an argument and seemed to deflate slightly when he realized there wouldn't be one. "Oh," he said. "Very well. Thanks for getting that done."

When Derek took off to rejoin the game, Leilani called Summer at the front desk to make the updated arrangements. I then noted the room change on my tablet.

"There he is," Leilani said with relief as she looked toward the entrance to the bar. She stood up and waved to get his attention.

I turned to get a look at my new photographer, prepared to give him a proper chewing out for being so late.

Oh my.

The person standing at the entrance of The Lava Pot turned out to be not what I had been expecting. For one thing, he was incredibly handsome in that tall, broad-shouldered kind of way, and for another, he was somewhere in his early to mid-thirties. I don't know why, but I'd been expecting someone a lot younger.

A tight black and green University of Hawaii Rainbow

Warriors T-shirt showcased the muscles of his chest and arms, while a pair of casual khaki cargo shorts showed off his well-defined legs. Even the man's feet were attractive in his leather sandals, and I usually am not the kind of person to check out a guy's feet.

He had the kind of deep tan that a mainlander gained by living on the island full time. But what really struck me were his curly dark hair and piercing blue eyes. The man was serious eye-candy.

"Sorry I'm late," he said, flashing me a brilliant smile as he walked up and extended his hand. "I'm Jake Hunter."

"Look, Jake," I started after we shook, prepared to lay into him. "If you're going to do this, I can't have you stroll in late to…"

"How much longer will everyone be out here?" he interrupted, pulling a high-end Nikon camera out of his bag and removing the lens cap. From the gold band next to the focus ring, I could see the lens was a professional model.

"About forty-five minutes," I said as I glanced down at my watch. "Maybe a little less. But listen, I can't have you…"

"Plenty of time," he interrupted *again*, even as he smiled at me with a lopsided grin. "By now, they've all had a drink or two, and no one will be shy about getting their picture taken."

Turning, he hopped onto the sand and made his way to the volleyball pits. Frustrated that I didn't get a chance to vent, I mentally crossed my fingers and hoped he at least knew what he was doing. A lousy photographer could leave a bride in tears and cause lasting problems for the wedding planner.

For the next twenty minutes, I watched as Jake wove in

and out of the group, easily inserting himself into the moment. Judging by his cocky attitude, I figured he'd be completely lame when it came to taking photos. Honestly, I'd dreaded the worst, like a puppy who's adorable but still destroys your house.

Instead, I was pleasantly surprised by how effortless he made it seem. His photography style appeared to be a combination of casually chatting with people and taking pictures.

Jake quickly worked his way through the entire group, making sure to get shots of everyone. Unlike some photographers I'd worked with who were intrusive, everyone seemed to be relaxed with Jake.

When he got to Flirty Roxanne, I couldn't help but notice she spent several moments positioning herself in some rather suggestive poses. Although she'd obviously tried to entice him, he'd waited until she relaxed into something more presentable before taking the photos.

Jake then gathered everyone together for a group picture as the players were switching sides. It didn't take him more than a minute or so to correctly stage everyone, complete with a breathtaking backdrop of palm trees and the beach.

I heard the rapid *ping-ping-ping* as he took a burst of eight or ten shots. He glanced at the back of his camera, then looked up with a dazzling smile. "Perfect. Thanks, everybody."

The group quickly scattered, everyone going back to the game. I was utterly amazed. Jake had done in two minutes what I'd seen other photographers struggle with for ten minutes or more.

As I watched Jake work, I noticed the way the light breeze coming off the ocean ruffled his hair. It looked so soft that I started to wonder what it would feel like to run my fingers through it.

Clearly, my lack of male companionship over the last six months had affected how I looked at men. I was starting to get hungry. I hated to admit that I hadn't been on more than two dates in a row with anyone since I'd arrived at Aloha Lagoon.

Chapter Two

Carly-the-bride wandered over to join Leilani and me at our table. In her early thirties, she was a pleasant-looking, somewhat curvy woman who seemed to be one of those people totally happy in her own skin.

Her smile was sweet, her brown eyes crinkling at the corners. I loved how the shag cut with curtain bangs and subtle highlights flattered her.

I'd met her in person the day before when she'd flown in with Justin Cooper, her husband-to-be. Fortunately, she'd been my favorite kind of bride to work with, realistic and organized.

Carly was decked out in full bride-to-be gear. She sported a white one-piece swimsuit that flattered her curves. Gold cursive lettering proclaiming *The Bride* was splashed across her chest. And a sparkly silver tiara graced the top of her head.

From her happy laughter, it was apparent she hadn't yet heard about the missing necklace. I briefly considered telling her, but the news would ruin her afternoon, and I didn't want to be the one to do that. I was confident her aunt would tell her soon enough.

"Kristy"—she beamed at me—"you were right about everything. The beach is fantastic. How are we doing on time? I have the schedule on my phone, but I left it in the bungalow."

So much for being organized.

I pulled my tablet from my bag and flipped it open. "We'll wrap up here in about fifteen minutes," I said. "That'll give everyone plenty of time to clean up, get dressed, and make it to the Ramada Pier for the luau by six-thirty. They'll serve dinner and start the show at seven. Tomorrow morning is sightseeing. We'll meet at the entrance to the lobby and leave at nine."

Suddenly, we heard a frantic scream. We looked up to see that Movie Star Alex had grabbed another bridesmaid. His latest victim was the maid of honor, Lauren Maxwell.

"Geez," Leilani grumbled. "What's up with that guy?"

"Kristy?" Carly moaned, looking at me like his actions were something I had control over.

Again, Alex had his victim slung over his shoulder and was effortlessly holding her with one arm, her slim frame making his job easier. His other hand held the remains of a Lava Flow.

He took a few steps towards the surf but then turned to smile back at the group. They all shouted out "boo" and "you suck!"

Somewhere along the way, Lauren had lost her oversized black plastic-framed glasses. She pounded on his back and kicked her legs in front of his face.

When I'd met Lauren the day before, she'd struck me as painfully shy. Now she was loudly shouting a string of profanities at Alex, something that surprised me.

The night before, I'd been amused to see her dressed in an aloha shirt decorated with colorful Pokémon characters. Today, her pink one-piece swimsuit sported a picture of the anime cartoon character Sailor Moon. I was starting to think of her as Anime Lauren. The cobalt-blue tips and highlights in her shoulder-length brunette hair coordinated well with her suit.

Unlike earlier, when Alex had snatched up Roxanne, it seemed like he'd grabbed Lauren simply for the fun of it. There was a wide goofy smile on his face before he laughed and tossed back the rest of his drink, flinging the plastic cup on the beach. He then turned and started walking towards the surf.

"Loser!" one of the bridesmaids yelled out to Alex.

I sighed and stood up, knowing that as the wedding planner, I needed to go out and have a heart-to-heart with Alex. I'd have to remind him he was here because of Carly and Justin, the happy couple, and he shouldn't do anything to spoil the occasion.

I'd just stepped onto the sand, and Alex hadn't made it more than five or six steps toward the ocean, when Jake stepped in front of him. Alex tried to go around, but Jake again blocked his path.

Alex absentmindedly let go of Lauren, and she landed on the beach with a thud. He casually stepped over her to get in my photographer's face. I was still too far away to hear what the men were saying, but after several moments, Alex got an icy look on his face and gave Jake a hard shove.

Surprisingly, Jake didn't budge. Instead, he returned the shove, and Alex was knocked back several steps before toppling to the sand.

No, Jake, you can't do that to a guest.

Alex quickly jumped up, rage on his face. His fists were tightly clenched as he readied himself for a fight.

The groomsman stared at Jake for a moment, breathing hard, before seeming to think better of it. He then turned to go back up the beach and almost ran into Lauren, who had climbed to her feet.

She stood, hands-on-hips, directly in front of Alex. She was also breathing hard, her face red from anger and embarrassment.

Without warning, she swung her arm and, with a resounding *crack*, connected with a solid slap to his face. It appeared he hadn't been expecting it and didn't have time to avoid it.

"Ka-Pow!" somebody shouted from the volleyball pit. Most of the men, and a few of the women, started to clap— some were also laughing.

The blow was loud enough to be heard over the pounding of the waves, like a branch that had broken off the side of a tree. It staggered Alex, and he fell back onto the sand again.

"Slimebag!" Lauren shouted at Alex before turning and stomping up the beach in the direction of the bar.

Alex climbed unsteadily to his feet, angry and apparently looking to continue the confrontation with Lauren. Jake again stepped in front of him and shook his head.

By now, the entertainment value had drained from the encounter, as Alex wisely chose to slink back to the volleyball game. I noticed everyone in the group avoided making eye contact with him.

"I'm starting to regret inviting Alex," Carly said with a deep sigh and a shake of her head when I returned to the table. "Lauren's right. He's acting like a jerk. I suppose he hasn't changed a lot since college."

"If you knew he was a bully, why'd you invite him?" I asked.

"Oh, he was Justin's roommate all through school. I couldn't invite everyone else and not ask him. I'm glad your photographer was there to stop him. He seems like a handy guy to have around."

I was starting to think I agreed with her.

Carly got up to retrieve Lauren's glasses, which had fallen on the beach. Then she followed the maid of honor, who'd stomped into the bar, obviously upset and wanting another drink.

I let everyone know they had time to relax for a bit and get ready for the luau. Several people seemed relieved as they packed up and headed back to their rooms. After what had just happened, many appeared to welcome the chance for a change of scenery.

* * *

The Ohana Luau was always one of the highlights of any wedding week. Ohana means family and people of all ages would attend the event. It was held at the Ramada Pier, an area of the resort on the beach set aside for larger events.

As I arrived, traditional Hawaiian music was being played on the main stage by a three-piece group featuring a steel guitar. The music was upbeat and foretold of a fun evening ahead.

Guests dressed in colorful aloha shirts and muumuus filtered onto the pier from the central part of the resort. They gathered around the bar and gradually filled the tables.

Several guests, most holding a complimentary beer or rum punch, had collected around the *imu,* the in-ground barbeque pit where a whole pig had been slowly roasting all day. With a great deal of ceremony, two shirtless Native Hawaiian men in colorful skirts removed the pig from the pit. They then carried it to an open-air kitchen along the side of the venue, where men in white coats and chef's hats prepared the pork in a style known as *pua'a kālua.*

I walked into the seating area and saw one of the groomsmen, Orson Cross, standing at the bar with two rum punch cocktails in front of him.

Orson was tall and thin, almost to the point of being skinny. As with most of the wedding party, he was in his early thirties. His skin was pasty white, and his long brown hair was pulled back into a ponytail, emphasizing his skeleton-thin face and oversized nose.

Orson's eyes were riveted on a video game he was playing on a handheld gaming console.

"Hi, Orson," I said as I walked up to him. "Can I take your drinks to the table?"

He briefly looked up and smiled. "Hi, Kristy," he said. "Hold on. I'm almost done with the level."

With a final flourish, his fingers danced over the buttons. The video game played a happy fanfare, and Orson relaxed.

"We issued an update to this game today," he said as he shoved the device into his pocket. "I was making sure it was uploading correctly."

"Carly said you design computer games. Was that one of yours?"

He blushed pink and looked down at his feet. "Yeah, um, I'm the lead developer at the company. We're about to launch volume seven in the *Orc's Apprentice* series. The last release won Fantasy Game of the Year, so we're hoping for some decent sales."

"Wow," I said, thoroughly impressed. "I had no idea."

"Are you a gamer?" he asked.

"Um, no. I haven't played video games since I was a kid."

"You should try it," he said with a knowing grin. "The

graphics and gameplay have come a long way since the old Nintendo Game Cubes and PlayStations."

I walked with Orson over to our table. Alex was off to the side, talking with Wealthy Derek. I noticed Orson went out of his way to avoid them.

Alex didn't look so much like a movie star anymore. The side of his face was red, and there was the start of a nasty bruise under his left eye.

When we reached our table, Orson delivered one of the rum punches to Anime Lauren, who also seemed to be actively avoiding Alex.

She'd changed into a short yellow dress with the Pokémon character Pikachu across her chest. I was glad to see she wasn't showing any ill effects from the earlier encounter on the beach.

"I'm here, on time," a voice behind me said. I turned to see Jake standing three feet away. He had a grin on his face, as if he'd pulled something over on me.

That man has the most dangerous smile.

He'd changed into a tight black T-shirt and was wearing some kind of sensual cologne. I caught traces of wood, musk, and leather. I could picture Jake as a cowboy, sitting in front of an open fire with a soft drift of smoke.

There were parts of me that were slowly starting to wake up, parts that hadn't been awake in a long time, maybe not since my divorce, now almost seven months ago.

"I'm glad you made it," I said, doing my best to keep my voice even. "We have maybe thirty minutes until the buffet opens and the show starts."

"No worries," he said with his lopsided grin. "Let me know if there're any specific shots you want."

"Tonight should be simple. Take some general memory photos of the luau and the show. I'll also need candids of everyone and some small group pictures. We have permission to use the luau stage for a group shot if you can get everyone up there, but don't force it."

"Okay, I'll see if they're in the mood for it."

"During dinner, they do the quieter part of the show," I said. "Nani Johnson does her ukulele numbers, and she sometimes has a singer with her."

"That should be easy. What else?"

"After that, the Aloha Lagoon Hula Wahines do some dance numbers with the guests. They already know about our wedding party. They'll pull Justin, our groom, up to hula in front of everyone, so make sure to get that."

"I'll shoot that in video," Jake said slowly as though he was mentally planning the shot. "If I stand behind the stage, I can rack focus to get some reaction pictures of Carly as he dances."

"Great idea. I can already imagine how well that'll work out."

"How late should I stay tonight?"

"Well, after the Hula Wahines, the Ahi Fire Knife Dancers come on stage. The house lights are then basically off for the rest of the show. You might as well take off after they start up."

"Perfect," he said as he nodded and gave me a wink. "I should have all the time I need."

Oh my god. He winked at me. I liked it, but who does that anymore?

"Don't forget," I reminded him. "We're meeting in the lobby tomorrow morning at nine o'clock for a group visit to the Fern Grotto. Make sure to get there a little early. The grotto's a beautiful place. It'll be a great setting to get candids and small groups."

"I'll be there," he said. "I looked at the raw images from this afternoon. Some of them are pretty good. I'll clean them up, and we can review them tomorrow whenever you have some time."

His cologne was starting to trigger thoughts that were definitely inappropriate for the workplace. I wondered if I could find out what it was so I could sprinkle a little on my pillow.

Jake started to circulate through the crowd. He worked the wedding party, chatting with people and shooting pictures. His muscles flexed and bunched as he turned the camera to capture different angles.

Geez, I really need to find a boyfriend.

While I was mesmerized by Jake's physique, Aunt Audrey walked up to the table. Rather than one of the complimentary drinks, she held a glass of the resort's high-end reserve pinot grigio.

Reluctantly pulling my attention away from the view, I asked, "How'd it go with the police? Is there anything they can do about your necklace?"

"It doesn't appear so," she said, clearly disappointed. "I'd place more faith in Jimmy Toki. He seems a little more on the ball. The detective I talked to, Ray something, says there isn't a lot he can do."

"I'll work with Jimmy to see if he's learned anything yet."

"Thank you, dear. That necklace has always been Carly's favorite piece of jewelry. As a child, I'd let her wear it, and she'd pretend she was a princess."

On the stage, a shirtless native Hawaiian man wearing a colorful lavalava skirt blew a loud musical note on a conch shell. The sound signaled the start of the feast.

* * *

In the relative calm between dinner and the main part of the show, I spent a few minutes chatting with bridesmaids Madeline and Victoria Trapp, a pair of identical twins. They were both tall and athletic, with similar hourglass figures.

Physically, the only thing that set them apart was their hair. Although both women had the same honey-blonde color, Victoria had long flowing tresses, while Madeline's locks were cut shoulder length.

"Hello, ladies," I said as I took an empty seat next to them. "You were both fantastic in the volleyball pit today."

"Thanks," Victoria said with a shrug. It was hard not to think of her as the sister with the long hair. "I thought we were terrible. We haven't played together since college. We were pretty good back then."

"Well, we *were*," Madeline said absentmindedly as she looked out at the rest of the wedding party. "But that was a long time ago. My serve is terrible, and I can barely set the ball anymore."

I caught a distracted tone from both women. I wanted to help if I could. "Is everything okay?" I asked. "Is there anything I can do for you while you're staying at the resort?"

"If you could turn back time about ten years, that would solve a lot of problems," Short-haired Madeline said in a wistful tone. There was a somewhat distant look in her eyes as her gaze lingered on Movie Star Alex and Wealthy Derek, who were now chatting with Carly and Justin, the bride and groom.

She turned and saw my puzzled look. She then gave a

small laugh and shook her head. "It's okay," she said. "We're good."

"It's sweet of you to keep asking," Long-haired Victoria said as she flashed me a beautiful smile. "But we're fine."

"Okay," I said, a little discouraged. "Let Leilani or me know if anything comes up. We'll take care of it."

I didn't want to be overly pushy, so I let it go. As long as nothing spilled over to the rest of the wedding party, I'd gladly let them keep their secrets and work out their problems on their own.

By now, nearly everyone in the group was smiling and laughing. The lone exception was Angry Eddy Martin. He stood near the bar, looking out at the ocean, so I went over to talk with him.

He didn't look as grumpy and intimidating as he had earlier in the day, but he still didn't look all that friendly. He now seemed annoyed and frustrated, as if something was gnawing at him.

"Hi, Eddy," I said. "How's everything going?"

"It's alright," he said in a quiet, steady voice. "The resort is gorgeous. Carly and Justin chose a great place to get married."

"Have you known them both a long time?" I asked.

"We all started out as freshmen together in the same dorm. Justin started dating Carly our sophomore year."

"That's a long time to know a group of people."

"Yeah," he said as he glanced over at Flirty Roxanne. "It's interesting seeing everybody again. I'd lost track of most of these people over the years."

"Do you know why Carly only invited people from college to be in the wedding party? I'm sure our bride and groom have family and friends they could have asked."

Eddy snorted out a laugh and nodded his head. "I hear it happened because Carly and Derek the billionaire have apparently stayed pen-pals for all these years. The rumor is that Derek said he'd come to the wedding and even be the best man, but only if Victoria and Madeline Trapp were bridesmaids."

"Why those two?" I asked.

"He used to date Victoria. I think he even dated Madeline for a while before that. So, since the first three people in the wedding party were part of the old circle from college, it snowballed from there. Carley has several sisters, and she used Derek as the excuse why they all couldn't be in the wedding party. I suppose it saved her from hurting anyone's feelings. As I understand it, the rest of the friends and family will show up later in the week."

"Deciding who to exclude from the wedding party is never easy," I agreed. "What did you think about how it happened?"

"Hey, we get to come out to paradise a week early, courtesy of Carly's aunt. I was all for it." He grunted and held up his beer. "One last time to get the old gang together."

* * *

When the Ahi Fire Knife Dancers took the stage, I was entranced, like the rest of the audience. The unique event combined athletic skill, unflinching bravery, and ever-present danger.

Jake spent a few minutes shooting the fire dancers then returned to the table. Since he was done taking pictures for the night, I expected him to take off. Instead, he pulled out an empty chair and sat next to me.

A whiff of his cologne drifted past, and his presence

pressed in on me. As the fire dancers transitioned from one scene to the next, Jake leaned in closer, his mouth brushing my ear, sending tingles along every nerve ending.

"Those guys are pretty good. Do they ever miss as they're tossing around those flaming knives?"

I turned so I could talk to him without having to raise my voice, which brought our faces to within a few inches of each other. As soon as I realized what had happened, my heart sped up a notch.

"In the six months I've been here, they've only missed a couple of times," I said. "Haven't you ever seen the show before?"

"I haven't been to a luau in years. But we were always going to them when I was a kid. Whenever family would come over from the mainland, my parents would take us to one of the luaus. I've always loved them."

"Same for me," I sighed. "The first time I went to one was on my honeymoon, seven years ago. The marriage didn't work out so well, but I'll never forget the fun I had at the luau."

"How long ago was the divorce?" he asked. His deep blue eyes met mine, and I could sense he was genuinely interested in my answer.

"It was final about six months ago," I said with a shrug. "There weren't any kids, and he wanted to move on with his life, so it was a simple process."

He looked at me for a moment, then nodded. He reached out and lightly rested his fingertips on my arm. His touch felt both exciting and comforting.

"I understand what you must have gone through," he said quietly, a somewhat distant look in his eyes. "It's not easy when someone you care about no longer wants you."

He seemed to realize he'd brought down the mood, and he pulled his fingers away. I was a little sorry to feel them go.

He again gave me that lopsided smile and spread out his arms. "But it's hard to be sad when you live in paradise, huh?"

"It certainly helps," I said with a laugh. "Not living in the same city as before helps as well. Too many things there reminded me of my ex-husband."

"How did you end up at Aloha Lagoon?"

"I was lucky. I found out about the job through an ad the resort put in a wedding planner's magazine. The interview process was quick, and I've been working here ever since."

He looked like he was gearing up to say something else when he seemed to change his mind. "Okay," he said. "I'd better take off and start to clean up the pictures from tonight. I'll meet you down in the lobby a few minutes before nine tomorrow morning."

He got up, and my eyes followed him as he left the Ramada Pier. I knew I'd be thinking about him tonight.

Chapter Three

I made it to the Aloha Lagoon Wedding Center a little before eight the following day. The office was just off the cavernous main lobby, past the concierge desk, between the gift shop and Gabby's Island Adventures.

As I walked in, the bell above the door jingled. It was a pleasant and happy sound that always made brides smile.

Dorothy Campbell sat at her white desk concentrating on a document while Leilani was standing next to the coffee pot, pouring herself a cup of Dorothy's custom roast Kona blend.

Dorothy had been the office manager at the Wedding Center for the last thirty-five years. Her parents had come to Kauai from Jamaica when she was a small girl. She pretty much considered herself a Hawaiian native, even though she'd managed to retain a slight Jamaican accent.

As always, Dorothy's clothes were neat as a pin, and her curly black and gray hair hung down to her shoulders. Her signature double-strand Mikimoto pearl necklace was draped around her neck, making the regulation resort polo look somewhat fashionable.

Dorothy's eyes were bright, her mind was sharp, and not a lot got past her scrutiny. She was one of the most organized people I'd ever known, and I was grateful to have her. She effortlessly took care of the hundreds of details that went into planning a destination event and could mentally keep track of twenty weddings at once.

I grabbed a mug of coffee and plopped down on the chair behind my desk. Unlike Dorothy's spotlessly clean workspace, mine always seemed to have several stacks of catalogs, magazines, and notebooks on it.

"How did it go yesterday?" Dorothy asked, her eyes shifting to Leilani. "How'd Jake do? I was a little surprised when you said he was a photographer. I didn't think he had any interests outside of computers and surfing."

"He seemed to do alright," Leilani said, maybe a bit annoyed that Dorothy would question her friend's abilities.

Dorothy didn't have a mean bone in her body. But since it was Leilani who had recommended Jake, Dorothy would be pinning his results on her.

"Jake did fine," I echoed. "But yesterday was a mixed bag. There was a little friction on the beach in the afternoon. And I suppose you heard about Aunt Audrey's necklace possibly being stolen?"

"Leilani was telling me about it," Dorothy said. "It seems to be quite valuable."

"The center diamond alone must have been four or five carats," I said, a touch of envy in my voice. "There were another dozen diamonds and rubies besides that."

"Oh, really?" Dorothy asked. Her eyes sparkled at the thought.

"It totally bites that some jackwagon stole it," Leilani said.

"Why didn't she have it in the room safe?" Dorothy asked.

"When I asked her about it, she said she didn't think the room safes were all that secure," I replied. "She also mentioned that she'd planned on giving it to Carly to wear at the ceremony with her gown."

"Geez, that would've made a nice present," Leilani moaned enviously. "I should've been born to a wealthy family." She then shrugged it off. "What's the schedule for today?"

"The group had breakfast on their own," I said as I pulled out my tablet. "I imagine most of them went to the Rainbow Buffet or the Loco Moco. We have about half an hour before we need to go to the lobby and gather everyone up for Gabby's shuttle to the boat for the Fern Grotto."

"I always like it there," Leilani said as she nodded her head. "Standing on the grotto overlook is an excellent place for selfies."

"After that is a group lunch back here on the Ono Terrace at noon," I said as I flipped through the schedule. "They have the afternoon off, and I imagine most of them will head back to the beach. Tonight will be dinner and karaoke at the Loco Moco, starting at six."

With a thrill of anticipation, I knew I'd be working with Jake again. Hopefully, he'd be on time today. I didn't want to give Dorothy any reasons to be disappointed with him.

As I thought about my photographer and how good he'd smelled the night before, I realized I was beginning to develop a bit of a crush on the man.

"Maybe it's time to start dating again," I mumbled to myself.

"What?" Leilani asked, surprise in her eyes. "I thought you said you were through with men. I remember about a month ago, you said they were all scum, and the world would be better off without them."

"Well..." I admitted, "Maybe I did. But I'm starting to rethink that position."

"Really?" she asked, confused. "With who? Are you

talking about Alex Adair? He doesn't seem like your type."

"No," I confessed with a guilty grimace. "Jake Hunter."

Leilani laughed and wrinkled her nose. "Really?"

"Why would you say that? He likes girls, doesn't he?"

"Oh sure, he dated a woman named Michelle for about three years. I figured they'd get married, but four or five months ago, she dumped him for a condominium developer from Oahu. I guess she had some daddy issues. The guy was close to fifty years old."

"So, what's wrong with Jake?" I pressed.

"Nothing's wrong with him. But I've known him since I could walk. It's hard for me to think of him as dating material."

"It won't creep you out if I talk about it, will it?"

"Go ahead," she laughed. "Knock yourself out. Jake's always been nice to me, and he seems like a decent guy. So, go for it. Drag him behind a coconut palm if you want to."

Dorothy shook her head and gave us an eye roll. Fortunately, she had a pretty high tolerance for the things Leilani and I discussed.

We started going over the week's events when something caught Leilani's eye, and she stared into the lobby. "Uh-oh," she groaned. "Management doesn't look so happy today."

I sighed, knowing what was coming after the problems we'd had the day before. Actually, I'd sort of been expecting it.

The door to the Wedding Center opened with a friendly jingle, and David Mahelona walked in.

David headed the resort's human resources department. He was a large man with islander heritage. Even after working at the resort for six months, I hadn't learned anything about him other than he was in a continuously lousy mood.

As he walked into the room, I could feel him occupying much of the office space. His shoulders were broad, his long dark hair was pulled back, and his expression was downright intimidating.

"Hello, David," Dorothy said, using her most soothing *dealing-with-a-client* voice. "What can we do for you today?"

"Good morning, ladies," he said to Dorothy and Leilani. He then turned to look at me. His smile was stiff and didn't make it up to his emotionless eyes.

"Kristy, we received a complaint yesterday afternoon from someone in your wedding party, a Mr. Alex Adair. He said he was on the beach when he was attacked by your photographer, Jake Hunter."

Leilani rolled her eyes and barked out a quick laugh. She quickly quieted when David glared at her. I sighed and shook my head.

"That's not what happened," I said. I knew I sounded annoyed, but I couldn't help it. David just rubbed me the wrong way.

"Alex had grabbed one of the bridesmaids and had thrown her over his shoulder. She wasn't happy about it and was screaming to be let down. Alex was walking down the beach, seemingly intent on tossing her into the ocean, when Jake stepped in front of him. Alex got annoyed and gave Jake a shove. Jake pushed him back. That was it. Jake actually resolved what could have turned into an ugly situation."

David stood impassively, but it was apparent he wasn't going to listen to anything I had to say.

"I do understand how guests can be, especially when there's alcohol involved," he said, trying to sound reasonable but completely failing. "Still, we can't have anyone associated with the resort involved with assaulting a guest. Next time something like that happens, he's out. If you're not able to control your employees better, you'll find yourself out as well."

David turned and left the office. The bell over the door jingled as he went.

"Well, he was more cheerful than usual," Leilani said.

"I don't know," Dorothy said, sounding worried. "He seemed pretty serious this time. You better keep Jake on a tight leash. I don't want to see anyone getting into trouble over something like that."

"Come on," I said to Leilani as I looked down at my watch. "Let's go find our group and our naughty photographer."

* * *

Leilani and I arrived at the front of the massive lobby, where we started to gather the wedding party. I imagine preschool teachers go through much the same process before beginning class.

The space was a hive of activity, as it always is in the morning. Bellhops were pushing carts full of luggage while people stood in line waiting to check out.

Flirty Roxanne and Gamer Orson had already arrived and were chatting near the lobby entrance. Leilani and I walked over to greet them as Orson noisily sipped on the remains of a Bloody Mary. Roxanne's long red hair looked especially fluffy today.

A few minutes later, we were joined by Victoria and Madeline, the blonde twins, as they entered the lobby from the direction of the conference center. They both wore matching outfits that showed off their long legs.

After saying hello to everyone, I stuck my head out to check the parking lot. I confirmed that Koma had the van from Gabby's Island Adventures waiting to take everyone down to the Wailua River to start the morning's excursion.

I've always liked Koma. At twenty-three, he and his twin sister Lana were full-blooded Hawaiians who worked for Gabby. He was handsome, muscular, and good-natured. All the ladies loved him.

I looked around, but Jake hadn't arrived yet. I hoped he wouldn't be late again. No matter how great he looked or smelled, I couldn't work with someone who didn't show up on time.

Aunt Audrey strolled into the lobby wearing a pair of white plastic sunglasses and an oversized sun hat. Walking behind her were the bride and groom, Carly and Justin.

Carly was wearing a sundress that flattered her curves, the sparkly silver tiara, and *The Bride* white sash. With his medium-length brown hair, medium height, round face, and slightly soft body, I was once again struck by how completely average Justin looked.

Angry Eddy came in and stood with the others. Looking at his solid build and the many tattoos covering his arms, he seemed somewhat intimidating. I noticed he surreptitiously eyed everyone and glanced around the lobby before joining the group.

At nine o'clock, Wealthy Derek and Anime Lauren wandered into the lobby. Derek's hair again looked like he'd towel-dried it and then forgot to comb it. Lauren had a nice outfit that showed off her fantastic figure and blue-tipped hair, but she also had a headband with pink cat ears. It looked like she'd even used makeup to place a large black dot on the end of her nose and had drawn cat whiskers on her cheeks.

I did a final headcount and noticed we were one short. "Does anyone know if Alex is coming today?" I asked.

Victoria Trapp, the sister with the long hair, gave a little snort to show she didn't care if Alex came or not. She was joined by some additional snickers and murmurs of agreement. *Loser* and *jackhole* were the two terms I heard most clearly.

"If we're voting, I'd say leave him here," Lauren said with a wicked grin.

"Or, why don't we take him but then not bring him back?" Roxanne suggested.

"I saw him earlier when I went to the gift shop," Derek volunteered. "But that was probably a half-hour or forty-five minutes ago. I think he was walking toward the meeting rooms," he said as he pointed down the hallway that led to the conference center.

"Alright," I said. "I'll give him another few minutes, then track him down. Has anyone seen Jake Hunter, our photographer?"

There were some blank looks along with a few mutters and shaking of heads. Roxanne's eyes sparkled, and she bit her lower lip, apparently in appreciation of Jake.

I looked over at Leilani. She gave me two palms up and a slight shoulder shrug.

I felt a surge of irritation. Although Jake was utterly adorable, he was starting to become more trouble than he was worth.

Geez, it's always one more thing.

We waited another five minutes while the wedding party milled about the lobby entrance. I walked over to Leilani.

She had a slightly guilty expression.

"Um, I'm sorry," she said as she scrunched up her face. "I don't know where Jake is. I tried calling, but he didn't answer. Maybe he wasn't such a good choice for a photographer after all."

I sighed and shook my head. "Let's not worry about him now. Run back to the office and grab the old camera. I'll get everyone to the shuttle. Go out with the group and take as many pictures as you can. I'll find Alex and drive him to the boat, assuming he still wants to go."

"Okay," she said as she beamed at me with her bright smile, eager to make up for Jake's tardiness. "I can do that."

As she turned to scamper back to the office, I led the group out to the van. I heard Carly telling Justin that the trip would probably be a lot quieter without Alex there to cause trouble.

Once everyone was settled, Leilani ran out of the lobby, holding the office camera bag. She climbed into the van, and I wished her luck with the excursion. As I headed back to the resort to start my search for Alex, I briefly paused to watch Koma maneuver the big vehicle out of the parking lot.

I sighed and shook my head. The wedding week had started out on a sour note. I only hoped it got better from here.

As I headed down the hallway that wound toward the conference and events center, I knew I only had about ten minutes to find my lost guest. If I couldn't track him down by then, the excursion boat to the Fern Grotto would leave with the wedding party, and Alex would miss the outing.

I passed the Kealia and the Alaka'i conference rooms within the conference center, and both appeared to be locked. I knew a door at the end of the hallway, next to the bathrooms, led out to the main pool, so I headed that way.

Traditional instrumental music played softly through overhead speakers as I quickly walked to the end of the hallway. I'd almost made it to the exit when I passed the Halelea conference room. Its door was slightly ajar, and the lights were on.

With a bad feeling, I stepped in and quickly glanced around, hoping to find a meeting in progress. Instead, I saw something on the floor and froze.

Jake lay crumpled against the back wall. He held his hand to the side of his head, and his leg was kicking out weakly. As I approached, I could hear him moaning, almost inaudibly.

Oh my God.

A colorful tiki statue lay on the floor near him. It appeared to be one of the cheap versions you can pick up in any souvenir shop on the island. It was about two feet tall and looked to be made of wood or maybe hard plastic.

I hurried over to him and bent down. My mind was racing, and my questions tumbled out all at once. "Jake, what happened? Are you alright? Who did this to you?"

Jake kept blinking, as though his eyes weren't focusing very well. He didn't seem to recognize me. I knew he was injured, possibly severely.

Jake pointed across the room before his arm dropped back to the floor with a thud.

I glanced in the direction Jake had indicated. There was a table with a white cloth sitting in the center of the room. Sticking out from behind it, I could see a pair of men's legs, ending at a pair of brown leather sandals on the feet.

Oh no.

About the Author

Halfway through a successful career in technical writing, marketing, and sales, along with having four beautiful children, author B A Trimmer veered into fiction. Combining a love of the desert derived from many years of living in Arizona with an appreciation of the modern romantic detective story, the Laura Black Scottsdale Series was born.

Comments and questions are always welcome.

Email the author at LauraBlackScottsdale@gmail.com

Follow at www.facebook.com/ScottsdaleSeries

LAURA BLACK IS LOOKING FOR A MAN, A DEAD ONE...

Laura has a client with a problem. She can't find her dead brother's body. As Laura searches, she stumbles onto an international ring of ruthless black market antiquity smugglers. With multiple groups hunting for ancient Egyptian treasures, Laura quickly finds she's over her head. Add to that, Max's housekeeper, Beatrice, has a problem. Every year she loses the Scottsdale Cookie and Cake Club's cupcake bake-off to a talentless woman called Kaitlin Kingston. Is this Devil Woman merely fooling around with the judge, or are there deadlier shenanigans afoot?

WITH PLENTY OF HUMOR, ACTION, AND MYSTERY, THIS BOOK IS A
Scottsdale Scandal!

Book #10 is full of heart, heat, and a healthy dose of hilarity!
Scottsdale Scandal!
The perfect book for a day at the beach or a night by the fireplace.

Made in the USA
Coppell, TX
04 November 2024

39617029R00201